LEGACY

LEGACY

James Steel

WINDSOR

PARAGON

First published 2010
by HarperCollins*Publishers*
This Large Print edition published 2011
by AudioGo Ltd
by arrangement with
HarperCollins*Publishers*

Hardcover ISBN: 978 1 445 85575 2
Softcover   ISBN: 978 1 445 85576 9

British Library Cataloguing in Publication Data available

Printed and bound in Great Britain by
MPG Books Group Limited

For my family and friends.

SUNDAY 21 SEPTEMBER, LUCAPA
DIAMOND FIELD, ANGOLA

The whisper came through the African night.

'Zero, this is Lima Three.'

He pressed the radio earpiece hard against his head, focusing on that quiet voice from the throat mike feeding him information. He clicked the transmit key twice to acknowledge his forward observer silently.

The voice whispered again.

'Sighting report as at two-zero-four. At junction of Gully Red and Gully Yellow now. Infantry. Estimate platoon strength. Moving south.'

He checked the map. This was what it was all about, everything he did: contact with the enemy. They had waited for the moon to go down and hoped to hit the diamond mine just before dawn.

He turned round from his command post, a groundsheet hung up under an acacia tree with the radio on a stack of empty ammunition crates. Its dim glow was the only light. Behind him was the mortar platoon, black shapes in the darkness.

'Fire Plan India,' he called in an urgent whisper to the nearest crew, who repeated it down the line. The men twisted the elevation screws and the tubes rose slightly to lengthen the range. The 81mm mortars stared blank-eyed up into the night, blind to the destruction they would cause.

Yamba, the platoon sergeant, scuttled down the line to check the four crews were ready. Then he came close so that his dark face could be seen in the glow from the radio set. He nodded.

1

'Zero, this is Lima Three. Fire mission.'

'Lima Three, this is Zero. Fire mission. Out.'

He waited for the details; pencil stub paused over a dog-eared pad.

'Fire mission. Grid: three-zero-eight-four-eight-one. Bearing three-two hundred mills. Infantry in gully. Destroy now. One minute. Over.'

He repeated the fire-control orders back to the observer. Then he stood up and turned to the mortar line. The time for action had come.

'Open fire!'

He barked the order out in a harsh voice that tore away the veil of silence that had cloaked them.

The mortars made their distinctive *thunk* sound and spat their metal loads up into the night. White flames shot up out of the tubes. Base plates slammed and rang with the recoil.

The crews turned away from them when they dropped each round down. They jammed their fingers in their ears, but still it did not stop the feeling of being kicked in the head by the propellant burst.

After the first rounds dropped down the tube he grabbed the mike and called urgently: 'Lima Three. Shot five!' to indicate the number of seconds before impact.

The response came equally abruptly as the observer took cover.

'Shot five. Out!'

They pumped round after round out at the stars. The forward observer, dug into a foxhole a mile away, could see the vivid flashes of orange in the night where the shells landed but he could not see the murderous swarms of metal splinters

2

that they unleashed through the air when they burst.

The observer called in a correction.

'Drop fifty! Over!' he shouted loudly now over the din.

Range screws were twisted on the mortars.

'On target! Over!'

Figures ran, stumbled and fell. They blundered around, shocked by the blasts. An officer's whistle blew desperate signals but then stopped abruptly as a bomb hit. Eventually no more movement could be seen.

'Cease loading!' The shout went down the line and the last rounds fired off.

The crews froze and stared at their officer. The silence that followed was as stunning as the terrible noise that they had just been making.

He shouted brisk commands at them as he swept on his webbing and grabbed his assault rifle.

'Col! You take Charlie fire team and a tracker, and sweep east of Gully Yellow. Yamba! Bring Delta fire team with me! We'll sweep west!'

*   *   *

Alex Devereux looked down at the bodies laid in a row on the ground.

There were thirteen of them, teenagers mainly, but a couple of men in their twenties and one who must have been forty, a UNITA guerrilla veteran from the Angolan civil war, and presumably their commander. They were either barefoot or wore an assortment of wellies and trainers, with ragged T-shirts and patched trousers.

In the follow-up sweep to the mortar ambush

their torches had revealed the carnage in the gully. In the confined space the blast of the bombs had blown the insurgents against the walls and ripped them apart.

The trackers had followed the blood trails from the scene. Dark splashes on the ground and smears on elephant grass stems led them to their quarry. Two had been injured and had crawled a few hundred yards before collapsing.

The trackers, Yamba and Sunday, knew their stuff. As the blood got fresher they signalled the squad to fan out in a line and switch off their torches. Eventually Alex's squad heard the laboured breathing and mumbling of the wounded man as he dragged himself along.

Quick stabs of gunfire in the dark and he went down. No rules of engagement and warnings given here. He wasn't in the regular army any more.

They went back and cast around for more tracks, but by the time they followed them up the survivors were long gone; the tracks showed them running wildly and crashing through bushes, terrified, desperate to escape.

The men dragged the bodies back to the gully and laid them out neatly. In the morning, the local Angolan army commander posed in front of them with a grinning thumbs up for the camera. He had the shots framed for the wall of his office back at the mine.

The captured weapons were laid out on the ground: nine AK-47s, four RPG launchers, three PKM light machine guns and some Claymores to cover their retreat. They were well armed.

All in all, a good night's work.

Alex stood with his hands on his hips and

frowned. Six foot four, broad shoulders, a strong masculine face—he looked very threatening like that. He ran his hand through his short black hair, rubbed the back of his neck and stared down at one of the boys; a mess of flies was fidgeting in a wound on his cheek.

Fourteen years old?

Major Alexander Devereux. Wellington College. Blues and Royals. Forty. Single. Child-killer.

A cold darkness of self-loathing settled over his heart.

1501; CONSTANTINOPLE

The dancers in the graveyard waited silently for the signal.

Their faces, lit by flames, stared at the huge man standing in the centre of their circle.

Abba Athanasius was a Nubian, dressed now as an Ishfaqi mystic. His body was a slab of black muscle, more like a force of nature than flesh and blood. He was naked but for a black loincloth and kudu-skin bands that decorated his arms and legs.

Sensing the hour, he held up his right arm and bellowed, 'Dance for the darkness in your heart!'

'Amen!' they roared, and the music began.

In the centre of the circle, black men drummed on hollow logs; staring unseeing at the flames. Light gleamed off the sweat on their muscles.

Other musicians played flutes and horns. The cult was of every creed and colour: Muslims, Christians, Druze, Alawites, Copts, Maronites and

Bogomils.

The crowd danced as if they were one. Concentric rings of people moved in and out like a giant organism breathing. Their stamping feet stirred up the dust in the moonlight.

The dancers ululated. They made sharp cracks with little brass hand-cymbals. The sound was deafening, a heavy cloth of noise draped over them, suffocating their senses.

Abba Athanasius ran to and fro in the middle of the rings. He held a small drum in one hand and struck it repeatedly with a stick. He bounded around the circle, leaped in the air and screamed at the crowd, urging them on.

A young German knight, Eberhardt von Steltzenberg, danced himself into a frenzy and opened his heart to a nefarious force.

The rhythm grew faster and faster. The crowd shouted louder and louder. The drummers beat harder and harder.

The witch doctor suddenly stood stock-still. Sensing a spiritual climax he threw an arm up into the air.

'Silence!' he bellowed, and the drummers and musicians stopped.

The crowd gave a great groan as though winded by a blow. A sorrowful sound; as if coughed up out of the recesses of their souls.

The silence was overwhelming. It pressed itself into their heads. Men cried out and fell down on their knees.

Abba Athanasius called out to the drummers, in a quiet voice, 'Softly,' and they began a gentle rhythm.

As they played, the black priest picked a large

metal censer off the ground. It was made of three heavy iron chains attached to the rim of a metal pan. A lid with holes in it slid down the chains to cover the pan. Abba Athanasius flung the container into the fire and scooped it out, brimming over with hot coals.

As he was doing this, a gang of huge Nubian men pushed their way in through the crowd. They were naked as bulls, faces as powerful and impassive as cliffs.

Four of them were holding staves with solid metal ends, which they used to push the crowd aside. Behind them came a man lugging a narrow iron bucket, and two more carrying a heavy chest between them. Another four held the poles of a litter supporting a three-foot-long lump of rock like black glass. The Nubian Deathstone. The men staggered under its weight.

It was so dark and shiny that it seemed to have a light inside it, as if it knew something.

They pushed their way through the worshippers. When they came into the clearing they set the litter down. The priest leaped onto it, straddling the Deathstone, silhouetted in the light of the fire. His hands grasped the shaft of a sledgehammer and swung it up over his head. With a cry he brought down a swingeing blow on the stone.

The sound rang out and a lump the size of a fist split off. The priest scrambled to pick it up. He held the rock above his head to show to the devotees. They groaned like cattle.

Abba Athanasius flung the lump into the metal mortar that the Nubians had brought with them. The men with poles arranged themselves around it and began to pound the rock to powder with

7

their metal staves, just like the women in their home villages pounded cassava. They drove the heavy poles down so that they thudded in a constant rhythm.

As they worked, the priest threw open the chest; using a trowel he heaped incense from it into the censer. Lumps of myrrh produced a cloud of sweet fragrance. Other spices threw up puffs of white smoke. Finally he poured in trowels of opium resin.

When the rock was ground to powder the priest stood up on the litter and raised the heavy mortar above his head. A Nubian held the censer up to him by its chains. Abba Athanasius bent down and carefully poured the fine black crystal powder onto the pile of ingredients and then slid the cover down the chains and over the pan.

Black smoke poured out of holes in the lid. The huge monk took hold of the chains and whirled the censer around his head, sending out clouds of sparks into the night whilst he chanted prayers.

He gestured to the crowd to kneel and made his way around the rings of worshippers with the censer, dispensing a strange benediction. As he moved along the lines of kneeling figures he held the chain so that the pan passed underneath each bowed head. Evil, black clouds of narcotic smoke poured out, and each worshipper took a deep inhalation.

Eberhardt kneeled and stared at the Deathstone. Its gleaming black depths mesmerised him; he could feel it reaching out to him, pulling him into its mystery.

What was its secret knowledge?

Where had it come from?

What was it saying to him?

8

He knew he had to find its source, hidden somewhere in the heart of Africa. It would be his purpose in life.

He heard the priest coming along the row. The young knight had been shaken by the worship; his broad shoulders trembled with each breath. He bowed his head as the priest neared; his long, brown hair fell around his face. Nervously he brushed it back behind his ears. The huge man was mumbling some blessing in a language that he did not understand, over and over again as he walked slowly along.

Eberhardt could see the red glow of the censer out of the corner of his eye and prepared himself.

The first whiff of smoke caught at his nose, intensely fragrant. He forced himself to take a huge gulp of it as it passed under him.

Hot, noxious vapour filled his throat and bronchioles. He felt a seizure in his respiratory tract under the powerful chemical assault.

His throat burned and convulsed. He could not breathe. The strong opiate hit his brain as the black miasma of the Deathstone worked its way into his body and being.

Darkness invaded his heart.

He felt both lifted up and cast down, overawed and appalled. He had been invested by something profound yet terrible.

He clutched at his throat but no air came in. He passed out and fell face down on the ground.

THURSDAY 6 NOVEMBER, LONDON

'Alexander, this is your father.'

The upper-class growl was slurred by drink.0

His father's use of Alex's full name was a danger signal. He was in a fighting mood, when the frustrations in his life boiled over and he picked fights with those closest to him to displace his anger.

It was three o'clock in the afternoon. Alex was at his desk in his family's house in Fulham. He did a quick mental calculation: it was after lunchtime so his father must be drunk. He could picture him now, wearing his old tweed suit, sitting in his worn armchair in the drawing room of Akerley, the family house in Herefordshire, where he lived alone, looking out of the big bay window over the parkland.

Sir Nicholas Devereux was an ex-cavalry officer and an alcoholic. The Devereux had been loyal servants of the Crown since Guy D'Evreux had fought for the Conqueror at Hastings. There had been one of the family serving in the Household Division every year since Waterloo—until Alex left without a son to replace him. Membership of the family might have its privileges but it came with its burdens as well.

Alex knew where his father's problems stemmed from: the source of all known evil—his grandmother. She was an intelligent, strong-minded woman trapped by social convention in the role of an aristocratic adornment. Her talents had turned sour and she took to displacing

10

her personal disappointments on others, dismembering their characters with a cold sadism. Her acidic remarks had been fired at her son from the end of the long dining-room table for years, and had knocked his confidence to bits, driving him to drink and then to taking out his frustration violently on his wife. She had told Alex later that the first time he had beaten her had been on their wedding night.

Alex sometimes wondered if he was next in line for this legacy. Whether he would simply repeat the pat-tern of negative behaviour, transmitted down through the generations in a cycle of anger and destruction. The Devereux might be an ancient, landed family but the poison and the privilege seemed to go hand in hand.

However, it was one thing to understand his father's problems, another entirely to deal with them. Alex's upbringing had been a painful one, surrounded by the conflict between the Devereux's supposed noble grandeur and wealth, and the crappy reality of the life around him—his father's drinking bouts and his attacks on Alex's mother. He remembered the fear that gripped him and his younger sister, Georgina, when the fights erupted. The two of them used to run off to a barn to hide until they guessed that their father had passed out. They had avoided those conflicts but George hadn't got away from the problem entirely. Anorexia had forced her to leave Wycombe Abbey and she was now married to a similarly vain, flashy man, Rory, a barrister who drank too much.

Alex and George's mother had struggled valiantly to keep their dysfunctional home together, until stomach cancer had overwhelmed

11

her when Alex was in his early teens. Things had started to go downhill soon afterwards. The electricity had been cut off regularly, and he remembered overhearing the shouting matches between his father and suppliers in the courtyard when they turned up at the house demanding payment.

The most humiliating episode for Alex had been when he was summoned to a meeting with his housemaster at boarding school, who explained in the kindliest tones that he was going to have to leave because his fees hadn't been paid. Alex had gone home for a week until another field had been sold off to pay the bill. He had burned with shame as he had walked into breakfast on his first day back amid the other boys' taunts and jeers.

Despite all this, Alex had been brought up to be loyal and dutiful. Wellington was an army school and had drilled the service ethic into him—although he couldn't help seeing the irony of its motto: 'Sons of heroes.' His father had insisted that Alex follow him into the Blues and Royals straight from Wellington, without going to university: 'You don't need any of that leftie claptrap.'

His father's reputation and his own lack of a degree had been key factors in Alex not being promoted from major to colonel. He had thus faced the prospect of becoming that stock figure of quiet ridicule in English society: the passed-over major. A Tim-Nice-But-Dim, a try-hard who had never made it. Traditionally they were to be found in retirement in the provinces, living off their pensions, running village fêtes or gymkhanas.

His upbringing had left Alex with a brittle

pride. This touchiness would not let him face the ignominy of hanging around the regiment to complete sixteen years' service before picking up his pension, so he had left and joined the world of private military companies. He was a romantic and hated the idea of joining his former colleagues in the usual safe jobs they went on to—insurance broking or estate agency—and so he had turned to becoming the original freelancer.

His father had objected virulently, spitting out the word 'mercenary' with contempt. In response Alex was quietly and bitterly angry at him for having ruined his chance of serving his country as he'd hoped. An intense suppressed tension had existed between them ever since.

'Hello, Dad,' Alex said now in a controlled voice. He tried above all things not to lose his temper. His father was pathetic but he was still his father.

'So, have you fixed that roof of yours then?'

The roof in the family home in Bradbourne Road was leaking. His father had a sixth sense for picking out the things that were bothering Alex most and challenging him on them. 'Keeping you on your toes', he called it.

Alex had been back in London a month now since his contract in Angola had ended. He had effectively put himself out of a job by finishing off the bandits who had plagued the Lucapa diamond mine since the end of the civil war.

Money was the other main issue chiselling away at Alex's heart. He had no new assignments lined up and his usual contacts in the defence business had not been able to pass on even the hint of a new project. It usually took several months to get a

13

contract sorted out and he was not sure how he was going to pay the bills and fix his leaking roof in the meantime.

Lists of figures would drift through his head at night. There was the exorbitant estimate to redo the roof, which, combined with all the other repairs to his crumbling home, was over six figures, and his neighbours were threatening legal action if he didn't get on with it. He had also recently received letters from another firm of lawyers, threatening him over his father's debts. The old man had obviously lost control of Akerley entirely, although Alex still didn't know the full extent of the problem.

He took a deep breath and tried to fend off his father's jab. 'Well, I'm working on it. I've got some quotes—'

'Working on it! What does that mean?'

'It means I'm not there yet but I will be.'

'Working on it, Alex, always working on it,' Sir Nicholas chuckled with derision. 'You see, you need to be a bit more bloody decisive, like me.'

'Hmm,' Alex muttered.

'Now look, the dry rot is getting very bad in the north wing here, lot of the roof timbers are about to go. Seeing as you're just back from Africa and flush with funds I expect that you can fork out a bit to help keep the place running.'

'Dad, I need to get Bradbourne sorted out first.'

'Bugger Bradbourne, child! What about looking after your alma mater!' This was a well-worn argument. His father knew that the family pile was no longer sustainable since he had sold off most of the farmland around it, but had made it his cantankerous cause célèbre to die in the house he

14

was born in.

Alex's jaw tightened. He stood up and began pacing back and forth in the living room. He pressed the receiver hard against his head and his dark brows drew together.

'Look, let's just get to the point here, Dad. We *need* to sell Akerley. Without the land the house is just a liability—we're living in the ruins of our history. We can't go on as if we're . . .' he raised his free hand in exasperation, '. . . in the Middle Ages or something. You know we—'

'And you know damn well that I never will, so don't you start that cant again! If you were earning some decent bloody money as a colonel, instead of pissing around with nignogs in the bush, you might actually be able to start putting something back into this family!'

Alex stopped pacing; his shoulders heaved and he put his head down, his eyes closed, as he summoned up all his strength not to retaliate.

With forced calm he said: 'I am trying my best, Dad.'

'Trying won't do, Alexander! If you weren't such a fucking failure the family wouldn't be in this bloody mess!'

'I am *not a fucking failure*!' His voice cracked into a shout of rage.

Provoked.

Exposed.

Defeated,

Humiliated.

He had failed.

He had been drawn into an argument, allowing his father to score the petty victory he had been looking for to make himself feel better.

Alex slammed the phone down but he could hear the braying, triumphant laugh all the way from Herefordshire. His father's uncanny ability to zero in on his weakness had worked yet again.

Alex was shaking with anger as he walked to the back of the living room and stood with his hands on his hips, staring out of the window at the overgrown back garden. He did not see or hear anything else as the scene played itself over in his head.

Murderous fury consumed half of him; the rest was simply crushed by his father's scorn and his own fear of what he was.

I am *not a fucking failure*!

The phone rang again.

He stared at it uncomprehendingly for a moment and then snatched it off the cradle and barked, 'Yes!'

'Mr Devereux?' asked a voice in a concerned tone.

Alex could not place the accent exactly, something Middle Eastern but with an American overtone.

He forced himself to sound more civil. 'Yes, this is Alexander Devereux.'

'My name is Mr Al-Khouri. I represent an organisation that is interested in doing some business with you, Mr Devereux.'

'Yes?' Alex replied cautiously.

'I realise that you cannot talk on the phone but I would be interested to meet you tomorrow to outline a project.'

'Right,' Alex managed.

'I have booked a table for tea at the Ritz at three o'clock tomorrow. Would that be acceptable?'

'Fine . . .' Alex said slowly, avoiding commitment

16

as he desperately tried to think if he wanted to go. He knew he did not have any alternative, and the Ritz was about as unthreatening a place as one could meet in.

'Very well, Mr Devereux. Just ask for my table, Mr Al-Khouri, and it's jacket and tie,' he said in a smug tone.

'Right, OK. Thank you,' Alex tried to end the conversation sounding as if he was in control.

*   *   *

As usual, Alex arrived early; army habits died hard.

He was wearing highly polished black Oxfords, his bespoke blue pinstripe suit with a crisply ironed white shirt, and his Cavalry and Guards blue and red striped tie.

He didn't like being so obvious about his regiment—'cabbage' was their derisory term for flaunting the connection too overtly—but this was business, and he knew it was one of the few British army symbols that foreigners in his line of work recognised and valued.

He walked up the side entrance steps on Arlington Street and was greeted by a smartly uniformed porter with white gloves tucked into one of the epaulettes of his overcoat.

He was shown along the broad entrance hall by an overly suave waiter in black tie and a white dinner jacket. The middle of the Palm Court tearoom was dominated by an enormous gilt urn decorated with palms. A lady in a sequined dress tinkled away at a piano on one side.

Alex cringed; the whole effect was one of stifling

17

fussiness. The sparse clientele included grandmothers being taken out on their birthdays, aspirational fathers fulfilling their dreams by bringing cowed wives and children out for tea at the Ritz. Conversation was reduced to a subdued level by the formality.

'Mr Al-Khouri is over there, sir,' said the officious waiter, his arm extended grandly to point to a table in the far corner of the room. Alex straightened his shoulders and walked over slowly, eyeing his potential business partner carefully.

On first sight Mr Al-Khouri looked the epitome of a wealthy playboy: about thirty-five, blow-dried black hair, average height, slim build and clean-shaven. He was wearing a white shirt with a black Armani suit and tie.

The man stood up as Alex approached, all slick smiles and competitive bonhomie. 'Mr Devereux. Please come, sit down, sit down.'

'Alexander Devereux,' said Alex unnecessarily, and gave his firmest handshake as he towered over the smaller man. It was all part of the male posturing, manoeuvring to show who was in charge.

'Yes, yes. Kalil Al-Khouri. Thank you for coming, Mr Devereux. Tea for two, please.' He signalled to the waiter hovering behind Alex. 'Your finest Earl Grey,' he added fastidiously.

'A nice location.' He swept his hand around the room.

'Splendid,' replied Alex.

'I like to come to the Ritz when I am in town; it has a very . . . established feel. I do a lot of business in London.' Kalil spread his hands and his voice dropped to a quieter conspiratorial tone. The word 'business' was deliberately vague, implying things far too important and secret to be spoken about in detail.

'Right,' Alex nodded, and waited for the posturing to stop.

'So,' Kalil tilted his head to one side, 'my contacts tell me that you've been in Angola recently.'

Alex was not sure who Kalil's contacts were but there was nothing secret in what he had said so far. Alex's work was sanctioned tacitly by the Foreign Office so he had nothing to hide.

'Yes, a contract on the Lucapa field in the north. Mine defence and security team training,' said Alex.

'And how did that go?'

'It went well,' he replied cautiously. 'We had good support from the government,' which was a lie, but he was always careful to sound positive about his employers. 'We did a lot of clearing-up ops on the bandit groups in the area. Counterinsurgency, some armoured recce work.' He wasn't prepared to go into any more detail, and looked at Kalil, who was watching him carefully.

'Well, that's very much the line of work that we are interested in.' He glanced around to see that the grandmother and her family two tables away were not taking notes. He steepled his fingers together and leaned towards Alex.

'Can I confirm, in the first instance, that you would be free to be involved in a six-month project starting with immediate effect? The compensation package will be,' again he paused for effect, '. . . extremely competitive.'

The waiter arrived with a triple-layered stand of cakes and a silver tea set on a tray. He fussed around laying them out and then left with a simpering smile.

Alex and Kalil resumed their conspiratorial huddle.

Alex nodded. 'It would depend on the nature of the project, but yes, in theory, I would be available.'

'Good.' Kalil poured tea for them both and then sipped it slowly. Eventually he put his cup down and leaned over the table.

'I represent a cartel of Lebanese diamond dealers,' he continued quietly. 'We are interested in hiring you to lead an operation involving a mechanised battle group in Africa. My understanding from your file is that this is your area of expertise?'

Alex stared him in the eye and nodded slowly.

Lebanese. They ran the diamond-trading networks in Africa and were famously secretive, but it sounded like a big job so in principle he was interested. The money would be good.

'The cartel was extremely impressed with your file. You understand our position in the trade?'

'In broad terms, yes.' Alex had been involved in the business for long enough to have a good understanding of their role but he did not want to prevent any revelations so he held his hands out in a gesture inviting further comment.

'We are the *comptoirs*—the middlemen on the ground—in Africa, who supply the markets in Amsterdam and the Far East. De Beers, Steinmetz and the rest have been getting very antsy about CSR and blood diamonds of late, but we're not too angst-ridden about all that.' He tossed his head dismissively.

Alex was pleased that Kalil was dropping the bullshit and speaking more openly.

Corporate Social Responsibility was a buzzword of all the multinationals. It was supposed to be about ethical behaviour towards indigenous peoples and the environment, and generally not behaving like rapacious capitalists. All well and good, but for small fry like Alex it meant that big firms were no longer prepared to operate in the sort of lawless areas where his skills would be in demand. He was not bothered to hear it denigrated.

'I mean, we can't afford to be.' Kalil looked at Alex with his eyebrows raised to see if he was going to get precious.

Alex shrugged to indicate that he was not bothered about exact adherence to the codes of practice that the larger security firms followed these days. He was not in a position to be picky.

'Let me be plain, Mr Devereux.' Kalil took on a serious expression. 'This operation would be illegal by all international law codes. Don't get me wrong, it's not about genocide, but it does involve an attack across sovereign borders. Not that that means squat in the parts of the world we're talking about. It's basically a dispute between two private enterprises over a diamond field in the Central African Republic. If you don't feel comfortable in that situation, please tell me now.'

Alex looked at him. He didn't know the man from Adam. Was he a plant sent to trap him into an admission of illegality? Was he wired? He couldn't tell. He needed the money. He shrugged again.

'I'll take that as a yes. Don't worry, Mr Devereux,

21

the cartel is a bona fide organisation and we are as concerned to protect ourselves from outside scrutiny on this as you would be, so we are doing things very carefully. I think that is about as far as we can go on the operational details for now.' He indicated the incongruous surroundings with an open gesture of both hands.

'Tell me about your time in the army,' he said, sitting back and switching topics. His hand hovered over the teacakes as he chose one. He ate it, catching the crumbs with one hand under his chin, as Alex detailed his career résumé.

'I was commissioned into the regiment and served with them in Northern Ireland, Cyprus and Bosnia. I trained for armoured recce with Striker, Spartan and Scimitar, and then main battle tanks with Challenger 2, so I am able to deal with all types of armoured warfare operations. We were also part of 5 Airborne when we were at Windsor so I have done paratrooper training and can handle infantry ops as well.'

'And you left as a major?'

'Yes.'

This was another tricky topic for Alex. He did not want to say that he could not face being a passed-over major.

'The British Army is the best in the world,' he went on, 'but I wanted to get more action and independence so I went into the defence business . . .' It was a downright lie but he was so used to telling it that he sounded like he meant it. What he had really wanted to do was to stay and serve his country as a colonel.

'And have served with companies in Sierra Leone, Congo and Angola?' Kalil dipped his head interrogatively.

'Correct.'

Now that Kalil had dropped the act he seemed to be much more down-to-earth. Alex was not exactly warming to him but at least he thought he was someone he could do business with.

The chitchat continued until they had finished their cups of tea and then Kalil stood up, swept his hand through his hair, chucked a fifty-pound note dismissively on the table and led the way out.

As they walked to the hotel lobby Kalil's quick eye caught the display of 'Ritz Fine Jewellery' cabinets arranged along one side. He stopped to look at the cases of rings, necklaces and brooches.

'You see, this is what it's all about.' He pointed out a diamond pendant to Alex and spoke with sudden enthusiasm. 'This is what *we* in the cartel do. This is a white diamond—yes?'

He looked at Alex, who bent down to inspect it and then nodded, wondering why he was asking such a question.

The immaculate sales manager stood up from her desk and came across to them. She was a suitably striking addition to the Ritz: tall, with long blonde hair and an elegant black dress.

'Can I help you, sir?' she asked Kalil in a voice as polished as one of her stones.

'Hey, how are you?' Kalil looked up, slightly startled, and fired off the standard American greeting rather defensively.

She had had enough American customers to know that the question was not meant to be answered and nodded in return as Kalil continued without pausing.

'I'm looking for a coloured diamond. You gotta coloured diamond?' His eyes were flicking over the displays.

'We have some over here, sir.' She led the way across to where a row of select-looking cabinets were set into the wall. The pieces in them sparkled alluringly under the lights.

'We have a natural Vivid Yellow stone set in a necklace here and this is a natural Vivid Green stone in a ring.'

'That's it! OK, lemme do a price comparison. Can you get me a white stone the same carat as that, please?'

The manageress walked over to the cabinets in the middle of the room. Kalil's black eyes flicked a quick glance over her svelte backside. He watched her intently as she paused to pull a pair of white cotton gloves onto her slender hands. She unlocked a cabinet, took out a ring, closed it carefully and walked back.

'This is a one-carat white diamond.' She held it up and it sparkled pure white light.

'Can we compare it to the green one, please?'

She nodded obligingly and unlocked the cabinet on the wall. There was a soft peep of an alarm as it slid open.

'Now, look at this, see?' Kalil held the new ring up to Alex and turned it back and forth so that it caught the light. At first glance it appeared clear but as the light played on the facets it sparked green.

Alex had never had much interest in the aesthetics of diamonds before but he had to admit that it was captivating how the colour appeared from nowhere.

'You see, same chemical structure as a diamond—it's *not* an emerald—but *totally* different effect. They're formed when the diamond is in the presence of radioactive minerals: uranium oxide, molybdenum, radon. You know, they get all hot and compressed in a kimberlite pipe, all that stuff,' he said dismissively, assuming Alex knew the basics of diamond formation.

'Hmm,' Alex murmured with genuine interest, continuing to peer at the stone.

'OK,' Kalil held up the two rings and turned to the manageress. 'What's the price comparison between them?'

'OK, well, this stone is—'

'It's a one-carat stone, ya?'

'Yes, they are both one-carat stones. The value of this white diamond is eleven thousand.'

'Dollars?'

'Sterling.'

'And the green diamond?' Kalil held it up in anticipation of the punchline.

'The value of this diamond is one hundred and fifty thousand pounds.'

'You see . . .' Kalil nodded and looked at Alex with a smug grin on his face.

'OK, so we're talking about a . . .' Alex paused to do the maths, '. . . a fourteen times price differential.'

Kalil nodded again in satisfaction at having made his point.

'OK. Thank you, ma'am.' He handed the stones back to her. 'We're just looking around at the moment.'

He gave her his most charming smile and led the way out of the hotel and onto the darkened street.

They stood under a streetlamp.

'Ya, OK, so apologies about that. Got a little overexcited.' Again the quick grin flashed. 'But the point *for us* is this.' He leaned towards Alex. 'The field we're gonna capture in Central African Republic produces *green* diamonds.'

11 P.M., THURSDAY 6 NOVEMBER, CENTRAL AFRICAN REPUBLIC

The man sat alone in the room watching the silent black-and-white film flicker awkwardly on the screen. The pictures jumped sometimes, the camerawork was amateur. The room was quiet but for the soft whirr of the projector and the whine of mosquitoes drifting through its beam.

The camera panned over a long table on a terrace; soldiers slouched around it on chairs. SS double lightning-flash tabs showed on their collars. The table was covered in the casual debris of a good lunch: messy plates, bowls of couscous, tagines, grapes and bottles of wine. The men were smoking. As the camera went closer and interrupted their conversations they smiled and waved good-naturedly.

The shot swung round to a tall man with blond hair, scraped down in a severe short back and sides. He was leaning back on a railing in front of a view—Tripoli harbour. The man in the room recognised it.

The soldier wore the field-grey tunic and insignia of a major in the Waffen SS. His tunic buttons were undone and he held a cigarette in an

26

off-hand way. He had the commanding but relaxed air of natural authority as he talked to the camera. Standing next to him was a pretty, petite woman in a tight-fitting, floral print dress. She had black hair pinned up in a 1940s fashion and was listening attentively to what he was saying, her eyes sparkling.

The officer began pointing out sights in the harbour. The camera swung awkwardly back and forth between him and the ships in the bay. He blew smoke out of the side of his mouth, said something, grinned cheekily at the camera and then looked quickly at her.

Handsome bastard.

The woman clapped her hands delightedly and flashed a black-eyed smile at the lens.

She was a looker as well.

Her gesture was all the more powerful for its complete lack of affectation. She was beautiful but modest with it. She kept her eyes lowered and the laugh only broke out when the girlish exuberance of her nature could no longer be contained.

The film continued with the woman listening to everything the major said and he touched her arm affectionately once. Eventually the film ran out and the scene cut off abruptly.

The man behind the projector continued to stare at the bright white square on the screen. His heart far away, his eyes filled with angry tears.

AUGUST 1522, STELTZENBERG, SOUTHWEST GERMANY

Eberhardt von Steltzenberg lay asleep on his four-poster bed in the tower of his castle, his barrel chest exposed. The canopy over the bed was worn and moth-eaten, full of dust and dead flies.

It was a hot night; a mass of cloud brooded over the single main tower of his cramped castle in the forest. It blotted out the moon and stars, pouring a thick darkness over the land. His bedchamber took up the whole of the first floor of the tower. The heavy old ceiling beams were hung with cobwebs. His accoutrements littered the room: a suit of armour, his lance, saddles, his chests of clothes.

On one side of the room was the trap door that led down to the great hall where his manservant and his ten hunting dogs slept; their excreta mixed with the rushes on the floor. The hot stench of it rose up through the gaps in the floorboards.

The tower was packed with heat. There had been clear summer skies for the last few weeks; the dark red sandstone had been baked like a kiln during the day and now emanated warmth. The main door was barred shut and no breeze could stir through the five thin arrow slits that punctured the walls of the knight's chamber. A heavy weight pressed on the air in the room.

The figure on the bed breathed in slowly, his eyes fluttering in deep sleep, and then stopped.

Dreaming furiously, Eberhardt saw a black spot appear in his heart.

He could see it against the deep red in his chest.

It grew slowly.

He watched it.

What was it?

It was getting larger and heavier. He could feel the weight of it beginning to strain the fibres in his chest, like heartburn. It was hard and jet black, cutting into his soft tissues.

The Nubian Deathstone had returned.

He knew it.

What was it doing there? Why had it come back to him now after twenty-one years?

Blackness swirled out of it like a mist and began branching out along the blood vessels in his heart. The tendrils were reaching across his chest like black ivy.

Confusion at first but fear coming now.

He could feel the strength of the strands clutching at him, squeezing him. He could not breathe. Terror built, pouring through his veins.

'I can't breathe!' he screamed.

The figure on the bed twitched and convulsed. It groaned and scrabbled at its chest with both hands.

His eyes flew open.

Now he could see it properly! He could see the Deathstone and the black miasma that was choking him. It was the smoke from the stone all over again—the cloud of it was now moving in and out of his body at will.

In the darkness he saw it clearly. The rock pressed down on him, forcing him deeper into the mattress. He struggled desperately against it, thrashing his arms and legs. He was a being of fear fighting a being of darkness.

A mighty effort and he was on his feet.

29

The darkness was all over him, both within and without, coiling around his body and weighing him down. The stone hung down inside him, the darkness wriggling through his blood vessels, penetrating out through his ears and his eyes, choking his throat. He had to escape it, he had to breathe!

He lurched across the room, blundered into a chest and fell onto his knees.

It had him on his knees now; he had to fight back.

He forced himself through the pain and straightened his legs. There in front of him was an arrow slit. He could sense the clean air outside. He could tear the slit open and escape the foulness that was forcing itself down his throat. His fingers gripped the thin stone edge of the slit where it narrowed in through the thick walls.

He tore at it with all his might. His huge shoulders knotted, the tendons tensed and sweat stood out on his skin.

It did not move. The stone blocks were ancient but well laid.

'The Deathstone is conspiring against me. It has seeped into the stones here.'

He lurched around the edge of the room, supporting himself with one arm against the wall. His fingers found the next arrow slit and he heaved on that. Again it stayed resolute.

'No!'

The figure blundered round the circular room, pawing at the wall and then tearing at the arrow slits. His fingers were torn and bleeding.

Five times he heaved and five times he failed. Finally he sank to his knees, wheezing for breath and clutching at his throat.

Above him the thunderheads were grinding against each other in the sky. Dark winds swirled around the tower. Lightning flashed, and then came an explosion of thunder that banged the room like a drum and shook the floorboards against his knees. The hunting dogs in the hall below started up, baying and howling.

The rain came in like a wave. It crashed against the stone, gushed off the guttering and spattered down the walls.

'The sky. I can reach the sky.'

He lurched to his feet again and blundered up the crude wooden steps that led to the trap door in the ceiling. Scrambling up them on his hands and knees, he hit the trap door with his shoulder and flung it open. It banged back against the floorboards and terrified the old woman, his grandmother, who lived in the upper chamber. She shrieked from behind her bed curtains. Seizing her horsewhip, she threw them open and flew across the room in her nightgown, a white-clad banshee shouting obscenities and flailing at him with the whip.

'A plague on you, you dog! Coming into a lady's chamber!'

The new onslaught combined with the coiling darkness that still squeezed him. He ran from her and charged up the final steps to the roof. Flinging the next trap door open, he at last emerged into the air.

It was hot and thrashing down with rain. He was soaked instantly. He ran to the edge of the tower and leaned over a gap in the battlements, seventy feet up, whooping in air. The pressure in his chest began to ease.

The old woman caught up with him and laid the whip squarely across his back. He jerked with the pain, turned round and caught the whip. Anger at his oppressor filled him now that it had taken human form; at last he could fight back.

Strength flowed into his limbs; he seized the creature by the throat and lifted it off the ground. He grabbed one of its legs with the other hand, held it above his head.

A huge curtain of sheet lightning lit up the sky. The figure standing high up on the battlements was momentarily silhouetted against it.

It held the oppressor over its head for a second and then cast it down, down into the darkness.

SEPTEMBER 1522, PFÄLZERWALD FOREST, CENTRAL GERMANY

Eberhardt gently slit the soft white flesh on the inside of his forearm with his knife.

He clenched his fist and let the bright red blood run out and drip off his elbow. He aimed the drops so that they splashed richly on a patch of earth on the roadside.

'Sir!' Albrecht, his steward, shouted in alarm and tried to restrain him.

Eberhardt was enraged. 'You swine!' he bellowed, and angrily brushed the smaller man away. 'Our blood cannot be separated from the soil that bore us! It will return! It will return again!'

He continued dripping blood, whilst he muttered through gritted teeth, 'Blood and soil, blood and soil, we will become one again,' like an incantation.

His hands held out, Albrecht wailed helplessly, 'Sir, what are you *doing*?' He screwed his eyes up and looked away.

'I am a blood sacrifice for the German nation!' Spittle flecked Eberhardt's beard as he shouted through the pain. 'I will become an oblation poured onto the soil. The soil that raised us, that has cradled us since our inception. Our father, our mother . . . our land!'

It was mid-morning, three days after the tragedy on the tower. Eberhardt was not sure what had happened to his grandmother. Her broken body had been discovered the next morning, cold and wet in the mud: did she jump or had he thrown her? He was unsure if he had experienced a dream or a spiritual visitation. Either way, his brush with the Deathstone had unsettled him. Why had it returned to him? What mission was it calling him to?

Albrecht had put it about in the village that his master's grandmother had taken fright at the thunder and leaped to her death, and few had enquired further. He was a middle-aged, worrisome character who peered out suspiciously at the world from under a thatch of brown hair.

In contrast, his master was a big man in his forties, an old roué whose appetites had overrun his frame; his gut bulged out over his hose. He had a mane of silvery hair, with a heavy beard cut off square just under his chin. His eyes were rheumy and the skin of his face sagged like the canvas of an old tent.

Eberhardt was a *Raubritter*—a Robber Knight—

33

although he preferred just to call himself a knight. He was from an ancient German family, but was really a bandit in charge of a cramped castle, a village and a few square miles of the Pfälzerwald.

The imminent Knights' War against the Imperial Princes had revived some of his youthful passion.

He shouted at Albrecht, cowering in front of him, 'The Pope and the Princes are ransacking the German people! The Emperor has banned our right of feud! The Knights won't stand for it. The German people won't stand for it!'

'Yes, but—'

'The good Dr Luther has raised the clarion call against the papists—Rome is leeching this country dry! We Knights will ride against the Princes. The time for sacrifice has come, Albrecht!'

They were two days' ride from home in a shady spot in the forest, on the way south towards Landau, where the Knights were rallying. Eberhardt had spontaneously made his blood gesture on a break in their journey, having brooded on their mission as they rode along that morning.

'Things can't go on as they are.'

With this statement of fact he calmed down at last and stopped clenching his fist. He held his arm out to Albrecht.

'Bind it up.'

Albrecht rummaged in the saddlebags of his horse for some spare cloth. He walked back over to Eberhardt and began binding his forearm. He was a simple man who focused on practical arrangements and left matters of national politics and religion to his lord. He was not even sure what Eberhardt meant by the concept of 'the

German people'. The Holy Roman Empire covered the area and was composed of hundreds of states run by Princes, and imperial free cities. Such ideas were beyond him.

The Knights had been able to hold their lands in this strange hotchpotch for centuries because they had the legal right from the Holy Roman Emperor to conduct armed feuds. This was supposed to allow the chivalrous art of war to be practised but was now just an excuse for murder and racketeering.

The new Emperor, Charles V, had tired of such anarchy and triggered the Knights' War by banning their right of feud. The Knights had been declining for centuries and saw this as their last-ditch attempt to hold on to what little status they had left.

'We'll teach them a lesson,' Eberhardt mused as he watched Albrecht tie off the white cloth.

'There you go.' His servant looked at his neat handiwork with satisfaction. Although he was used to his master's outlandish manner, he was relieved that Eberhardt had calmed down.

He had known Eberhardt since he was a boy and he had always been a romantic. As a student at Heidelberg University he was an enthusiastic Renaissance man: a knight but a scholar as well, one who had joined the German intellectual revival that was shedding light into the Dark Ages. He was so inspired by the new thinkers that he'd begun writing his own *magnum opus* entitled *The Quest for Glory*, and had developed his own motto, *Lumensfero*!

However, these lofty ideas had been undermined when he was caught in bed with a professor's wife. He had to flee, and travelled south where he fell in with a company of *Landsknecht*, German mercenaries, heading down to the Italian Wars, where he proved to be a brave soldier.

He journeyed on to Constantinople and fell in love with its exoticism. People of all creeds and cultures passed in front of him in a kaleidoscope of colours, languages and scents.

He felt preternaturally alive. His skin was taut; he could sense his body pushing against it, straining to take in all the new experiences. It was a wild, mad, beautiful time.

With sensations such as these it was no wonder that he had been writing like a fury. Every spare minute he had, he would sit and transcribe his adventures. He accumulated so many books that he had to bundle them up and send them back to Ludwig Fritzler, an old university friend working in the Heidelberg library.

When he thought back to those times, Eberhardt often wondered what had happened to Abba Athanasius, the Nubian mystic who led the Ishfaqi cult. He was such an odd mixture of religions. 'Abba' meant Father in Aramaic and 'Athanasius' meant immortal in Greek—both came from his background as a Coptic Christian priest. But he had then formed a cult that mixed elements of Islam and Christianity with animism, the worship of spirits. In this case the spirit was inside a large piece of black rock found in the heart of an extinct volcano in central Africa: the Deathstone.

The strange priest was the biggest human being that Eberhardt had ever seen, as forbidding and impenetrable as the Deathstone itself. With his bald head and black flowing robes he had a charisma as powerful and brooding as the volcano that the Stone came from.

He preached that the mountain was the new Mount Sinai and that it held the keys to the gates of death. The people there feared the Stone; those who had worked in mining it had all died of strange diseases.

Eberhardt was enthralled by the cult and took part enthusiastically in its ceremonies. In the Deathstone he was sure that he had discovered the nexus between life and death; an object that had true meaning.

The German had become a trusted follower of Abba Athanasius, with Latin their common language. His curiosity led him to ask the monk for the whereabouts of the holy mountain. Eventually he was given the task of organising an expedition to find the origins of the Stone.

He had set about planning avidly, obtaining directions from the monk and Arab traders that went into the area. Using rivers to mark out his route, he sketched a map along the Nile through the deserts of Egypt and Sudan and then southwest, cutting down right into the heart of the Dark Continent.

It was all planned out and he was getting ready to set off on his new odyssey when he received a letter from his mother. His father had died and he was summoned to return immediately to inherit his estate before other greedy relatives tried to claim it.

It was a bitter blow; his heart had been set on the journey. In a daze he had walked into Abba Athanasius' bare cell, clutching the letter, and with great sadness explained that he had to go home.

Eberhardt stared longingly at the sketch map he

had drawn before folding it up and tucking it into his journal. Then he took a last look into the heart of the Nubian Deathstone, bade farewell to its mighty keeper and left.

But the Stone remained lodged deep inside him.

Eberhardt had gone back to be lord of his little patch of backwoods Germany. He had donated the remaining notebooks of *The Quest for Glory* to Ludwig and the library, and then for the past twenty years he had lived the life of a country squire in a damp and crowded castle, forced to stay put to retain his inheritance whilst going quietly mad, dreaming of foreign lands and the freedom of his youth.

Now though, the thrill of the campaign was beginning to awaken him once more as he mounted up and rode on south through the woods.

He could feel his skin tightening, his pulse quickening. The Deathstone was calling him for its purpose; he did not know what it was but he spurred his horse on to the coming war.

PRESENT DAY, 17 NOVEMBER, LONDON

'OK, so here's the plan for our war.'

Kalil stepped up to the projector screen and circled an area on the satellite image with his finger. Today he looked even more of a playboy than he had before. His black hair was neatly coiffured and he wore a pearlescent white shirt, designer jeans and expensive loafers.

'This is the target area for the attack. The extinct volcano where they actually do the mining is here;

the blue circle is the caldera lake in the crater.'

He smiled excitedly as he turned back to face Alex and Colin—'Col'—Thwaites, a former sergeant-major from the Parachute Regiment, who were sitting on chairs in the plain meeting room. They watched him attentively, notepads on their knees. Kalil had provided a small rented mews office in Mayfair for them to work from. He apparently lived five minutes' walk away but still drove to work and parked his silver Porsche Carrera in the basement garage.

'This shot covers a four-hundred-square-mile area and as you can see there isn't exactly a lot going on in the neighbourhood.'

Apart from some rivers, the lake was the only thing that broke the green carpet of jungle that filled the rest of the picture; the sharp cone of the volcano stood out from the flat terrain by its shadow.

'OK, so if we zero in on this you can see some more detail of the actual buildings.' Kalil clicked the remote and the image zoomed in.

'These are very good shots.' Alex nodded appreciatively. 'Where did you get them from?'

The remark was well meant but Kalil reacted uncomfortably. 'The cartel has ... connections.' He looked evasive and turned back to the screen.

Alex had not meant to be intrusive; he was just grateful to be back in work and was trying to show willing. He was in a much better mood than he had been lately. His restless mind needed to be constantly engaged, and sitting around at home fretting about bills had been driving him mad. With his first two months' pay in advance in his bank account, and the promise of a lot more to come, he had been able to arrange for some builders to do the roof. Lavinia, his neighbour, was speaking to him again and had called off her lawyers.

However, he had also had a call from the bailiffs in Herefordshire saying that his father would be evicted in a month if bills for services and debt interest weren't paid. Alex had handed over enough cash to fend them off for a while but he was anxious to get the project completed so that he could pay them in full. Despite everything, he was not going to see his father turned out onto the street and, strangely, now that the responsibility was his, he didn't want to see his ancestral home lost either.

Apart from helping with his domestic problems, the project was also his chance to prove himself; to throw something to the dark wolves of self-doubt that had been biting him for so long. I can't be a failure if I am responsible for all this? he thought.

It was the biggest thing he had been called on to organise—his own private army. Finally, his own independent command, the chance that had been denied him by the army. He furrowed his dark brows and concentrated on what Kalil was saying.

'So, the mining goes on up here in the volcano. They have also built a little hydroelectric plant here, in this break in the crater wall, where the lake overflows. Smart way of getting power. The mine seems to be a pretty primitive setup, though: just shafts dug into the side of the crater by hand. We assume they must be using slave labour from somewhere as there is almost no local population in the immediate area apart from some Pygmies.

'The ore from the mine gets dumped into a system of chutes down the side of the volcano

40

here.' Kalil traced a blurry line cut through the dense jungle on the mountainside. 'Alongside them there seem to be ladders that they use to get the slaves up and down the slope. They then truck the ore along the road about a mile west to this complex here on the flat ground. This will be the actual focus for the attack.'

The photo showed a collection of buildings on the south shore of a small lake, which was fed by the stream flowing from the hydroelectric plant.

'We're not quite sure what all these buildings are—probably barracks for the slaves and soldiers.' Kalil pointed to a series of evenly spaced long buildings. 'There are two key areas for the assault—this factory structure here is where the power line comes in from the volcano plant and is presumably where the ore refining goes on.' He turned back to face the two soldiers and raised an index finger for emphasis. 'It is *essential* that this is seized *intact* at the first opportunity.'

Alex and Col nodded and noted this on their pads.

'The second focus of the assault must be on these houses along the lake shore, where we guess the command and control element live.' Kalil paused. Then:

'I must emphasise to you that the cartel requires that you neutralise this command and control element *permanently*.' He looked at Alex for a long moment.

Alex looked him straight in the eye and then nodded.

There was no point in being squeamish about it; killing people was his job. What else did he expect if he agreed to start an illegal private war?

41

Alex stood up and tapped the map with his Biro. 'It's got to be a helicopter assault.' He stepped back and crossed his arms. The three of them looked at the detailed satellite photograph.

'Hmm, I don't fancy dropping into that lot with a parachute.' Col pointed at the dense jungle foliage around the mine. 'Might catch me bollocks on a palm tree.'

Col Thwaites was in his mid-forties and had been working with Alex through all his operations in Africa. Sharp, tough and a stickler for military professionalism, he was the mainstay of the group of freelancers that Alex was currently assembling for the job.

Like many Paras he was short, stocky and wiry; aggressive energy making up for what he lacked in size. He was balding on top, with close-cropped grey hair, a coarse-boned face with gimlet eyes, and a small moustache. Tattoos of Blackburn Rovers on his right forearm and the Parachute Regiment badge on his left completed the picture of a Northern hard man. Wry comments and an endless stream of poor-taste jokes were delivered in a harsh Lancashire accent.

He had been born on a council estate in Blackburn with a restless natural intellect that failed to achieve anything at school. Drifting into a life of glue-sniffing and petty crime, he had signed up for 2 Para with a mate one day because they had been watching *The Professionals* the night before and knew that the lead hard man, whom they worshipped, was a TA Para.

As with many wastrels before him, the strictures of army discipline had provided the channel to focus his energies. He had fought in Northern

Ireland, the First Gulf War and Bosnia. He had risen to be a sergeant-major in the Pathfinders, the Para's élite reconnaissance unit, and done stints all over the world, training and advising Special Forces.

Alex and Col had been through a lot of combat together in Africa. Ordinarily toff officers from posh cavalry regiments were not respected by hardened Paras; 'Ruperts' was the standard dismissive name they used for them.

However, Col had grown to respect Alex as an intelligent and focused commander. He realised that he had some personal demons, whatever they were—and Col had never asked—but they never got in the way of his work. Rather they were controlled by his upper-class English reserve, so that they fulminated under his black brows only emerging through his vigour and intense looks.

The Lebanese turned to Alex now. 'You think helicopters would work?'

The tall major nodded. 'Hmm, we'll probably need about a hundred men altogether. Insert them here, here and here.' He pointed to landing sites around the complex.

He looked at Col, who stood next to him with his arms folded, staring hard at the photo.

'Aye, it's double all right. Yeah, get some Mi-17s, twenty-two blokes in each, say...' he cocked his head on one side, '...five? Bit of an air force but...' he shrugged.

Kalil turned to Alex. 'Whatever you think is necessary to get the job done, Alex—the cartel will pay for it. We just want that mine.'

'Hmm,' Alex nodded thoughtfully. 'We'll need a gunship as well to suppress ground fire when the troops land.'

'I've heard there's a Shark going in Transdneister,' said Col chirpily.

'A what?' Kalil frowned.

'A Kamov Ka-50 Black Shark—NATO codename Hokum. Fooking beast of a thing: 30mm cannon, rocket pods, automatic grenade launcher, you name it—it's got it. Evil-looking, an' all. It's got two contra-rotating main rotors on top of each other so it don't need a tail rotor.' Col made excited twisting actions with one hand over the other. 'Russian Army uses 'em. Heard about it from Arkady—a mate of ours what works for a Russian transport outfit. The Fourteenth Army Group in Transdneister . . .'

Kalil had obviously lost him here so Col broke off, realising that the enclave was not well known outside the mercenary community. 'It's a little strip of land on the border between Ukraine and Moldova—the Russkies have been there since some dodgy deal that Yeltsin did, and sort of run the area as a criminal country, like. They don't get paid much so the general keeps "losing" kit.' He wagged his fingers to indicate the irony.

'Anyway, Arkady reckons he could get it for one and a half mil US, plus parts and ammo—fooking bargain. He ships stuff out of there the whole time to Africa in them big Ilyushins—no questions asked. They'd sell their granny for a pack a fags, they would.'

'OK, sounds good.' Kalil nodded uncertainly; he could only understand half of the words in the heavy Lancashire accent, and his American English meant he was confused by the expression 'pack a fags'. However, at the same time he was impressed

44

by the detail.

'Yeah, you'll have to come shopping with us there sometime. It's sorta like a military Dubai really,' said Col enthusiastically.

Kalil laughed nervously.

Alex chipped in, 'Pretty much all the kit we'll use is Russian.'

'How so?' Kalil asked.

'Because it's cheap, it's robust and it kills people. It's the standard equipment used in Africa, so we won't need to train the soldiers to use it. But we're going to need to do a CTR first,' he continued, before they got too carried away; he knew it was not going to be that simple.

'A what?'

'A close target recce, mate,' Col filled in for the Lebanese's lack of British Army jargon. 'That means me and 'im doing the sneaky-beaky bit on foot round the mine.' He made wiggly motions with one hand to indicate creeping about. 'You know, like carrying our own shit and not farting for a week in case we make a noise. Fooking love that, me.'

Kalil looked at him confused; he didn't get the standard-issue British Army sarcasm either. 'Erm . . .'

'We'll have to do it.' Alex folded his arms authoritatively. 'There's no way we can stake this much on some maps and satellite shots.'

'Well, they're pretty good, aren't they? It took a lotta trouble to get them for you guys, you know.'

'I'm sure it did, but success in these operations is all in the detail. I mean, what's this?' He traced a blurry line around the edge of the complex with his finger.

'Perimeter fence?'

'Yes, but is that all? There's a large cleared area either side of it that could contain a lot of nasties. There are also these checkpoints on the approach roads and these little covered huts dotted around the perimeter; we don't know what's under the cover. I'm not going to risk this many blokes on it; we're going a hell of a long way from anywhere safe and if we mess up we're all dead.' He paused. 'Plus you said *you* wanted to come on the op,' he smiled.

'OK, OK. You're the experts; I've never been to Africa. You do the C-whatever,' Kalil smiled and capitulated. 'Just don't get fucking caught! I don't think they like visitors.'

He picked up the projector remote control again. 'Right, so that's the target set up then. Let me just take you through some of the background on Central African Republic.'

The other two sat down and resumed taking notes. Kalil clicked up a map of the country and its neighbours on the screen.

'OK, so as you can see the country at the heart of Africa is roughly triangular, with the Democratic Republic of Congo running along its base here, the Ubangi River forms much of that border,' he traced it with his finger, 'Sudan up here to the northeast, and Chad over there to the northwest. We're going to be here in the southeast bit in Mbomou Province.

'Now, as I am sure you are aware, like a lot of failed states, CAR is not so much a country as a platform for criminal activity. It is *completely* wrong to apply the idea of a nation state to it because the central government has virtually no control outside the capital and a few of the main

46

towns. The rest of the country is controlled by rebel groups, criminal gangs and tribal militias.'

He looked down at his notepad to check his facts.

'So, in the shitty country stakes CAR is right up there with the best of them: the IMF ranks it a hundred and sixty-eighth poorest in the world, out of a hundred and seventy-five. A lot of that is due to there being either civil war and no government, or peace and a government that steals everything.' He shrugged at the irony. 'Total population of about three million and a lot of them are around the capital, Bangui, giving the country a very low overall population density. To put that in context for you Brits; it's five times the size of England but with fourteen times fewer people living in it.'

'So basically, what yer saying is that it's a whole lot of fook all,' said Col, scratching his jaw thoughtfully.

'I guess that's right.'

Col wrote something down on his pad.

Alex kept his face straight but winced internally. He valued Col for his direct nature but he wished he wouldn't let it rip during their client's introductory briefing.

Kalil got going again.

'The terrain is mainly flat with semi-desert in the north, then savannah and finally dense rainforest in the Ubangi River basin in the south. That's us,' again he smiled at his audience, 'nice and hot and humid.

'Economy is nearly all subsistence farming although it does have a lotta diamonds, gold, uranium, and other minerals, but these are largely unexploited because transport links are so poor . . .

47

apart from our friends here.' He tapped the area of the map where the mine was.

'And finally, some relevant recent history: French Equatorial Africa got its independence in 1958 and then there was the usual story of one crappy dictator replacing another, although,' he held up an index finger to mark the point, 'from 1965 to 1976 they did succeed in having one of the more entertaining guys—Emperor Bokassa—saw himself as an African Napoleon—spent twenty-two million dollars on his coronation, including twenty-four thousand bottles of champagne.' He raised his eyebrows. 'Some party.

'Eventually, even the French got pissed with him and pulled their troops out, so he turned to Colonel Gaddafi for money and military training— the Libyans themselves were after his uranium deposits.

'After Bokassa was overthrown there was a long civil war with heavy fighting, diseases and banditry spreading across the country. Troops from Libya, Chad and rebel groups from the Congo all got involved. Ended up with General Bozize toppling Ange Patassé and declaring himself President,' he shut his notebook decisively, 'of what was left.'

Alex leaned back in his chair and looked at Kalil. 'So, what you're saying is it's a bloody mess?'

Kalil was suddenly ashamed of his flippancy. He nodded. 'Ya . . . it's a mess. OK, that's enough to start planning the campaign on. Let's take a break there.'

The other two nodded. Col needed a cigarette and Kalil had declared the office no smoking. Alex didn't smoke but wanted a chat with him so they went out into the narrow mews.

'Col, can I just have a quick word?' Alex asked as they moved away from the office to confer. 'There's something Kalil said that's bothering me.' He looked at the short sergeant quizzically. 'If he's running diamonds out of Africa for his job, how come he's never been there?'

17 NOVEMBER, MBOMOU PROVINCE, CENTRAL AFRICAN REPUBLIC

There is no more mournful scene than the aftermath of a fire.

The morning air was still. Wisps of smoke twisted up into it from the ashes of the torched village. Everything was burned black and white: the stumps of the hut walls, the kapok tree in the centre, the men and women who had resisted the attack the night before.

Colonel Ninja looked at the burned-out village but was no longer capable of feeling anything for it. He took a slow drag on his cigarette; the sound of a child crying was coming from somewhere nearby; there was a burst of machine-gun fire and it stopped.

His real name was André Kakodamba but that belonged to a person who was no longer alive. He was eighteen now but André had died aged ten when his home village in Congo had been raided by MLC militia. They took away all the children and brutalised them into soldiers; forced to mutilate and murder; each action a blow falling on his soul until it was numbed and his eyes frozen into blocks of ice.

He had killed his own soul. Now all he knew was how to force others to do the same. He had learned that fear was the key to life: fear of being hungry, beaten or shot. Gradually he had learned that it was best to *be* feared—fear gave you first pick of the food, the drink, the drugs and the girls. Fear was now his friend—the more the better.

He cultivated it in the gang he led: the Muti Boys.

Muti: *La Science Africaine*, Black Magic. His child soldiers were captured on raids like this and forced to murder their relatives to make them complicit in the gang. They dreamed that in their sleep they would travel to a demi-world to kill and eat human flesh. Awake they were not much better.

He shouted in Sango at a boy dawdling under a tree smoking a joint. 'Hey, hurry up! Get in the ute!' and pointed him over to the Toyota that was waiting to drive out of the village ahead of the truck with the prisoners.

The boy was sixteen and dressed in combat trousers, dirty white singlet, round mirror shades and a woman's curly blonde wig. Muti charms and amulets hung around his neck—Colonel Ninja had told him that the bullets of their enemies would flow off them like water. Ammunition belts for his light machine gun were wrapped around him. He hefted the gun on its sling and stumped over to join his eight friends in the back of the truck. Its windscreen was shattered by three bullet holes and the bonnet had a collection of filthy teddy bears strapped to it as charms.

The boys sat in the back with their legs sticking out over the side, displaying a collection of bare

50

feet and flip-flops; they bristled with RPGs and AK-47s. Tired after their night of destruction and slaughter, they slumped against each other and passed round a plastic bottle of home brew.

Colonel Ninja was tall and heavily muscled; he deliberately fought stripped to the waist to show off his physique to the younger boys. As he slung his PKM machine gun over his shoulder the veins stood out on his biceps. He flicked his cigarette away, scratched his head and walked over to the blue truck behind the Toyota.

It was a battered container lorry specially adapted for its new job with the addition of airholes shot through the sides. They didn't want anyone suffocating on the way back home. The Boss had said that they needed more labourers; for some reason they kept dying in the mine; coughing up blood and wasting away.

'They all in?' he asked the boy standing at the open rear doors, pointing his rifle at the prisoners inside; the terrified faces of the men and women stared at him out of the dark.

The boy nodded.

'*Bon, allez!*' Colonel Ninja swung the heavy door shut in their faces and locked it.

SATURDAY 22 NOVEMBER

Here we go again, Alex thought as the plane swept in over the rusty iron roofs and palm trees of the shantytown around the Aéroport de Bangui-M'poko in the capital of Central African Republic.

It was midday and as soon as the door opened,

51

hot African air swept into the cabin like a slick of warm oil. By the time their Air France flight from Paris had disembarked and they had walked over the burning tarmac to the arrivals shed, Alex's shirt was plastered to him with sweat.

The 1960s terminal was dilapidated and filthy. Windows were broken and chewed sugarcanes, nut husks and litter were piled in corners. The noise from the press of people battered him. The air was thick with the strong smell of body odour.

When he got to the customs desk the uniformed officer looked at him with the quiet stare of a hyena eyeing a gazelle on the savannah.

He tapped the table in front of him with the end of his large truncheon and Alex dutifully dumped his rucksack down. He glanced across to where Col was getting the same treatment at another desk.

Welcome to Africa, he thought, as his baggage was unpacked and items of interest removed. The new MP3 player and bottle of whisky that he had deliberately placed at the top disappeared behind the desk; then Alex accidentally dropped a fifty-dollar bill out of his breast pocket and was through.

'How'd ya get on?' said Col as they met up on the other side of customs.

'Didn't get anything we need.' The important kit for the mission was buried at the bottom of their bags.

They scanned the brightly dressed scrum of Africans milling around them.

'Bienvenue à Bangui, Monsieur Devereux.'

A large black face with three tribal scars cut down each cheek emerged out of the throng. A gigantic hand extended and gave him a soft handshake. *'Je m'appelle Patrice Bagaza.'*

A huge man with an understated manner, as if he was embarrassed by his size, he averted his eyes as he shook Alex's hand. He was wearing a long red and green print shirt, jeans and flip-flops.

'Bonjour,' said Alex carefully.

'Monsieur 'Waites.' Patrice didn't attempt to pronounce the 'Th' at the start of his name and shook Col's hand as well. He then turned and shouted in Sango to make a path through the crowd.

Patrice's bulk forced a way and the two men followed in his wake, loaded down with rucksacks. Their visa said they were here to go big-game hunting and they were dressed in lightweight outdoor gear: boots, walking trousers, slouch hats and tan waistcoats with lots of pockets.

Once they were through the chaos of the terminal, Patrice led them across the road to an old yellow Peugeot estate in the car park.

They stashed their bags in the back with the equipment that Patrice had assembled for them. As he shut the boot he turned to Alex and smiled. 'Don't worry, Mr Devereux, I'm not going to make you speak French the whole way. That was just for the plainclothes security police in the crowd; they take an interest in whites coming in.'

Alex was caught off guard by the switch to American-accented English. Kalil had said they would be met by the cartel's contact but Alex had not been sure what language they would be speaking. Besides, his French was passable from previous ops in Congo.

'That's fine,' he smiled, conscious that he was reliant for now on this man.

They drove into town but Patrice didn't seem to want to talk; he concentrated on steering them through the manic traffic. Old Peugeots, Renaults and Citroëns wheezed and limped alongside newer Toyotas and Mitsubishis. Trucks and buses were piled up with people and goods, and slouched on their axles; driven at top speed, they swerved around the worst potholes. Patrice was unfazed by it all, and weaved through them on the wide Avenue de l'Indépendance.

Alex and Col opened the windows to try to get a cool breeze but it was like having a hair dryer turned on your face. They looked out at the town; it had the rundown appearance of somewhere that had been taking a battering since its heyday in the 1960s. Most of the houses and buildings dated from then; their peeling whitewash was stained brown with red dust from the earth verges and were pockmarked by bullet holes. All the houses were heavily fortified against the outbreaks of rioting and looting over the years, with crude bars welded over windows and doors. Rubbish was strewn everywhere: plastic bags, newspapers, wrappers and cola nut skins. Sitting on beer crates at the roadside were 'Gaddafis'—youths selling stolen petrol from large jars; named after the oil-rich Libyan president, who had interfered in the country so often.

Driving through the centre, they circled the main traffic island. Alex saw it was covered with the distinctive spiky leaves of cassava plants; it had been turned into vegetable plots by civil servants used to being unpaid for months.

They headed out of town on Boulevard de Général de Gaulle, along the north bank of the

Ubangi River. Alex looked out across it; it was over a mile wide, a great brown snake coiling through the heart of Africa.

Patrice drove them out east into the bush. The buildings gave way to vegetable patches and then the jungle began to take over. Dirt replaced tarmac, and they bumped past the mud huts of the village of Damara with red dust trailing behind them. A kilometre on and Patrice turned right up a small track to a football pitch surrounded by trees; long grass grew across it and the goal posts sagged at either end.

He parked in the shade out of the fierce sun. The three men got out and began unpacking the kitbags.

'MP5s, as requested, with silencers,' said Patrice, as he handed them machine guns. Both men checked them deftly, before pulling off their civilian kit and putting on camouflaged combat jackets and trousers. Alex prowled off round the field to make sure it was secure whilst Col went through the compasses, radios and homing beacons.

Patrice sat and smoked a Gauloise. When Col was satisfied that the kit was in order he sat with his back against a tree and read a biography of CAR's former ruler, Emperor Bokassa, called *Dark Age*. Alex waited in the car with his long legs stretched out of the door and read through his maps and notes for the mission.

The hundred-degree heat sat heavily on the field. Nothing had the energy to make a sound. An hour passed and the men waited; Alex occasionally looked up at the sky and checked his watch.

When the distant noise of the helicopter broke

the stillness he flicked his eyes at Col. They picked their kit up and readied themselves. Patrice grabbed his holdall out of the boot, then pulled a jerry can out and shook petrol over the inside of the car.

The camouflage-painted Mi-17 roared in; treetops thrashing in its wake. Alex never got over the shock of seeing such a huge, ungainly object hanging in midair, as if a bus were hanging over his head. Sunlight flashed off the cockpit windows as the pilot swung it round into the centre of the field and flared to hover two feet off the ground. Alex glimpsed Arkady Voloshin at the controls, cigarette clamped in the corner of his mouth as ever; his eyes narrowed as he scanned the tree line.

The door in the side was open; Yamba Douala crouched in combat gear with a 7.62mm machine gun poking out of the door in case they needed cover.

Grass and dust billowed crazily in the downwash as the two whites ran out through it, hunched under their packs.

Patrice stood back from the Peugeot and flicked his Gauloise into it. The petrol whooshed and then the fuel tank exploded as he ran to join them in the helicopter. Yamba hauled him and his bag inside as the big turbofans lifted them up.

The huge aircraft disappeared east over the trees towards the next phase of the operation.

14 JANUARY 1525, NEUHOF FOREST, HESSE, CENTRAL GERMANY

Dark clouds hung threateningly over the snow-covered forest. A shaft of bleak winter light slid in under them, cold as a knife.

Eberhardt shifted the axe in his hand and stared at the figure slipping between the frosted tree trunks. Everything was still around him; all he could hear was his breathing. Each breath pulsed out, froze in the still air and then descended gently. His beard jutted out, thick with frost.

The weight of the axe felt reassuring. He and Albrecht could not see clearly who was coming along the track that merged with theirs up ahead. In such a remote spot as this, bandits and outlaws were his first fear. He could see only one man, but could there be more? Was he a scout for a gang of brigands coming along behind?

It was two years after the Knights' War, and Eberhardt and Albrecht's circumstances had changed greatly.

The war had been a disaster. The Knights' desperate attempt to try to preserve their status in society had merely hastened their demise. The Imperial Princes had united and crushed them in a few short battles. Eberhardt had fled and lived now as a woodcutter to escape the punishment inflicted on his fellows.

The Princes assumed he was dead and, as he'd been a traitor, his castle and lands had been sold off. If they ever found out he was alive, far worse would be visited on him. He and Albrecht travelled around, surviving on day labour: cutting wood and ditching.

The pair of them wore heavy winter clothing: sheepskin jerkins, broad peasant hats and *Bundschuhe*, the peasant boots made of strips of leather bound together with thongs. On their backs were their worldly possessions: bedding rolls, cooking pots, and tools. Albrecht stood nervously behind his master, his cooking knife in hand, unsure what to do. He had stayed despite everything. He had no family in Steltzenberg, and with the seizure of Eberhardt's lands his job was gone as well. His whole life had been one of service and he could not think of any other way. Stoic and dour, he plodded on, focusing on getting his master through one day at a time and trying hard not to think about their problems.

The whole country was in similar dire straits. The growing population led to land shortage so the ordinary folk starved and turned to crime. Riots and attacks on the nobles were common; Germany was in turmoil, hence Eberhardt's fear as the man approached in the wood.

Eberhardt would not have taken this track by choice but he still feared discovery by the Princes. With the climate of fear, checkpoints had been put across the main roads to look for suspicious characters.

He gripped the axe and filled his deep chest with air, summoning his most commanding tones, and bellowed out at the stranger: 'Who are you?'

The bellow echoed through the still woods. It died away and silence hung in the air like the clouds of his breath.

'Thomas the Carpenter, good day to you!' the

man called through the trees, and walked towards Eberhardt and Albrecht. He approached at a steady pace with his hand thrust out in greeting.

Eberhardt was relieved to see that the man looked like a travelling artisan. He was short and slight; wearing undyed woollen hose and a shabby leather coat down to his knees. He had a broad-brimmed felt hat with a grey cloth wrapped round his head against the cold. A satchel was slung over one shoulder with a bedding roll and a cooking pot over the other.

Eberhardt was, without realising it, impressed by the confidence in the strong clear voice and the man's open-handed approach. The hand he shook was small but the grip was sharp.

'Eberhardt the Woodcutter,' he said.

Albrecht could not look him in the eye but muttered, 'Albrecht the Steward,' whilst looking down at the man's hand. He was used to appraising men for work and judging their capabilities. The thin-boned hand had no scars or calluses; it had never plied its trade as a carpenter.

'Good day to you both. A fine day to be out walking across this great German land of ours,' breezed the stranger, waving an arm at a shaft of light catching in the snow-laden treetops.

Eberhardt was puzzled by the man's accent: the cadence was the flattened *Schriftdeutsch* of the educated élite, not some carpenter's burr.

The man also had an intriguing face. He was in his mid-thirties, but seemed much older. His face was thin and pinched with hunger; it looked burned out, with large bags under his eyes that had been drawn down where his cheeks had shrunk in

59

the cold. Yet the eyes themselves showed no signs of exhaustion. Indeed, quite the opposite: his glance was quick, taking everything in, his movements rapid and decisive.

'There is, however,' he continued, 'rather a lot of our German nation.' He indicated the path with an ironic smile and dip of his head. 'It looks like our paths have joined—shall we?' He held a hand out to indicate the road ahead.

'Hmm,' said Eberhardt, realising that there was no alternative and that the three of them would have to walk together for some time. He handed his axe wordlessly to Albrecht, who strapped it onto his pack and shrugged it back onto his shoulders.

They set off down the path. Eberhardt glanced at the stranger as he tried to work out what he was about. Albrecht tagged along behind. The tension of their sudden coming together made them all edgy and they plunged into conversation to relieve the awkwardness.

'So where are you headed for?' Thomas took command of the discussion.

'Leipzig—I have friends there from . . .' Eberhardt was about to say university, but realised that did not fit with his cover story so finished lamely, 'from before . . . The German nation, you said,' he blustered, trying to think of a way off the subject. 'What do you mean by that?'

This was not just a diversion; the subject was of great interest to him. He had been trying to think who could be the new saviour of Germany ever since the Knights had failed.

'Well,' Thomas laughed, 'Dr Luther and his Protestants would have us believe that we are the new nation of God,' he said mockingly, 'rising up to throw out the Whore of Rome!' He laughed again.

'It's not a bad thing to give those Italians a taste of the *Bundschuh*,' muttered Eberhardt.

'No, they haven't made themselves many friends,' agreed Thomas, flicking a quick glance at Eberhardt to gauge his expression.

Albrecht had been walking along behind his master, fearing that his lack of discretion about the Knights would give them away. 'That Luther's bad news,' he muttered.

Thomas chuckled again as if he didn't really understand it all. 'Well, he says he wants to reform the Church, to take it back to its roots.'

'Yes, but he says there's something special about Germans,' continued Eberhardt, immune to his servant's subtleties, 'that God has chosen *us* to reform the Church and bring light into the darkness that has grown up under these popes.'

'And what do *you* think?' asked Thomas. He shot a sideways look at Eberhardt.

Instinctively he knew who the leader of the pair was, despite Albrecht ostensibly outranking him socially. A steward should not have been deferring to a woodcutter. Equally a woodcutter should not be discussing politics. None of the three of them was fitting his story well.

'Well, he's certainly stirred up the whole country,' Albrecht cut across the question, trying to override Eberhardt's tactlessness. 'Stirred 'em up good and proper down south last summer, he did.'

There had been riots, rent strikes and refusals to pay tithes by the peasants in Franconia, and open rebellion had broken out in the Schwarzwald.

'Yes, but that's not *Luther*, is it?' Eberhardt turned round to look at Albrecht scornfully. '*He's* not running round stirring up the peasants, is he? God knows who's been doing that!' He looked at Thomas for support.

'Malefactors!' said Thomas, and laughed. His tone mocked the term used by the authorities in their proclamations issued against the rebels.

Albrecht fell silent in the face of the rebuke from his master. He had tried what he could to keep him from self-incrimination but he seemed hell-bent on it. Albrecht retreated to following on behind the other two.

The track now turned left up the side of the valley and so the conversation slowed down as they leaned into the gradient and took breaths between sentences.

'The peasants are just jumping on his cart. They don't know a bloody thing about his theology, they just think it's an excuse to get rid of their lords,' Eberhardt continued. '...But we're all just buggered as long as the Princes keep running the country. *They're* the real problem! I would challenge any man to disagree, be he big Hans or little Hans.'

'You're no friend of the Princes then?' asked Thomas.

'The Princes betrayed the Knights in their attempt to cleanse the realm of Popish trash! May the Devil shit on them!'

Albrecht groaned inwardly. This was the rant that Eberhardt had brooded on since the war. The steward had heard it often enough, he just wished that the knight would be more careful about who he said it to. The Devil only knew who this man was.

'Only the Knights could have saved Germany . . . but now their cause is lost . . .'

Eberhardt suddenly felt a strange need to confess all. He was big and could put on a show but inside he was a hollow man; Thomas was the more confident.

He stopped and turned to the carpenter. 'I should say that I am not what I appear,' he said hurriedly.

Thomas stared at him patiently as if he had been expecting some revelation.

'I am a knight . . . Eberhardt von Steltzenberg. I fought in the Knights' War. I wanted to serve the German nation—this land.' He repeated Thomas's phrase self-consciously. 'Albrecht was my steward . . . We escaped the Princes and have been wandering ever since . . .'

He dried up as Albrecht stood behind him, aghast.

Thomas stared at the knight for a few seconds and then looked down. He bobbed his head, looked up at Eberhardt and said quietly, 'I too am not what I appear. My name is Dr Thomas Müntzer.'

The name of the infamous rebel crashed into Eberhardt's mind, stunning him.

PRESENT DAY, MONDAY 24 NOVEMBER, MBOMOU PROVINCE, CENTRAL AFRICAN REPUBLIC

'So how are they doing then?'

Yamba pointed to the Blackburn Rovers tattoo on Col's forearm. He had a heavy Angolan accent, with a rising and falling cadence.

'Er . . . not right up there like we were, you know . . . middling, like.'

'Ah, but you are telling me *forever* that they are the *best* team in the world.' Yamba rolled his eyes and chuckled, pleased to get one over on his friend.

Yamba was sitting in the passenger seat of the Land Cruiser and Alex was driving. Col had been leaning forwards in between the seats when Yamba had seen the tattoo on his arm and decided to break the monotony of the journey.

After their uplift, Arkady had flown them east to Gbadolite, just across the border in the Democratic Republic of Congo, where Patrice had arranged a meeting with the local militia group on a crucial part of the plan. They had then flown on to Rafaï, the nearest town to the mine, about a hundred kilometres south of it. Patrice had supplied the car and then waited in the town as the others set off north to complete the recce mission. They could have flown up there but Alex wanted to be careful not to create any disturbances in the vicinity of the mine. He guessed that helicopters were unusual in such a remote area and could set off alarm bells.

They were now thirty kilometres away from the mine but it had taken nearly two days to force their way along the appalling jungle road, a line of rutted red earth that made its way through the tunnel of green vegetation that was trying to overwhelm it. They were not expecting any contact with the mine forces this far out but were in combat gear and had their MP5 machine pistols within easy reach.

'Now, look 'ere, you cheeky booger,' Col wagged his finger at Yamba, 'they're still better than bloody Soweto United, Joburg whatever . . .' He waved his hands, trying to think of an insult.

But Yamba was cackling, rocking over away from him with laughter, his hands clasped together: he had him on another point.

'Ah, but you see, my friend, I am *not* a South African, you know that! I am from *Angola*.'

'Yeah, well, you know, whatever.'

Yamba was a former sergeant-major from 32 Battalion—The Buffalo Squadron—in the South African Defence Force. He had been born in Angola and as the brightest boy in his village had been sent to a strict Jesuit mission school run by Portuguese colonialists. Despite the beatings, he had done well and became head boy. Academically gifted, he had been dead set on becoming a surgeon and using his talents to save the lives of his countrymen.

It didn't work out like that.

The country fell to the communists and his family were massacred. He was forced to flee into exile in the South African dependency of Namibia. Aged sixteen, he followed many other black Angolan refugees into the South African Army to fight for his adopted homeland.

He was now in his forties but still very lean and muscular; his bony head was shaved bald and his face had the hawk-like look of a disciplinarian. He had worked with Alex's team for years.

Yamba was scarred by his experience in the crucial battle at Cuito Cuanavale, the largest battle in Africa since the Second World War. His unit had fought a combined force of tough East German, Cuban and Angolan troops. Neither side won, but by simply staying operational Yamba's unit prevented the fall of neighbouring Namibia. The action took its toll on him, and his men often regarded him as a narrow-minded stickler. He could not care less; he understood that military victory required obsessive attention to detail in planning. He was never going to be in such a desperate position again in his life.

Alex grinned at the exchange going on next to him, but his mind was busy turning over their mission. He was responsible for making an accurate survey of the target and Kalil's initial briefing had worried him. Whoever was running the mine seemed very concerned to keep people out. Given its isolated position he couldn't understand the heavy security precautions; he had never seen such measures in all his time in Africa.

'Whoa, third gear!' he called jokingly to the others as the road suddenly became less rutted and they actually stopped bumping along in second for the first time that day,

' 'Bout time too—bloody Africans can't build a road for love nor money . . .'

'Ah, my friend! Now suppose we are in the United Kingdom, and I am a *guest*! A guest in your

66

house, am I going to be going about saying things like, ah . . . you know, "Ah, this queen of yours, you know, she is getting a bit, er . . .'" he fished for the right idiom, '"long in the tooth"? Am I going to be—'

'Shit!'

Alex hit the brakes as they turned a corner and the Toyota skidded over the dust. He managed to stop them from crashing into the bushes but the engine cut out and they stalled in the middle of the road. A cloud of red dust blew out from under them and everything became very quiet as the noise of the engine died away.

As the dust cleared Yamba and Col could see what the problem was. A large log had been laid across the track to stop traffic. If that was not enough physical impediment, a psychological one had been added: a naked body was hung by the neck from a tree on the right-hand side, its intestines strung out and hooked into a bush on the other side. Flies swarmed inside the man's abdominal cavity and along the purple strands, making them into a living barrier.

Figures emerged from the bushes ahead of them like predators stirring as they sensed blood. They were teenagers and wore an assortment of T-shirts, outsize combat fatigues and wigs. Alex took in six assault rifles pointed at him. They were still thirty yards off and moved slowly forwards; hesitating at the unusual sight of whites in such a remote region.

Alex's experience and training kicked in. He stared at the slowly advancing child soldiers and thought fast. He couldn't restart the truck and reverse in time without being riddled with bullets.

He sat still but spoke quickly and quietly out of the side of his mouth to the other two: 'Don't move. Wait until they've all come out of cover. When we're ready, Yamba take the two on your side, Col take the middle two, I'll take my side.'

Col and Yamba slipped their hands onto the grips of their machine pistols, thumbed the safeties off and clicked them to automatic. Alex slowly put his hand up out of the window. The boys' eyes flicked onto the movement and they halted in their gradual advance to the truck. Alex slowly leaned himself out of the window, trying to make eye contact with them. They stood still, watching intently. He gently pulled the door lever, swung it open and got out so that the door shielded him. The MP5 that had been tucked down the side of his seat was in his hands. He stood for a second looking at them; estimating distances and angles.

'Now,' he said calmly and fired a long burst through the door panel. He dived to the side of the road, rolled and came up on one knee firing again on auto.

Col and Yamba opened up from inside the car; bullets punched out through the windscreen. Then they were out as well, diving into the dense bush.

The gunfire crashed against the silence, birds erupted out of the trees. Short aimed bursts snapped out from the mercenaries against wild chattering salvos from the boys that veered off overhead as their oversized guns kicked up. Bodies jerked and spun in the road; arms flung rifles haphazardly away from them and then it was over.

The mercenaries moved forwards quickly and purposefully through the bush at the side of the road; hunched over the sights of their weapons, scanning ahead of them. The sound of the shots died away into the forest and the smell of cordite drifted past. No other fighters emerged from cover and there was no sound of any panicked flight into the jungle. Alex nodded across the road at Col, who ran out to check the bodies as the others covered him. Their marksmanship had been accurate, the shots were tightly grouped around the chest; none of them was alive.

They quickly moved on and searched the area around the roadblock. There was a crude shelter of banana leaves set back from the road. The earth floor was littered with screwed-up blankets, plastic bowls of cassava bread, bundles of dagga—the powerful local marijuana—and a lot of plastic bottles of home brew.

With the immediate danger over, Alex's brain switched to figuring out the next problem. Were these child soldiers linked to the mine? Had the contact just blown the recce mission?

Overall, he figured they were still too far from the target, and it was hard to believe that a normal commercial mining operation would use such unorthodox troops. Also, they had got too close now just to turn back—he couldn't return to London and face Kalil without at least trying to go on.

An idea occurred to him and he barked out orders. They dragged the bodies back around the basha and scattered them as if there had been an argument and a shoot-out in the group. They placed bottles of liquor around the corpses and emptied some more so that the place stank of alcohol. They then wrapped two bodies in blankets and put them and their weapons in the back of the car as the 'ones that got away'. They would dump them in the bush further on.

Alex wrapped a shirt round his face, took a forked stick and unhooked the intestines from the bush; they exploded with flies and he nearly threw up but he forced himself through it. At the same time, Yamba heaved the log aside so that Col could drive through. The two of them then replaced their respective barriers.

Col cut some branches and swept the vehicle tracks off the road whilst the others picked up their 9mm shell casings from the firefight, leaving only the boys' 7.62mm ones. It was by no means perfect but Alex was banking on the fact that whoever commanded these guys probably did not have advanced ballistic forensic skills.

They drove on in tense silence.

Eberhardt reeled from the words—Thomas Müntzer! A man whose prophecy of the end of the world had recently set Germany on fire.

Associations flashed past him: a brilliant theologian, a firebrand preacher, an early associate of Luther's who had split from him and was now leading the radicals against both him and the Catholic Church.

Zwickau.

Back in 1521, after Luther was condemned as a heretic and had had to go into hiding, the extremists took over the Protestant movement. They made the town of Zwickau the centre of the radical Reformation. The Zwickau Brethren were led by Müntzer and had been forced to leave with him by the town council, who had become fearful of their growing fanaticism.

Eberhardt had seen them: mad saints wandering the highways dressed in rags. They mumbled to themselves and jerked their arms wildly; staring and shouting as they imagined the millennium: the end of time that Müntzer said was coming soon.

Eberhardt looked at him now. The sallow face prematurely aged by the intensity of the prophecy he had made to bring about the Kingdom of God on Earth.

'How...? But...I thought...' Eberhardt mouthed frantically, trying to think how he came to be there.

Thomas nodded and explained calmly, 'You probably last heard of me back in the summer, when I had my pulpit in Altstedt. I preached to the Princes and called on them to prepare the way for

71

Christ's coming. But the Devil stopped their ears and they would not hear me, the Dear Lord forgive them for they will burn in the hottest Hell. They chose to join with Satan because of their love of wealth.' He shook his head at their folly. 'So they drove me out and I had to flee into hiding. But through this trial the Lord showed me that the true Elect, His most faithful angels, will be the common man. They will be the new saviours of Germany.

'I was organising secret meetings of the Elect in the Schwarzwald last year.' He looked at Albrecht. 'Those were the first stirrings you were referring to,' he said, pitying him for his lack of understanding of the working of God in this world.

Albrecht nodded awkwardly.

'I am now on my way north to Mühlhausen. You should join me,' he said, looking intensely at Eberhardt. It was an instruction not a question. 'We did not meet by chance. The Lord wanted you to hear His message; to be part of His movement—it is your destiny to be part of it!' He held up a warning finger and hissed, 'The end of *this* world is nigh!'

Eberhardt stared back at him, gripped by the certainty in the man's eyes. He was presently a wanderer searching for a saviour for his nation and now he had found one.

He nodded slowly. 'Yes . . . destiny, it is my destiny to join you, Thomas. We will save Germany!'

PRESENT DAY, TUESDAY 25 NOVEMBER, MBOMOU PROVINCE, CENTRAL AFRICAN REPUBLIC

At first light the next day Alex twisted the focus on his binoculars and stared at the perimeter fence of the mine.

It was eight foot of razor wire with a coil of the stuff on top. Watchtowers with an armed guard in each were spaced along it, and a twenty-foot-wide swathe in front had been cleared of vegetation and covered with brown gravel.

Nice touch, he thought. We can't sneak across that without making a noise. But it's still not going to stop us if we drop in behind by helicopter.

Beyond the gravel strip, the trees had been cut down for a hundred yards into the jungle to clear the field of fire; clumps of tall grasses and bushes had grown up in their place and Alex was lying in a bush thirty yards from the gravel. The smell of damp earth and rotting vegetation was in his nostrils and he was soaked in cold dew from lying motionless on the ground for two hours waiting for dawn to come up. His body kept shivering and he fought to keep still.

The three of them had crawled into their observation post under cover of darkness in full combats, heavily camouflaged with cam cream on their faces and vegetation stuffed into their webbing and cam-netting head covers. Throat mikes on their radios meant they could communicate but radio silence was to be observed for all but emergency situations this close to the enemy.

They had wriggled forwards on elbows and knees with their weapons held in front of them; they had fitted their rifles with silencers, and had radio beacons to call on Arkady for emergency uplift, but Alex hoped to God that they did not have to make contact.

They were lying on the ground in a triangle shape, facing outwards. Yamba and Alex watched different sectors of the complex, whilst Col maintained a guard behind them. One foot lay over each other's ankles so that a silent tap could alert them to any danger.

They were on the first leg of what Alex hoped would be three approaches to the perimeter; going in and out in a classic flower-petal pattern around the site to see it from all angles. He wanted to check the enemy's defensive positions and weapons, their routines, and also to get some idea of what calibre of troops he was up against. Alex knew that a long day of discomfort lay ahead—it was going to be twelve hours before he could move enough to have a piss.

They were at the east end of the complex, where the road and the power line came in from the volcano. He had been able to see the outline of some of the buildings through the blurry green vision of his nightsight: the ends of a row of barrack huts and behind them the huge grey corrugated-metal shed they had to capture. However, he really needed daylight to get a detailed look at things.

As daylight seeped quickly into the air he pushed the night-vision goggles up onto his forehead so that he could use the binoculars. He twisted the focus again to zero in on the perimeter defences.

Shit, he muttered in his head. He was looking at one of the covered structures that had shown up on the satellite photo in Kalil's presentation. From the air it looked like a simple square banana-leaf-roofed hut but underneath it was a concrete bunker.

Who the hell builds that kind of thing out here? he wondered as he looked at the squat hexagonal concrete structure. He could see that the walls were a good two foot thick from where the firing slits went through them. The long barrel of a heavy machine gun pointed out uncompromisingly from each of the three concrete pillboxes that he could see along the perimeter.

After that it just got worse. At seven o'clock an empty oil barrel was bashed with something metal as the camp wake-up call. Alex scanned the barracks as soldiers emerged from the long huts; they were mainly the same sort of teenagers that they had encountered at the roadblock, armed with a mixture of automatic weapons and grenade launchers.

So the boys at the roadblock *were* from the mine.

At first sight they looked dishevelled and scruffy, wearing a mixture of combats and ghetto-style Western fashion, but someone obviously had a grip on them. He noticed that they had jumped pretty quickly at the sound of the reveille and were hurrying across to a parade ground that he could just see between two huts. It was probably the tall, muscular guy stripped to the waist, who walked into his field of vision; he was shouting at the boys, urging them on.

What now?

Alex scanned on to two uniformed, middle-aged

officers, who were now going from hut to hut checking that everyone was up. He didn't recognise the camouflage pattern of their uniforms and caps, which was strange, as he had come across most nationalities.

White mercenaries?

He focused in on them. Swarthy and dark-haired, they didn't look European.

Middle Eastern?

He couldn't tell from this distance.

Yamba's foot tapped his left ankle.

He looked round.

The black sergeant pointed to another wide hut structure halfway between two of the pillboxes, set back from the perimeter. Alex had skipped it in his initial scan. As he looked closer he could see more of the troops in proper uniforms get hold of the posts, lift up the ends in the ground and walk back with them so that the roof split neatly in two. As the camouflage netting pulled back he tensed.

The twin barrels of a Russian ZSU 23mm anti-aircraft gun rose up smoothly from the horizontal position to the vertical and swept the sky in an early morning anti-aircraft drill. Any Mi-17 helicopter that got within a thousand yards of that would simply become a twenty-two-man coffin.

There goes the plan.

He put the binoculars down and rubbed his tired eyes; this was not going to be easy. He stared down at the ground in front of him for a while, deep in thought.

Eventually he looked up again at the complex but this time something outside the perimeter caught his eye. He hadn't seen it before because he was either using the nightsight or the binoculars; he squinted and craned forward, peering at it for a minute.

Across the stretch of gravel he thought he had seen a slight shimmer just off the ground in the low dawn sun. He picked up the binoculars and twisted the focus all the way back to the nearest possible range. He peered at it again and then put the binoculars down and rubbed his forehead; the swathe of gravel was not just there for making a noise.

Yamba heard his sigh and twisted round to look at him. Alex rolled on his side so he had both hands free and put his fingers and thumbs together to make a large 'O' shape—the hand signal they used for mines.

The shimmer that he had seen was the early morning sun catching on droplets of dew that hung on tiny transparent rods and trip wires sticking up out of the gravel: spring mines. Once tripped, they shot up out of the ground to stomach height and then exploded in a shrapnel burst that left any man within fifty yards dead or writhing in agony. He could also see the tiny, pronged spigots of anti-tank mines mixed in with them.

The thick layer of gravel stopped the usual tropical plant growth from setting off the trip wires and disrupting the mines—weeding in a minefield was not something that you wanted to be doing every few weeks. Whoever was running this place was very organised.

How the hell were they going to do this?

That evening the flickering fire lit the exhausted faces huddled around it.

Eberhardt, Thomas and Albrecht were sitting on the earth floor of a tiny wooden hut on the edge of the forest with its owner, Joachim the Weaver, a follower of Thomas. The tiny fire did not succeed in heating the hut—their breath froze in the room— but it was better than being out in the snow.

Joachim was forty but looked seventy. His face in the firelight had deep creases cut into it by the strain of his life. Stoop-backed from his weaving, he was gap-toothed and bald, with shaggy grey locks hanging down the side of his head. Weighed down by suffering, he rarely spoke.

His wife and three remaining children were cramped in around the hut. Four others had died that winter already: tuberculosis and measles. The children were tucked in the bed head to tail, and a heavy racking cough came occasionally from it. They wouldn't last long either.

These then were the poor.

Eberhardt had seen a lot of them since his fall, but such poverty still shocked him. Their faces were twisted by hardship, they stank of sweat, their hands were grubby and stained; their fingernails like claws with black grime under them.

Thomas seemed in his element. They had just shared a meal of thin gruel; he smiled and said graciously, 'Joachim, you are too kind, too kind,' gripping the man's forearm.

With some dinner inside them now they perked up. Eberhardt looked at Thomas questioningly. 'So you have prophesied that the end of the world

78

is nigh?'

Thomas smiled. 'The Lord has given me the gift of prophecy and interpretation of dreams, from which I can see clearly that the most right and ancient prophecy of Daniel is upon us.'

Eberhardt looked at him agog. Thomas's eyes shone in the firelight as he wound himself up, his voice rising and his hands gesturing, following the words of a sermon in his head.

'The Prophet did dream that there would be Five Empires overthrown before the Coming of Our Lord in Glory.

'The first Empire was the Babylonian, the second that of the Medes and Persians, the third was the Greek, the fourth the Roman and the now the fifth is the one we see before us. This is the greatest evil, this so-called *Holy* Roman Empire, patched with dung and the vain schemings of hypocrisy.

'The work of ending the fifth Empire is now in full swing. The spirit of God is revealing to many elect and pious men at this time the great need for a Full and Final Reformation in the near future.'

Eberhardt nodded in amazement—the Bible itself was coming true!

But Thomas was just getting going.

'And to whom should we look for the source of our oppression? Who is the fount of this current injustice? The rich.'

Joachim grunted in assent. His wife was nodding her approval in the darkness behind them. Albrecht looked at them in alarm.

'Those whose teeth are swords and whose jaws are set with knives to devour the poor from the earth. All in the name of their wealth and glory!

79

Thus have the masters themselves created this situation in which the poor man, against his goodwill, is forced to become their enemy! The poor must come to a full realisation that they have to do God's work before He can return. For they are the Elect—the hands and feet of God. They must cleanse the world and set all to rights before it is fit for Christ to come again. They must rise up and establish the Kingdom of God on earth. A Kingdom where all work and all property must be shared in common, and complete equality will reign. A union of the people has to be organised to realise this commonwealth, not only throughout Germany, but throughout the entire Christendom!'

Thomas's voice became a shout as he reached his climax.

'*Christ* can only return to the earth in His Glorious Second Coming when all existing authorities have been destroyed. The Princes and nobles are to be invited to join, but, should they refuse, we will overthrow and kill them, with arms in hand!'

THURSDAY 27 NOVEMBER, MBOMOU PROVINCE, CENTRAL AFRICAN REPUBLIC

Two nights after their first approach to the mine, and the team were on their final night across the lake, north of the complex, on a hillock overlooking it. They still whispered; being on a covert recce was a state of mind you had to maintain.

'What do you think?' Alex asked.

'We're gonna need armour to get through that lot.' Col's face was close to him but invisible in the pitch-black jungle. Alex could hear the despondency in his voice, though. 'I mean, what the fook is it in there that warrants all that malarkey? It's like the Maginot Line or sum'ut.'

They had just finished their third sortie into the complex to observe it. After starting at the eastern end they had looped round to the western side and then finally come back in from the north. Having observed all day, they had set up a small basha of groundsheets strung between two trees to give them some respite from the dripping foliage overhead.

They were tired, hungry and soaked to the skin; they had hardly slept during three days of constant vigilance. Alex sighed and rubbed his hand on his short black hair; it was sticky and plastered down flat with sweat. He had insect bites all over him and felt filthy, layers of greasy camouflage cream on his face blending in with a week's worth of tropical dirt.

This muttered conference was the first chance

that they had had to discuss their findings after the three days of observation. They had at least learned a lot more about the site. Alex estimated the total enemy fighting force at about a hundred and thirty men: fifty of the uniformed soldiers who seemed to be the more professional troops in charge of things and about eighty of the *kadogos*—the child soldiers. The bare-chested guy seemed to be their commander.

They had also seen a lot more military hardware: two DAF trucks with ZSU 23mm AA guns mounted on the back. These guns were mobile so it would make it very hard to destroy them before helicopters could come in, hence the abandonment of the air assault idea. A Russian D-30 122mm howitzer had been spotted poking out of a bunker next to the main road entrance from the south, and another in a bunker by the back gate from the mine. There were also five pickup trucks with 12.7mm Dushka heavy machine guns and two large Unimog all-terrain vehicles with massive 106mm recoilless rifles on the back. These came and went regularly during the day, from which Alex deduced that there would be a number of heavily armed checkpoints on the approach roads.

They had also got a feel for the camp's daily routine. After the soldiers had their morning parade, men and women slave workers in rags and leg irons were dragged out of three large barred huts in the east of the complex and put through their own roll call. They were then pushed and shoved into trucks and driven off east to the mine through a large razor-wire gate. An hour later the first dumper truck roared back in through the same gate and dumped its load of black ore onto a conveyor belt that disappeared into the factory shed.

This was run by a group of technicians that they saw on the previous day from across the lake. The fifteen men slept in a long dormitory block along the lakeshore next to the refinery. Alex had seen them emerge at eight o'clock and amble along the shore, chatting and pulling on white lab coats. He was astonished to see that they were Asian. Chinese? Again, he couldn't tell.

'Flippin' UN going on down there,' was Col's whispered comment from their vantage point.

At nine o'clock someone had joined them from one of the three houses further along the shore from the factory. These were single-storey white clapboard affairs with little gardens and verandas looking over the water. The two nearest the shed belonged to uniformed officers, but Alex had watched curiously as a man wearing smart trousers, a blue blazer and tie had left the one on the end and walked down the beach. He couldn't get much more detail because of the range across the lake but he thought he walked rather stiffly, either because he was old or because of something in his manner.

The loud whirr of machinery had started soon after this man had entered the building and continued all day. The technicians had emerged at regular intervals for tea and lunch breaks, chatting and smoking on the lakeshore, for all the world like factory workers in any city.

At five o'clock they knocked off for the day and the plant shut down. They all walked back along the beach. Some of them had supper on the dormitory's veranda, watching satellite TV, whilst others swam in the lake; apart from some floating patches of vegetation washed down by the river it was very clear.

All very civilised, and no crocs, for once. How nice, Alex thought to himself.

On the afternoon of the second day the three of them had glanced up as the distant sound of rotor blades reached them. A Mi-8 transport helicopter flew over their heads, circled and then landed in the middle of the site next to a large hangar shed. From across the lake they could see equipment and crates of food being unloaded from the cargo ramp into pickups and driven off to the barrack huts. There was then a wait until a squad of armed soldiers came out of the refinery, accompanied by the man in the tie. One of the soldiers was in civilian clothing and carried a briefcase chained to his wrist; he saluted the man in the tie, got into the helicopter and flew off again. Alex guessed he was on the weekly diamond run to meet whatever *comptoir* outfit trafficked their produce.

In the darkness Yamba reluctantly agreed with Col's assessment of the difficulties they faced.

'Well, at first I was sure that we could do this but now I am not so sure.' He ticked off the options on his fingers. 'We cannot go across the lake because there are two bunkers at either end that cover the whole thing with machine guns. We can't do an aerial assault because of the anti-aircraft defences. A frontal infantry assault is out of the question— we are mercenaries not, you know, suicide bombers or something. There's no way a mercenary force would sustain the casualties necessary to get through those defences. The only way is to have overwhelming armour superiority.'

'Hmm.' Alex nodded as all of them contemplated the obvious next problem—how the hell do you get an armoured force all the way to such a remote mine?

You couldn't just drive a column of tanks hundreds of miles across Africa. They had no territorial base to start from. Even then, an armoured assault would be risky—tanks were not invulnerable: there was the howitzer by the main gate, the anti-tank mines, the recoilless rifles, loads of RPGs. Any one of them could destroy or disable even a main battle tank.

All of this was going through their heads as they sat in the dark.

Col was the first to break the thoughtful silence: 'I mean, I don't want to put a dampener on it, but you know, we could just say sod this for a . . .' he was about to say 'game of soldiers' but then realised the inappropriate nature of his comment and concluded awkwardly, '. . . you know, we don't have to take the job?'

Alex glanced towards where Yamba was in the dark; his silence said it all. He had been with the two men through many firefights and he knew that neither was afraid of combat. They were seasoned professionals who took only carefully calculated risks. That was why they had been around so long. He knew they were right to express these doubts. They weren't fighting for Queen and Country now and had no moral obligation to finish the job; it was not unknown for mercenary commanders to turn down operations that were just too risky.

They had come to a tipping point. Alex was cold, hungry and exhausted; it was dark and something buried underneath his heart was telling him to give

85

in.

Yet he had staked so much on this. It wasn't just that he needed the money—he would find that somehow—it was his pride. *'If you weren't such a fucking failure!'* His father's words sounded loud and clear in his head.

Could he do it?

Could he actually pull off something big when it really came to the crunch? When the chips were really down?

He rubbed his face with both hands, massaging his tired eyes with his fingers and taking a deep breath at the same time. 'Look, we don't have to take a decision on it now, let's just . . .'

The others were already grunting their assent, glad to release the awkwardness. They had made their views clear. They trusted Alex to make sensible decisions when the time came; he was glad of their tacit sympathy and changed the subject.

'Col, you're on first stag, OK?'

'Aye.' He began moving about, setting himself up for the first two-hour sentry duty.

'I'm going to go down to the lake again; I just want to have a think for a bit.'

'Right-on.'

Alex picked up his MP5 and night-vision gear and moved off down the slope. Yamba was already drifting off to sleep, curled up under his poncho. Col sat under the groundsheet, putting on his night-vision goggles and preparing himself for the task of staying awake for the next two hours when everything in his body was screaming at him to lie down and collapse. He listened to the rustling noise of Alex disappearing through the bush down to the lake.

He mulled over their conversation. He hated being negative about any project. Must have sounded a right Jessie, he thought to himself, but equally there was a time and a place for expressing doubts, and this job did look like a pig's ear.

Suddenly there was a crashing noise from down the slope. His head flicked round and he was on his feet; machine pistol coming up to port. Yamba instantly sprang up, his MP5 in his hands.

Alex ran up the slope, panting from exertion and excitement at the same time.

'Col, Col—I need you to cover me, I've got an idea.'

Eberhardt was the first person in the hut to recover from Thomas's prophecy of the coming war; his imagination had been set on fire by his apocalyptic words.

'So you can interpret dreams like Daniel's?'

Thomas was annoyed at being interrupted and glanced at him fiercely.

Eberhardt blurted, 'I had a dream once.'

'Yes?' said Thomas sharply.

'There was a darkness. It started in my heart, then it spread all over me . . .' Eberhardt moved his hands around his chest as he tried to think how to describe the feeling of the Deathstone. He was not sure how much about the Deathstone cult he should tell Thomas—it was hardly Christian and he didn't want to risk his wrath. '. . . A while back—I was young—I joined a group in Constantinople. There was a priest—a man of God—Abba Athanasius. He did something,' he waved his hand vaguely, 'with a black stone—he called it the Deathstone. I breathed it in and I think it entered my heart and stayed there. It came from the heart of Africa. I was going to go on an expedition and find where it had come from, but then I inherited my lands and I had to come back to Germany. But now it's come back. Well, I mean it came back in a dream I had,' he looked at Albrecht, 'before the Knights' War, back in 'twenty-two.'

Albrecht shrugged and looked away, not wanting to be party to the strange story.

Eberhardt thought back to his hot, stinking chamber that night. He remembered the thing writing in and out of him.

'I felt it . . . it was in my heart and all over me. It was a darkness, a heavy stone in my heart. I fought . . . I prayed!' he said inventively. 'I struggled five times against it,' he remembered tugging frantically at the five arrow slits in his chamber, trying to escape it, 'and then eventually I broke free of it. It was a terrible thing and it ended in a great flash of light and death.'

He decided to omit the matter of his grandmother's death.

Thomas looked at him and nodded. 'So, this dream started in your heart and it's a thing of darkness and fear?'

'Yes.'

'And you struggled and prayed against it five times?' Thomas was attracted to the similarity with Daniel's dream of Five Empires.

'Yes.'

'And it ended in a flash of blinding light and death . . .' Thomas nodded, struck by the strange mixture of imagery. He was a brilliant scholar with a wealth of biblical knowledge. He was fired up and in a prophetic mood. With his utter conviction in himself as a prophet, he began to speak in an authoritative tone.

'I believe that the Bible passage that relates most directly to this prophecy and your dream is Job, chapter twenty-eight, verse three: "Man puts an end to the darkness; he searches the furthest recesses for ore in the blackest darkness."

'Your dream carries with it a threat to the German nation if it is not resolved.' He looked down as he considered the weight of what he had just said. 'There will be five great struggles against this threat and if it is not defeated then it will come in a flash of light and bring great destruction!'

Eberhardt stared at him entranced. Thomas raised his index finger and stared back at Eberhardt to make sure his point had sunk in.

What else could it mean?

Those Bible words written so long ago had finally delivered their message. They were meant for him.

Eberhardt looked at Thomas wild-eyed. He opened his mouth to say something but his voice cracked. His body was racked by sobs, his shoulders shook.

'Darkness . . . To defeat evil. To save Germany!' He coughed to clear his throat, sniffed and spat into the fire loudly. He wiped the tears from his eyes. 'At last—you understand. You see . . .' he cleared his throat and glanced at Thomas, 'that dream . . . that prophecy . . . has been in my heart for so long . . .' He broke off again.

In his mind, though, he could hear the words: 'Man puts an end to the darkness.'

Man. Him. Eberhardt.

Who else could it be referring to? His motto—*Lumens fero!* I bring the light! Light in the darkness! To be part of the Enlightenment process of the Renaissance that he had always dreamed of as an idealistic youth at Heidelberg.

The word 'ore' struck him. The Deathstone.

'Searches the furthest recesses . . .'

'The furthest'—the ends of the world—central Africa; 'recesses'—the heart of a mountain. It was all so obvious, so clear.

Just as Thomas would free Germany and the

world from papal domination so Eberhardt had his special mission in life.

Why else would he have drifted apparently so haphazardly into Constantinople just at the time when Abba Athanasius was there with his nomadic cult? Why else had he partaken in their ceremony as a young man, and then suffered the recurrence of the Deathstone so recently just as the Reformation was breaking loose in Germany?

These events were like dots scattered across the blank page of his life. A line had now connected them into a meaningful shape. At last he could see it all for what it was.

The apparently random nature of the events became all the more compelling when they were seen in this light. The more random they had at first appeared, the more purposeful they now became.

All the suffering, his fall from power, the apparently aimless wandering of the last year; it all had purpose now. He bent his head down with his face in his hands and wept.

Thomas was used to such emotional outpourings and saw it as further evidence that he had got the prophecy right. He placed his hand on the top of Eberhardt's head and prayed in a solemn voice.

'O Lord, bless Your servant who You have commissioned with this prophecy. We give You thanks that You have spoken Your Word into his heart. We pray that Your servant Eberhardt would contend valiantly to save the German nation from whatever this terrible peril will prove to be, so that we will see the defeat of this,' he paused, 'Dark Heart Prophecy.'

Alex crawled down the beach and into the black water.

Sharp stones dug into his knees. He reached out gingerly with a hand; felt it go into the cold water and then through the layer of slimy mud and onto the gravel underneath.

He had removed his boots and stripped off to his combat trousers. Around his neck and hanging down his back he had strapped an empty magazine bandolier. His torso was covered with green and black cam cream; he looked like a pagan warrior. Even the soles of his feet were covered; he didn't want their pink flesh showing up when he swam back.

If he swam back.

The water was cold as he slipped in; it came onto his chest and then his groin. He looked across the surface of the lake, flat like a piece of wet slate. Heavy clouds meant that the darkness around him was thick. All he could see of the complex on the other side, from this low angle, were dim lights in the windows of the dormitory block and the three houses along the lakeshore, and then, further away, from the watchtowers around the perimeter behind them.

Once he was immersed he pushed off and swam quietly out to the floating patch of vegetation that had given him this idea in the first place; he had watched them all day whirling aimlessly around in the currents. Treading water, he lifted the equipment off his neck and onto the bundle of branches and tangled lianas. It was a few feet across and he found he could push it quite easily;

92

he began heading out across the lake.

Col and Yamba crouched in the bushes on the shore and watched him anxiously. Their guns pointed out towards him but there wasn't anything they could do if he got into trouble. Alex had given them strict instructions to escape if there was a contact: 'There's no point in all three of us going down.'

Col had seen the white flash of his grin in the dark. What's he so bloomin' cheerful about? he thought as he watched Alex go.

And what's he doing now? He saw the black shape stop and dive down into the water at regular intervals. He was going deep each time, down for a minute or more.

Alex was encouraged by his discoveries and decided to push on right over to the other side. All was quiet in the mine; he had seen a sentry walk past along the beach but the man would take a while to get to the far end of it and back.

He wanted to have a closer look at the houses where the mine directors lived. He paddled his raft to within twenty feet of the house belonging to the man in the tie and peered at it through some liana leaves. The clouds were breaking up and moonlight was coming through; he could see neat flowerbeds in front of the bungalow. The door onto the veranda opened and light spilled onto the lake.

Alex froze.

It was the man; he was still wearing his smart trousers and tie but had taken off his jacket. He pushed open the door with his foot, carried a tea tray out and began setting the things on a white plastic table. Then he leaned over the veranda rail and looked directly at the raft.

Alex stayed stock-still, not daring to move. He stared at the man for a couple of minutes. This close he could see that he was in his sixties with white wavy hair scraped back in a neat short back and sides. He was small but with a paunch that he tried to hide by pulling the waistband of his trousers up over it. He had a swarthy complexion that could have come from anywhere in the Mediterranean. The face was fine-boned and sensitive but had the peevish expression of a disgruntled old man.

He turned round and poured his tea. He then went back inside and brought out a short-wave radio, which he put on the table and began tuning in. Static and interference crackled until he found the right wavelength and then settled back in his chair to listen.

Alex heard a German announcer's voice carry clearly across the water: *'Deutsche Welle, Rundfunk aus Deutschland. Es ist elf Uhr—die Nachrichten,'* followed by the news. The man drank his tea and listened to items about German politics; he tutted and talked to himself.

Halfway through the broadcast the reception began to deteriorate. *'Scheisser Apparat!'* he shouted shrilly, and picked up the radio to retune it.

When the news was finished the man reached over and dismissively switched off a light entertainment programme that was just starting. He was discontented, muttering to himself, and gesturing angrily with his hands. Eventually he packed up the tea and went inside; the lights went out and quiet returned to the lake.

Alex exhaled with relief; he was cold from having to be still for so long in the water. He turned and started swimming back across the lake, dragging the raft awkwardly after him.

The other two greeted him with smiles of relief; he had been gone over an hour. They crept down the beach and helped him scramble up it and into the bush, carrying his bandolier with him. He was dripping and shivering but he couldn't stop grinning.

'What' *the fook* were all that abou'?' Col asked in an angry whisper.

Alex lifted up the bandolier; the magazine pouches in it were full of something. He grinned silently at the other two as he stuck his hand into one pocket after another; each time pulling out a handful of gravel. He grinned and whispered, 'Got the bastards!'

6 FEBRUARY 1525, MÜHLHAUSEN, CENTRAL GERMANY

Eberhardt peered over the heads of the crowd around him. He stared at the bishop sitting on his throne ten feet up on one side at the front of the huge Marienkirche cathedral.

It was Sunday morning but Bishop Frederick von Linden was not happy.

He was terrified.

Facing him in the raised pulpit twenty feet across the other side of the nave was Dr Thomas Müntzer. Apparently he had been in the city secretly for a month and von Linden shuddered to think what he had been up to in that time. The slums of Mühlhausen were riddled with his supporters.

Von Linden was only twenty-two, and good-looking in a smooth, boyish way. His cheeks were blushing pink now. He was the youngest son of an aristocratic dynasty and had only agreed to take up the appointment to the wealthy see last year for the good of his family. He was terrified of the situation in front of him and was regretting accepting the post.

The bishop glanced away from his enemy and down the aisle of the cathedral. The vast space had no pews and was packed with people standing between the lines of soaring stone columns. The folk of the slums had walked up the hill from their hovels to hear their hero preach.

Von Linden could smell them from where he sat. The stink of their sweat and foul breath rose up in a cloud of steam into the cold air of the nave. It was lit in shimmering blues and reds by the sun coming through the stained-glass windows. Men and women, old and young, were all shabbily dressed and babbling excitedly.

Eberhardt was in the middle of the crowd. He had become one of the party of God now, and had marched to the church with the faithful. With his aristocratic genes he stood out six inches above the crowd but he felt part of them now; he did not even notice their smell any more.

Squeezed amongst the mob outside was Albrecht. He had become separated from Eberhardt in the walk up the hill as they jostled along. Truth was that he had not wanted to be with him in the forefront and had been very content to drop behind.

Despite the cold, the hinged wooden flaps at the bottom of the main windows had been propped open, people had placed ladders against the walls outside and were hanging over the windowsills to try to catch Thomas's words.

Inside, the crowd milled around in the huge space in an unruly fashion. The council had ordered the town guard to attend. Their bright blue and yellow striped doublets and hose formed a thin barrier in front of the choir stalls. Holding their halberds horizontally in two hands in front of their chests, they strained to push the crowd back.

The only people allowed beyond their line were the rulling oligarchs, along with Müntzer and the man he called his 'reader', Manfred, a huge man with no neck; his shaved head just disappeared into the folds of muscle and fat of his broad shoulders. It stuck out on top of his body like a large turnip, his long moustache drooped off his upper lip like a cluster of roots. He stood with his arms folded at the bottom of the steps to the pulpit and stared at the oligarchs with open contempt. Von Linden was unnerved by his lack of deference towards a prince of the Church.

The bishop twitched at his robes nervously and kept adjusting his mitre. He was conscious of the difference between the brilliant red silk and gold that he was wearing and the dun-coloured clothes of the plebeians in front of him.

He looked down at the jewelled crosses stitched onto the backs of his white kid gloves and pulled them tighter onto his hands. He had hoped to overawe the masses with the splendour of his rank; but he realised now that he had merely drawn attention to the class war that was dividing the town.

He had been alarmed by Thomas's radicalism and had expelled him from Mühlhausen the previous autumn. Since then an uneasy truce had reigned between the conservative town élite, the merchants and wealthy burghers, and the religious radicals, support for whom had been growing ever since. Although they had temporarily defeated Thomas, the town council realised that it was now not strong enough to remove its enemies by brute force; they had too many supporters in the slums.

The young bishop looked down at Kramer the *Bürgermeister*, who was seated in the choir stalls beneath him with the rest of the town council, all dressed in their furs and gold chains of office. He was a thickset man with heavy jowls. Under pressure his expression went blank; he kept glancing dully at the crowd as it pressed in on him.

This made him seem even more stupid and hateful to von Linden now, who directed an angry question at him in his head: What are we going to do with this mob now, you fat arse? It was your idea to give in to their demands for him to preach!

At the council meeting last week Kramer had confidently asserted: 'They'll calm down as long as they can hear Müntzer again. It's just a temporary concession until we can rally our forces and drive him out once more.'

Joachim the Weaver, though, had no intention of being driven out. He was at the front of the church, pressing his chest up against a pikestaff. He had used his sharp elbows to squeeze his old frame through the crowd and now he waited for the golden words of God to fall into his ears from the high pulpit.

He stared up at Thomas, his head bald and his mouth open and gap-toothed. His three remaining girls had died since Thomas and Eberhardt had eaten in his hut, so there was nothing left to keep him and his wife from coming to Mühlhausen to seek salvation. Thomas and his message were now their only hope.

The great preacher was back in his pulpit by popular demand and loving every minute of it. He stood in his ordinary workman's clothes, with his feet apart and his arms folded, a bag of tools at his feet. He looked out over the throng from on high. He was calm; he knew his hour had come.

Thomas had been allowed to preach on the understanding that he would respect the sanctity of the church and not stir up the mob. Looking at the faces of the crowd staring at him now, von Linden did not have much confidence that the promise would hold.

The outcome was predictable. The people had been filled with Thomas's ideas of a Christian communist revolution for months beforehand in the poor churches and in pamphlet readings in their houses. An orator of his power could not help but rouse such a hungry audience.

He smiled at them and held up his hands. The crowd fell deathly silent and this spread to the people outside as well. Eberhardt strained forward so as not to miss a word.

'Brothers and sisters! German folk! Hear me!'

His voice rang in the vast church. Von Linden winced at his populist tone.

'Are you all good Christian folk?'

There was a murmur of assent. Every face was looking up at him, eyes fixed on the small figure with his arms open, leaning over the edge of the pulpit to them.

'Are you the folk of this land who are *hungry* to obey God?'

'We are! Yes!' shouted out some hotheads.

'Do you hunger and thirst for *righteousness*? Do you yearn for *justice*?' He snatched the word out of the air and held it in a raised fist.

'Yes!' more people shouted.

'Then *what is justice*?' He hammered each word home and then paused to let them think about it.

'Is it justice that we have a Church led from a foreign land? By the Bishop of Rome? A Church that does not speak to us in our own tongue but mumbles to us in foreign with its back turned to our people.'

He swept his arm and looked over at von Linden as he said this, referring to the way the priest in Mass turned his back on the congregation and whispered the prayers in Latin.

Von Linden's soft face went red under the accusing gaze of the mob.

'*Our* language is not good enough for him! Why won't he speak prayers in *our* tongue—like a good honest *German*? Why must we bow and scrape to foreigners? Who decorate our churches with so much Popish trash!' He swept his arm around at the statues of the Virgin and the saints that decorated every alcove along the walls.

'We must cleanse the realm of this and all that stands in the way of freedom!' he shouted. The word '*Freiheit*' rang in their minds, with its promise of release from all their earthly torments.

Thomas had found his stride now.

'We are prisoners but God made all men free with His precious blood-letting! Christ died once, and for all sinners—to set us *free*!'

The crowd pushed on the guards; straining to be free of them. The council members stood up in alarm as the burly guardsmen stumbled back into the choir stalls.

People around Eberhardt began shouting, 'Freedom! Freedom!' like it was the culmination of everything they had ever wanted in their lives. It was getting hard for him to hear what Thomas was saying.

Outside, the crowd murmured and stirred at the sound of yells from inside the church. 'What's happening?' they called up to the onlookers at the windows.

Thomas continued, his voice rising to a shout,

101

'*How* shall we be free? We must look to Christ our saviour for guidance. *Christ* was a carpenter. *I* am a carpenter.'

He bent down, rummaged for something at his feet and then stood up.

'What is the symbol of the carpenter? The hammer!' He brandished it above his head. 'And what should we use the hammer for? To *smash* down the old, and build up the new! To build the Kingdom of God on earth!' He banged the hammer hard on the edge of the pulpit.

The violence of the blow went through the crowd like a whip and they responded with a roar. Von Linden leaped to his feet in fright.

In the crowd Eberhardt could hardly see the pulpit for all the arms up in the air in front of him.

'In these last dangerous days when the fifth Empire is ending, the children of light must march against the children of darkness! We must rise up and slaughter the rich, just as Elijah slaughtered the prophets of Baal. We must build the new Jerusalem!'

The crowd was enraged now and tore through the line of guards. They were overcome, punched and beaten down amongst the choir stalls. Townsmen scrambled over the wooden divides. The councillors tried to extricate themselves and reach the sanctuary of the altar but angry men grabbed them and dragged them back.

Joachim ran up the steps of the bishop's throne, filled with energy as if he were a young man again. He grabbed the bishop by the throat and shouted at him.

All the pent-up anger of forty years of grinding labour, misery and death had at last found an enemy to vent itself on. Von Linden went rigid at the sight of the screaming, gap-toothed man, his withered face weirdly rejuvenated by hatred.

Thomas continued to lash the crowd, leaning over the pulpit, sweeping them on with his arms, though few could hear him now amongst the uproar.

'Arise! Arm yourselves for the Lord's battle! The time is ripe. Strike while the iron is hot! Do not allow it to cool off! Do not allow it to become feeble! Arise! Arise!'

His voice was growing hoarse with shouting. Those who could not reach the front of the church looked around them for things to attack. They seized the idolatrous statues on the sides of the church.

Eberhardt was carried away with the anger of the mob and joined in with them. He seized the feet of a Madonna and rocked her back and forth until she tumbled out of her alcove and smashed on the flagstones.

Peasants picked up pieces and threw them at the hated decorative scenes on the beautiful windows. Red, blue and green bursts of glass showered over the crowd outside, who roared in reply. Albrecht looked on horrified at the noise and the explosions of glass coming faster and faster, as if the church were going to erupt.

Joachim dragged the terrified bishop down the steps by the throat and the crowd seized him at the bottom.

'The sinners are cowardly dogs. Spare not! Pity not the suffering of the sinners! Harden your hearts! The time of the harvest is at hand. Behold! I have sharpened my sickle!'

Joachim's knife was the first to be whipped out of the sheath on his belt. He stabbed the bishop wildly in the back. The blow glanced off his shoulder blade but he spun round to stare at his attacker in shock.

A fist caught him on the side of the face. He staggered and his mitre fell off. Another knife glanced off the back of his head and then he went down under a mill of fists and *Bundschuhe*.

'Arise! Arise, my brothers! Begin the war and destroy the ungodly while you still have the light!'

SATURDAY 17 JANUARY, GBADOLITE AIRPORT, EQUATEUR PROVINCE, DEMOCRATIC REPUBLIC OF CONGO

Its lights glaring and its engine snorting, the T-72 tank emerged like a dragon from the back of the huge transport aircraft. It looked ferocious, the long gun thrusting out in front, the turret bristling with heavy machine guns, smoke-grenade launchers, searchlights and infrared fire-control systems.

'You're OK, you're OK!'

Alex had to shout over the noise of the plane's four idling turbofans and the grunting of the tank's 1200. diesel, as he gave directions down the cargo ramp of the Ilyushin Il–76.

The driver, Tshombe, a black Angolan comrade of Yamba's, sat in the driver's hatch under the main gun and flicked his eyes back and forth between his guides, Alex on his right and Arkady on the left. Other soldiers in Alex's new company stood around waching the vital operation. The main battle tank was twelve feet wide and weighed forty-five tonnes. It fitted into the plane with only inches to spare; if he tipped it off the ramp he would wreck it and the aircraft.

Kalil stood at the side with his hands in his pockets, feeling overwhelmed. He had flown in Gbadolite only with this final delivery of equipment to the Battlegroup; Alex had wanted to keep him out of theatre until everything was ready. It was Kalil's first time in Africa and there was too much for him to take in: the heat, the smell of the bush, the huge tail of the aircraft that soared over his

105

head with its gaping clam-shell doors.

The tank finally squeezed out, edged down the ramp and made it onto solid ground. Tshombe smiled with relief as Alex and Arkady jumped up onto the sloped armour of the hull to slap him on the shoulder.

'Good job! Well done!'

Alex leaped back down and came over to Kalil.

'Isn't she a beauty?' he said, looking at the black and green camouflage-painted monster admiringly. As an armoured warfare expert he was very excited about the tank; she was also the key to the whole plan to take the mine.

'Ya, looks great.' Kalil didn't share his excitement but made an effort to sound like he did. He was feeling distinctly out of place: the only person not dressed in green camouflage fatigues. He had hoped that chinos, Timberland boots and a brown leather jacket would look sufficiently rugged.

'Alex, you've done a great job here! This is amazing.' He held his hands up to indicate the scale of the operation going on around them. 'I'm completely overwhelmed—'

Arkady ran over and interrupted him in a heavy Russian accent. 'Maximum payload! Forty-five tonnes!' He jabbed his cigarette at the tank, exhilarated at having got it onto the ground. 'Big fucker!'

He was short and stocky with a mousy crew cut, pale skin, stubble and a chunky gold necklace. He had a broad Slavic face with a slight narrowing at the corners of the eyes. He normally wore a sullen expression but became more energetic when oppressed. He was ecstatic now, having just

106

completed the tough task of delivering all the equipment that Alex and Col had bought on their buying trip to Transdneister.

Alex realised that Gbadolite was far from perfect when he chose it as the Battlegroup airhead. It was five hundred kilometres from the mine, but he had a plan to get the armour to the target. The fact was that they had to use the dilapidated airfield because it was the only runway in the region that was capable of taking the huge jets. Crucially, it was also outside the control of any government.

It was actually just a village in the middle of the jungle at the northern extremity of the Democratic Republic of Congo, just south of the Ubangi River, which formed the border with CAR. The runway had been built there because it was the birthplace of President Mobutu who, when he ruled Congo, had wanted an international airport so that he could fly in 747-loads of guests for parties at his huge palace nearby.

Mobutu had died and, in the wars that then ripped the country apart, his palace had been looted, the airport buildings smashed and five million people killed. A local tribal militia now ran the area; it was over a thousand kilometres from the government in Kinshasa. They made money by refuelling illegal arms flights across the continent.

Patrice had bribed the local commander when Alex's group had flown through on their way to do the recce. He had not told the militia what equipment would be flown in, but had promised that it would not disturb them at all. The commander had agreed to look the other way and future payments were arranged to ensure continued co-operation.

To increase security for the operation, the landings had been scheduled at night. With all the runway lights out of action this was tricky, as they had to make a flare path out of oil drums filled with sand and petrol. As they had driven down the side of the runway dropping these off a truck, Alex was reminded of a joke and had turned to Arkady. 'Hey, got a question for you! What did they used to use for light before they had candles in the Congo?'

Arkady looked at him blankly.

'Electricity.'

Confronted with Alex's amusement at his own joke, the Russian had had to crack a smile; but it was a serious point about the retreat into darkness in the heart of Africa that had happened over the last few decades.

Alex was definitely feeling on better form and it showed. He loved being on ops; the shared endeavour with his team to overcome obstacles bred a huge camaraderie.

Before taking on the task he had felt defined by his failures. His whole life had felt cordoned off and penned in behind watchtowers marked: 'Money for the house repairs', 'Lawsuit from neighbours', 'No job'. His natural dynamism and good nature had been trapped inside this pen, becoming soured and angry like a caged animal prowling up and down behind the wire.

Now the watchtowers had toppled and his vitality was out and running free. His natural talents were considerable when they were focused on getting the Battlegroup ready to win. With his height and his broad shoulders, he was an imposing commander.

He had a sharp mind, great field experience and an intelligent manner with his men. His good mood carried them along and smoothed over the conflicts of opinion and quarrels that always arose between the strong characters around him.

So they had lit the petrol flares and the huge jets had roared in every night for the last week. They taxied to the end of the runway away from the old airport buildings and disgorged tons of vehicles, ammunition, equipment and men. They kept their engines running as they refuelled and, as soon as the loads were off, closed their cargo ramps, taxied and roared off back to Europe. The vehicles then drove away into the night to the forward assembly area twenty miles into the bush by the Ubangi River.

The tank was the last item to be delivered because Arkady had been worried that it would damage the aircraft and halt the flow of supplies. He slapped its massive armour plating now. It felt like hitting a cliff: there was no reverberation from the metal at all.

'Good Russian engineering, eh?' He looked at the others.

'Sure is,' said Kalil, feeling completely out of his depth now that he was in the military phase of the operation. 'That's what we pay you guys for.'

Alex had spent a lot of money on the tank and felt the need to justify the cost to his employer, although Kalil had not balked at any of the bills presented to him. Alex was beginning to wonder where the cartel got its money from; it was going to take them a long time to earn the investment back from the mine.

'It's the new upgraded T-72S export version,' he

said, laying a hand proprietorially on the front glacis. 'This is a 125mm smoothbore gun.' He stretched his other hand up over his head to tap it. 'It's got a new SAVAN fire-control system. Those are the optics you can see sticking out by the commander's hatch.' He turned round and pointed to the top of the turret.

Kalil nodded, not understanding a thing.

'It gives me panoramic vision and a thermal imager for night fighting.' He was itching to try it out. 'With the laser range finder and guidance system we can fire on the move and pretty much hit anything up to three kilometres away.'

He hopped up onto the hull and stood next to where Tshombe's head stuck out from the driver's hatch. 'That's the 7.62mm, which is coaxial with the turret.' He pointed to the machine gun sticking out alongside the main armament. 'On top of the turret is the 12.7mm anti-aircraft gun. With this new upgrade I can lay and fire the gun from my position inside the tank—which means I don't have to get my head shot off . . . which is good,' he grinned.

'These are the eight smoke-grenade launchers at the front here.' He tapped them with his foot. 'Oh, yes, and this stuff is ERA—explosive reactive armour.' He thumped the small bricks that were stuck on every surface on the top of the tank. Kalil flinched. 'Don't worry; you need to hit them with at least an RPG before they go off.

'Umm,' he pursed his mouth and looked around trying to think if there was anything else, 'upgraded command radios for controlling the squadron, smoke unit at the back there . . . oh, yes—of course!' He had forgotten it in his excitement. He squatted down next to the left-hand side of the turret and slapped a large tube attached to it. 'My secret weapon!' he laughed.

14 MAY 1525, FRANKENHAUSEN, CENTRAL GERMANY

'Gunners are coming,' Eberhardt said.

He was standing with Albrecht on the edge of the Hausberg, an outcrop, four hundred feet up, looking out south over a broad river valley at the advancing Imperial forces. It was late evening but the long summer days kept blue sky above their heads and larks trilled over them in the warm air.

It was three months since the riot in the cathedral that had sparked the Peasants' War. Eberhardt's military experience meant that Thomas had appointed him as commander of a ragged army of eight thousand peasants, which had set out from Mühlhausen three days ago to seek a final battle with the Princes.

'Hmm, pikemen coming as well. Look, down there.' Albrecht shielded his eyes from the low westerly sun and pointed down the slope to where a column of lands-knecht mercenaries marched through the cornfields. They shouldered their weapons so that, from a distance, the hundreds of eighteen-foot-long poles held upright made them look like a huge box inching its way across the land, the long blades flashing in the sun.

The fields around them were so riddled with poppies that they looked like they were stained red. The distant noise of the column's drummers drifted up the hill.

Manfred was with them as well; his shaven-headed bulk looked even more threatening than usual because he wore a coat of scale mail over padded leather, which he had taken from the Mühlhausen town guard.

'Well, I've got just the thing for them,' he said, hitching the massive *Zweihänder* that he rested on his shoulder. The sword was five feet long, double-bladed and designed for cutting off the pike heads of an advancing phalanx. The 'cat-gutter' short sword hanging at his waist was for when he reached the men behind the pikes.

'Hmm, that'll sort them out,' Eberhardt grunted, and carried on trying to count the number of handgunners in the other column converging on the hill.

The Hausberg was an outlier from a ridge that ran east–west and marked the southern edge of the dense Kyffhäuser woods behind them. The hill itself was a misshapen lump a mile wide. It was covered in uneven ground and dotted with woods and gorse bushes. A few large meadows had been cleared by local farmers for grazing sheep.

On the valley floor below them lay the village of Frankenhausen. From this height its church tower, manor house and scattered farms seemed like children's toys. All were deserted and still in the gentle evening light.

The Army of God was made up of peasants on foot mixed in with a ramshackle collection of two- and four-wheeled farm carts pulled by oxen. It had been passing through the village at lunchtime when their scouts, the term Eberhardt used for the boys on carthorses, whom he had sent out ahead of them, had come clattering back down the road saying that they had seen the Imperial army up ahead. A cavalry force had been sent to cut the peasants off and force them into battle with the main army of Prince Philip of Hesse and Duke George of Saxony, coming up behind them. They were two and a half days' march from Mühlhausen and their great battle had finally found them.

Eberhardt had ridden quickly up the Hausberg and surveyed it; he wanted a good defensive position to fight from. Hurriedly he ordered the peasants to haul their fighting carts up the steep tracks and corral them into a laager in one of the large meadows on the hill.

The carts were to be adapted for war with the addition of heavy wooden boards down one side with loopholes cut in them for small cannon to fire out of. The tactic of laagering them into a defensive circle had been used to good effect by Hussite heretics in Bohemia against Imperial cavalry in the last century. Eberhardt was hoping to be able to do the same thing again.

He glanced back over his shoulder at the laager. The carts had not formed a long enough line to encircle the whole force so he had had to order the construction of defences in the gaps between them. Gangs of peasants were digging like fury now to create ditches and earth ramparts topped by cut gorse and stakes.

The carts themselves were being turned into wooden castles as peasants nailed boards and barn doors onto them on the outside of the circle; the dull banging of hammers reached their leaders' ears.

The gaps under and between the carts had been blocked up with bushes and pieces pulled from nearby fences. A few of Eberhardt's men had gunnery experience from time served in landsknecht regiments and they were hastily instructing peasants how to load and fire the cannon that were pointing out of embrasures in the sides of the carts. These were simple devices: thick metal tubes strapped to blocks of wood and packed with powder and a variety of stones and scraps of metal that would simply be blasted out as a crude form of shotgun. It was all far from perfect but it would have to do.

Despite his outward hearty assertion of divine victory, Eberhardt could feel fear gnawing away inside him. He looked back down the hill at the advancing Imperial forces and frowned; his heavy beard sank onto his chest. With its streaks of grey and the bags under his eyes he looked exhausted. All across the river valley, columns of men, horses, carts and guns were converging in on them, thousands and thousands of soldiers trailing shimmering clouds of dust.

They were a mixture of forces: feudal levies and paid landsknechts. He could see knights riding at the head of the columns. A pang went through him at the sight of their bright armour flashing in the sun and the coloured plumes waving on their helmets. All over the plain, bright heraldic colours had sprouted on banners and shields like early summer flowers: blues, reds, greens, blacks and yellows in a myriad of patterns.

Alongside them flew banners with the symbols of aristocratic power: lions, dragons, boars, bears, eagles and unicorns—rampaging, snarling, roaring and baying for his blood.

The foot soldiers were a mixture of pikemen

and handgunners. Their arquebuses—matchlock muskets—were slow to use but were still effective, not just because of their heavy lead slugs but also the psychological shock of the torrent of fire and smoke that they belched out.

Eberhardt could see that no expense had been spared in the bid to exterminate the peasants. The army had a good number of the latest field guns. From this distance their long barrels and light limbers looked too delicate to do any harm but he knew the reality of this new development in artillery from his time in the Italian Wars. Adapting the power of mighty siege guns to be mobile enough to fit onto the battlefield had been a big advance in an army's killing power.

Finally he glanced at the few columns of heavy cavalry. They were increasingly being replaced by infantry in warfare these days but they would still be deadly against his amateur army. Men and horses encased in armour, with lances, maces and swords, were hard for peasants with home-made weapons to damage.

What could they do against all this?

The pit of fear yawned under him; he could feel himself slipping down the slope into it. He closed his eyes, breathed in and out heavily through his nose and remembered their secret weapon.

Thomas had had another word from God the night before and prophesied that He would save them. Eberhardt had already witnessed the accuracy of one of his prophecies and now he believed in this one.

The priest had proclaimed to his simple peasant soldiers that they would catch the bullets of the enemy in the sleeves of their shirts. The wide cuffs of peasant smocks were used for holding seed when they scattered it on the fields and the simple image had stuck in their mind, so convinced were they by the truth of his teachings.

Eberhardt glanced down again and saw a screen of infantry skirmishers with crossbows moving carefully up into the woods on the lower slopes of the Hausberg, ahead of the main columns. They were moving from tree to tree, using the cover to probe forwards, searching for the outer peasant defences and any stragglers.

'Come on, we'd better get back inside the laager,' he muttered nervously to Albrecht and Manfred.

*   *   *

Urs Schwartz narrowed his eyes and peered at the peasants' laager over the sharpened stakes in front of his company's position. It was dawn the next day and misty.

Across the uneven ground the outline of carts, ditches and rickety fences was still. He could hear a few noises from the peasants: coughing and spitting as they roused themselves.

Urs was forty-five and an *oberster feldwebel*—regimental sergeant-major—in a landsknecht regiment. He wore a scarlet sash of office over his yellow and black striped doublet.

His men referred to him as *der Eber*—the Boar—partly because of his manner and partly because he looked like one. He had small piggy eyes set in a fleshy face and a permanently suspicious look that said that he had not got where he was in life by trusting people. He was heavily built and his jowls

116

wobbled when he shouted. His landsknecht moustache drooped down either side of his mouth onto his chest and he had a sabre scar across the brow of his nose and down one cheek.

He did not like these campaigns against the peasants. He was from a good German peasant family himself, and proud of it. He was also a Lutheran and sympathised with their anger against the foreign control of the Church.

However, Luther himself had turned against the radicals. Urs had read his pamphlet 'Against the Thieving, Murdering Horde of Peasants'.

'Let everyone who can: smite, slay and stab the peasants, secretly and openly, remembering that nothing can be more poisonous, hurtful, or devilish than a rebel. It is just as when one must kill a mad dog; if you do not strike him, he will strike you and the whole land with you. Listen to me: stab, knock and strangle them, there should be no mercy. Let the guns roar amongst them!'

Urs could not make sense of it all.

All he knew was that he was a professional mercenary and that he was being paid well to kill all the peasants that he could; the regiment's bonus payment depended on it. Their aristocratic paymasters wanted nothing less than savagery or they would hold back the majority of their cash. That was the capital he needed to buy himself the farm of his dreams and get out of this brutal life.

He glanced up at the sky to check the weather. Although it was cold now, the clear sky presaged a hot day. He looked back towards where his men were bivouacked. Gustav and Hans, his two sergeants, were going round kicking them awake. They would be up soon and ready to do the job, he would make sure of that.

Gradually the Imperial troops roused themselves. They had encircled the peasant laager during the evening, two hundred yards from its perimeter. The handgunners and pikemen of Urs' company wolfed their breakfast under his impatient eye. Artillery crews stood ready in their batteries with powder and shot stacked next to them, linstocks smoking gently. The gunners had drawn their artillery up into four batteries evenly spaced around the laager, ready to unleash a torrent of shot.

Screened behind trees, knights were buckling on their plate armour and reaching for their lances. Their mounts tossed their heads and protested as squires led them into line.

Eberhardt woke up to the smell of dew.

He had spent the night under a cart on the perimeter in case of a night attack. He looked out over the field; eight thousand men had slept under scraps of tents or in the open under sacking. There was the sound of coughing and hawking, the smell of fires getting going and lines of men trooping to and fro from the makeshift latrine trenches.

He rubbed a hand over his face, greasy with sleep, and knew there was not much more that he could do. Their battle plan was basic: no lines of outer field works to break up and direct attacks into carefully prepared killing grounds with interlocking fields of fire. No strategic reserve of cavalry to hold back for the final charge to annihilate the enemy after it had been worn down by manoeuvres. Just a bunch of peasants huddled inside a laager.

He gulped water from his canteen, swilled it round his mouth and spat it out on the grass next to him.

Joachim the Weaver woke up feeling as excited as a child on Christmas morning. Today was the big day—God was coming. Today was the day when it would all come together; he would earn his just reward for a life of obedience and faith. He was soaked with dew and his bones hurt from his arthritis but he was still ecstatic.

He was proud of the work that he had done yesterday, digging an earth embrasure, and of the halberd that he had taken from the Mühlhausen armoury. It was an axe on a six-foot pole with a spike on the top and a hook behind it for pulling knights off their horses.

He thought about his wife back home in the hut on the edge of the forest; he was doing it for her good. He hoped he would be brave and do his duty.

Thomas was in his main tent in the centre of the laager next to a large hay cart, which he had used to address the troops from, the day before. He had been praying late into the night and his thin face was ashen and unshaven, his eyes red and puffy. His thick brown hair was greasy and stuck up on one side where he had slept on it.

'Thomas, you should eat something,' Heinrich Pfeiffer, his personal priest, encouraged him.

Absentmindedly he gnawed at a hunk of bread and stared off across the meadow.

He was too febrile with excitement to eat heartily. He fully expected to be meeting God face-to-face that day.

Once all the Imperial officers had checked that their men were armed and in position, runners took the reports to the tent of Prince Philip and Duke

George. The two commanders were decked out in beautiful hand-painted armour of finest Milanese steel; they walked up to one of the four main batteries arranged on the front line. A nod from Duke George's plumed helmet and a single signal gun fired.

Eberhardt heard the dull thump as he was bending over, overseeing the loading of a cannon on a cart. He was startled by the sound and looked up. His eyes met Albrecht's on the other side of the gun.

There was a pause and then the bombardment began.

Fire and black smoke crashed out of the woods. Shot screamed overhead or banged as it hit wagons, knocking their wheels off, smashing the wood panels on their sides. Men were blown back, eviscerated and maimed.

The peasants were terrified by the noise. The metal howled as if the Devil himself was setting about them with glee. Many stood paralysed with fear or flung themselves on the ground with their hands over their ears. A few cannon banged out from the carts in defiance but the shot scattered uselessly and the gunners were too terrified to cope with reloading.

In the Imperial batteries the cannon recoiled back on their wheels before the gun crews threw themselves against their limbers and heaved them back into place. They were sponged, loaded and fired again as fast as they could. The air became heavy with the saltpetre stink of gunpowder.

Half an hour of relentless pounding followed. The batteries concentrated on four points until large gaps had been blown in the defences. The carts in the way were smashed into jagged pieces, which were scattered over the grass, and the areas around them swept clear of defenders by grapeshot.

As the bombardment went on, the knights stood next to their mounts, holding their bridles and stroking their heads to calm their nerves. Both animals and men were dressed in heavy metal plates. Intermittently the riders hefted their swords or studied their lances, thinking about how they would use them.

Urs was now wearing his metal breastplate and armour like a lobster's scales over his stomach and legs. His large steel helmet was open-faced, with a peaked visor, and he held a halberd in one hand. The cat-gutter at his waist was in case things got messy.

He looked intensely at his handgunners. Were they ready for battle?

He had been at them since first light, making them clean their matchlocks, inspecting their powder horns and musket balls. He then ran over to his company of pikemen and strutted up and down the column, getting them in line.

Once the guns had blown four large gaps in the defences, the shout came to cease fire. The silence filled the air after the percussion of the bombardment. Smoke drifted away from the batteries.

Taking his cue, Urs turned to the boys standing next to the pike company. His red face bellowed at them: 'Drummers!'

Their thunder filled the void of the guns and drove the men on. Files of pikemen emerged from the Imperial lines and, in response to shouts from their

121

officers, paraded, turned and faced the enemy. An *Igel*, or hedgehog, was formed—a column fifteen men wide and thirty deep. Huge poles swayed precariously above them as the front eight ranks lowered their weapons. With these pikes down and those behind held upright it looked to the peasants as if the forest itself had come alive and was advancing against them in a glittering steel-tipped phalanx.

Eberhardt had loaded and fired the cannon in his cart twice at the batteries opposite him. This defiance had drawn their attention and retaliatory fire. The first cannon ball punched through the boards above his head, spraying splinters over the gun crews inside.

A spike of wood whipped across his forehead, gashing it open. A heavy round then caught the frame of the cart, knocking whole boards loose and throwing him back out of it. As the hailstorm of shot broke upon them, Albrecht dived after him and they huddled on the ground beneath the screaming madness. The cart was knocked off its wheels onto its side and smashed to sticks.

In the pause as the pikes paraded, Albrecht lay shaking with fear on the ground. He could see Eberhardt next to him; his face was covered in blood. It was seeping down into his beard and curling it as it dried. Eventually, the lack of gunfire calmed him and he looked up.

The sight of the *Igel* approaching threw him back into terror. The pikes were so dense that he could not see the men holding them, just eight rows of metal spikes lowered and advancing at the brisk walking pace that gave pikes their shock factor.

Albrecht was galvanised. He stood up, and, with

strength from fear, grasped the dead weight of Eberhardt under the arms and hauled him back, away from the advance of this strange monster, towards the pavilion in the centre of the laager.

Urs ran forward along the side of the pike phalanx, leading a file of forty handgunners with their muskets held at port in front of them. Once in range of the carts he hastily formed them into two ranks, one standing and one kneeling, and fired a salvo into the defences to suppress any fire as the pikes neared it.

He need not have worried, the peasants were too terrified and disorganised by the bombardment to fire on them.

Then the pikes were at the breach. Urs spotted a gap blown in the fence at the top of the rampart next to it. Shouting commands, he formed the ranks into a double column and led his gunners down the ditch and up through the gap.

Manfred ran over from where he had been on the perimeter. His bare head bulged out of his bulky metal shoulders. He shouted at the peasants around him:

'Stand fast! Stand fast!'

He cuffed them into rallying to confront the pike column as it nosed its way in through the gap in the wagons. Holding his huge sword in both hands in front of him he looked steadily at the wall of approaching metal spikes. Screaming defiance he ran at it with his huge *Zweihänder* sword swinging. He cut into the pike heads; splinters of metal and wood went flying as he carved a path into them and was swallowed up in the forest of poles. The peasants cheered wildly and followed in the gap he made, bashing away at the hated pikes with swords, axes and halberds.

On other side of the laager, Graf Wolfgang von Frundsberg wanted revenge for the burning of his *Schloss* and the murder of members of his family by rebels in Franconia. Cavalry might not be able to dominate the battlefield as it used to but he was determined to do his bit against the bloody peasants where he could. As the artillery ended he yelled, 'Charge!' to his bugler, then snapped his helmet visor shut and led the way.

He had selected a tract of land that allowed the horses to get up speed before breaking cover from behind a copse. As the smoke eddied across the battlefield, the ground under it began to tremble.

The column of four hundred heavily armoured knights broke cover at full gallop, banners flying and lances levelled. Nothing was going to stop them.

Joachim emerged shaken from behind the earth bank where he had cowered with his fellow defenders. He had felt the ground shudder as metal had thumped into the embrasure. Several men had stood up and fled in fear; one lay beheaded a few yards behind him now.

Once the firing stopped, others took the chance to flee more safely. Joachim's gut felt watery with fear and his hands shook as he grasped the heavy pole of his halberd. He wanted to run but his sense of duty held him. Thomas had said that Jesus had felt fear but had not flinched from the cross.

'Stay with it, lads, stay with it,' he called to the youngsters around him.

The cavalry charge was aimed directly at a gap blown in the line of carts. One wagon next to it was still on its wheels and Joachim clambered onto the flatbed wielding the polearm.

The huge horses jumped the wreckage in the gap, their eyes wild. Bright colours and plumes flashed by as the armoured stream poured into the centre of the camp. The noise of their thunder was tremendous and the air was torn by their passing.

Standing on the edge of this Joachim was able to raise his halberd and swing it in at a knight on the edge of the torrent. The hook caught in the gap between his shoulder plates. He was jerked back in his saddle, lost his balance and toppled off the horse.

The halberd was yanked out of Joachim's hands and he fell off the cart. Both of them lay in a tangle on the ground.

Joachim staggered to his feet and picked up the weapon. The knight had landed on his back and was winded; he struggled feebly to breathe through his closed visor. Joachim held the pole halfway along its length in both hands and raised it over his head. He drove the foot-long metal spike on top of the pole through the grille on the man's helmet.

A companion of the knight had seen him unhorsed but had been swept along with the charge as it poured in through the narrow gap. However, once in the laager he was able to break away from the stampede, peel back round and turn to face Joachim, his lance levelled.

He spurred his horse into a gallop. Narrowing his eyes, he squinted through the visor slit. His narrow field of vision shook with the thunder of the charge but he saw the peasant yank the spike out of the fallen knight and straighten up. He concentrated on the bright red pennant dancing on the end of his lance, guiding it in to the peasant's back.

As he neared, he stood up in his saddle and moved the lance away from his body. It speared into Joachim, the momentum drove it through his frail ribs and on into the ground.

The impact snatched the lance back and away from the knight, he released his grip and let his arm wheel. He rode on, leaving the old weaver skewered and propped up in midair like a strange statue.

Thomas stood on the flatbed of the big haywain in the centre of the camp and looked around him. He could see three phalanxes of pikes pushing in through the carts at different points. Then his head jerked round as he heard and then saw the charge of the column of knights. They streamed into the sanctuary of his army, and to him they seemed like the hounds of Hell. He grabbed a banner with the *Bundschuh* symbol of the peasants and ran towards them.

The cavalry charge spread out as they entered open ground. Stragglers from the perimeter ran in panic from them and were lanced. By the time Thomas intersected with them most of the knights had already used their lances and drawn their swords or unhooked their maces.

He shouted and waved his white banner at them furiously.

'The gates of Hell shall not prevail! The children of light shall overcome you, Satan!'

Several huge beasts thundered by him, riders intent on hacking down fugitives.

Thomas staggered and turned as they whirled past him. 'The Lord said to Beelzebub, "I bind thee in the name . . ."' A blow from a mace caught him across the back of the head and he fell.

The battle broke down into a series of confused fights. Some peasants rallied and fought in beleaguered groups. Bands of knights rode around hacking at them from their high saddles. Herds of fleeing humans were driven hither and thither like sheep.

The cart wall became a liability as terrified rebels tried to climb over, under and through it, but got caught in the crush and were trapped. Gunners poured grapeshot at those who did make it out. Crowds built up behind the wall, which the knights rode through with their swords, slashing to right and left.

The corral of cart horses and oxen in the centre of the camp broke open and more carnage exploded. Terrified beasts blundered around, wild-eyed and bellowing in fear. Oxen trampled on peasants and soldiers alike, crashed into knights and unhorsed them.

The pike columns broke into smaller squares that charged across the open space, impaling anyone in their way. A mad scrum of humanity developed with one half trying to butcher the other.

Urs Schwartz led his company of handgunners in through the mayhem. A young man running in fear crashed headlong into him. The heavy old sergeant shouldered the blow and punched him out of his way. He was looking for a decent target for his men to shoot at.

Eberhardt came to, lying on the ground under the haywain where Albrecht had dragged him. His face was a mask of dried blood. White bone showed where his forehead was gashed until Albrecht bound his head with a ripped cloth. All around them was the furious bedlam of the battle: screaming men, thundering hoofs, bellowing livestock.

A crowd of peasants had taken shelter under the haywain and in the tent next to it. They cowered from the havoc around them. Eberhardt jerked into consciousness and saw Albrecht kneeling over him. He struggled to sit up and looked around frantically.

'The victory? What's happened to the victory?'

All he could see were peasants cowering or running in fear.

Albrecht dropped his eyes. 'God is coming. *God is coming!*'

Eberhardt's eyes were wide with fear. What if God should come and find him wanting? He struggled up and crawled out from under the cart.

'Brothers!' he shouted at the peasants hurrying around him. 'We must make an offering to Our Lord!' He was terrified that the Second Coming might not happen. He realised that he needed to restore events to their rightful path. He turned and bellowed at the men under the cart in his most commanding voice, '*Get on this cart now!*'

All his natural authority and fury went into bending those men to his will. They were dragged out of their stupor and clambered onto the haywain, cringing from the mayhem. He stood on the ground in front of them.

'God will not come unless *we* show Him our devotion and praise! We *must* make Him hear our prayers! Scripture says that the people of God will sing and make music to their Lord!'

Hymn singing was one of the defining features of

the popular Reformation. Radical preachers had taken Latin songs from church choirs and actually allowed the common folk to sing them in the vernacular.

He thought for a moment. 'We shall sing "Now we pray the Holy Ghost".'

Initially they looked at him aghast but his certainty was so domineering that he swept them along in front of him like leaves in a blast of air.

Forty men were clustered on or next to the wagon. Eberhardt raised his arms to start the singing. He bellowed in his full-throated voice:

'Now we pray the Holy Ghost
For the true faith, which we need the most,'

Their voices were thin and faltering but gradually picked up confidence from each other.

'That in our last moments He may befriend
    us
And, as homeward we journey, attend us.
Lord, have mercy.'

Urs Schwartz saw the group forming around the wagon and led his men in towards them. Here at last was a target that was standing still and worth shooting at.

When he got nearer, he heard that they were singing. He caught the tune and realised that he knew the hymn—it was one of his favourites.

He stood and stared at them. What the hell did they think they were doing? This was a battle. This was no place for singing. He felt a mixture of incomprehension, outrage and pity.

He was a hard man who had done a lot of killing in his life. His orders instructed him to kill them. But shooting a group of his fellow countrymen as they sang hymns seemed too much. What should he do with them?

He would give them a chance to surrender.

'Peasants!' he bellowed in his huge field voice, trying to make himself heard over them. 'Surrender yourselves!'

Eberhardt had his back to him as he conducted the singing but looked round at the huge shout. In front of him was an agent of the Devil, his saggy red face poking out of its helmet, raging with anger.

He ignored him and turned back to the singers. 'Sing on, brothers! The gates of Hell will not prevail! Thomas has said that we will catch the bullets in the sleeves of our shirts!'

He laughed and held out a wide cuff. The simple image came back to him now and he was certain in the strength of the prophecy. He jumped up onto the cart facing the gunners and held his arms up so that his sleeves fell open. The other singers did the same.

Eberhardt shouted joyfully, 'Sing on! Sing on, brothers!'

They began the second verse.

'Shine in our hearts, O most precious Light,
That we Jesus Christ may know aright,
Clinging to our Saviour, whose blood hath
    bought us.
Who again to our homeland hath brought us.
Lord, have mercy.'

Eberhardt's arrogant gesture infuriated Urs, his face flushed. His orders were clear. The peasants were agents of the Devil and as such must be exterminated. He had given them a chance. He roared out commands to his men as they sang on.

'In two ranks! *Fall in!*'

The gunners hurried forward and formed two ranks, facing the hymn singers at thirty yards.

'Make correct your ranks! Make correct your files! In post! *Fall in!*'

The front rank kneeled and those behind stood, squinting along the heavy barrels of their arquebuses. Their matchlocks smouldered.

Urs stood to one side of them and took one final look at the singers. The peasants had closed their eyes and were lost in their own world, carried away on an ecstasy of faith. They were standing with their arms raised, faces shining with the joy of their singing and belief in their salvation.

Fellow Protestants, fellow Germans, fellow human beings.

He looked back down the rank of his gunners and forced himself to think about his dream farm. He tried to sustain the pressure of his righteous indignation.

Damn them, they had asked for it!

He raised his arm, it trembled slightly, then he brought it swingeing down.

'Front rank! *Fire!*'

Fire and smoke crashed out.

Arms jerked and figures spun as the heavy rounds hit them at close range. Bodies bounced back into the living or tumbled backwards off the cart.

The singing faltered for a second but then sprang

back louder than before.

'Thou sacred Love, grace on us bestow,
Set our hearts with heavenly fire aglow
That with hearts united we love each other,
Of one mind, in peace with every brother.
Lord, have mercy!'

Urs was enraged. Luther was right—they should be killed as a rabid dog!

As they started the next verse he screamed, *'Fire!'* and the second volley of smoke and flame boomed out.

More men were dashed backwards and fell twitching on the floor of the cart. About twenty singers were left. Eberhardt was unscathed so far and sang on with his eyes closed. Some of the gunners were deliberately firing high and none wanted to aim at the commanding choirmaster in the centre of his flock.

Urs was red in the face. His scar flamed and his jowls shook with fury. He raised his arm again and brought it scything down.

'Fire!'

A third volley blasted into them. The man singing next to Eberhardt was struck in the face and knocked over.

Urs stared at the twelve men left. Their singing had dropped in volume but their intensity was unchecked. The cart was draped with bodies. The wounded moaned and cried out; adding a terrible accompaniment to the hymn.

He had hoped to teach them a lesson, to scare them. He wanted them to break and run after the first volley but they had stood undaunted and offered no resistance. There was nothing for him to keep fighting against; to maintain his righteous head of anger.

Now *his* will was breaking. He loved a hot fight: the salvo, the charge, the clash of pikes. But this was madness. This was cold-blooded slaughter.

They began the final verse. He followed the words in his head, anticipating them. Their meaning cut into his heart.

'Thou highest Comfort in every need,
Grant that neither shame nor death we heed,
That e'en then our courage may never fail us
When the Foe shall accuse and assail us.
Lord, have mercy!'

Urs raised his arm again to bring death down on their heads. He held his hand up, fingers flat and rigid like the blade of a knife. He looked at the bleeding pile of corpses on the cart and the maniacs standing amongst them singing.

His fingers crumpled like a leaf withering. His arm drooped and fell limply to his side. He turned away from the singers in disgust. Tears of anger and frustration started in his small eyes. A lump of pity stuck in his throat; he tried to give the correct orders to disengage and break formation but his voice cracked.

His whiskery face reddened. He walked along in front of the rank of his men with his face turned away from them, making a repeated sweeping gesture with his arm.

*   *   *

133

Thomas had created an apocalypse of truly biblical proportions.

The whole of the Hausberg outcrop was covered in a battling mass of humanity. Fifteen thousand men wrangled with each other: knights charged, peasants screamed, guns boomed. Maddened carthorses galloped, tails high, eyes rolling, blundering from one mêlée to the next.

Where gaps could be broken in the cart wall the peasants streamed out and ran. More cavalry were waiting in the woods around the camp and were thrown into action. The ground drummed as the heavy horses cantered forward. Fleeing footmen had no defence against the long lances that sought out and skewered them.

Then came the awful business of the knights riding through the crowds, bludgeoning left and right with sword and mace. They inflicted terrible wounds as they slashed back into the faces of the fleeing men.

The nobles had none of Urs' scruples about killing their countrymen. The peasants had sought to overturn their entire God-created world order: for that they would be damned and it was the knights' duty to send them on their way to Hell. It was tiring work but their status in society had been threatened and they were determined to regain it.

The peasants ran in blind panic. They banged into each other, fell into ditches, blundered into trees and bounced off, knocked senseless.

The main track down the hill went through a small gully. So many fugitives tried to get through that they got crammed together and blocked it; many were crushed underfoot.

Landsknecht gunners took up positions on the

slopes of the gully and fired down mercilessly into the press, driven on by their officers' batons if they slacked off from the appalling slaughter.

Some knights dismounted and stood across the track, wielding their heavy swords on any who squeezed their way through. Eventually they were so exhausted with hacking that they could cut no more. They staggered off into the woods and threw themselves on the ground. Ripping open their visors, they lay on their backs and gasped for air. The cloth surplices over their armour were sodden with gore.

Some peasants did escape into the dense Kyffhäuser woods where it was hard for the cavalry to chase them. However, of the eight thousand souls who left Mühlhausen, over six thousand were killed on the outcrop, which became known as the Schlachtberg—Slaughter Hill.

Of those who escaped the mêlée in the gully and made it down to Frankenhausen, many were taken prisoner by the Imperial forces that streamed after them. Three hundred were summarily executed; their bodies hung on every available beam and tree around the small village, as if it were celebrating some strange summer festival.

Eberhardt lived, with eleven members of his choir. When the ranks of the firing squad broke, he opened his eyes and saw his enemies turn away and disperse before him in confusion. Amazed, he ordered the survivors of the bloodbath to kneel down amongst the bodies piled on the cart and give prayers of thanks to God for saving them through their faith.

In the midst of the mayhem going on around them their kneeling forms became one with the dead and were ignored. The Imperial forces gradually dispersed as they chased the peasants down the hill, until none was left in the laager.

Quiet returned to the hilltop, the only movement smoke from the burning lines of carts. It formed a gentle, mournful shroud as it drifted across the carpet of broken bodies.

Birdsong returned to the sky.

Albrecht emerged terrified but unharmed from under the cart.

'Come on. God has saved us,' said Eberhardt gently, as he took his steward's shaking hand and helped him to his feet. He held up the sleeve of his shirt to show the bullet hole in it. With the rest of the band they picked their way over the wrack of bodies and walked unharmed into the Kyffhäuser woods.

Thomas had been knocked senseless by the blow to his head. He came round to find himself part of the graveyard covering the camp. Heinrich Pfeiffer and Manfred were also in it. Half out of his mind, Thomas fled with the remnants of his army, stumbling down the hill, and hid in the cowshed of a farm on the outskirts of Frankenhausen. He was discovered by soldiers conducting house-to-house searches for fugitives and hauled out of the straw where he had hidden. He was put on the rack and tortured in front of Prince Philip and Duke George before being beheaded on a scaffold in the royal camp outside Mühlhausen.

With its spiritual leader dead the Peasants' War was doomed. Eighty thousand died in a series of battles, and the punishment campaigns that followed. Some were slow-roasted over fires but most were hanged. The summer of 1525 was remembered for the smell of their corpses that hung over the landscape.

The Peasants' War was the largest uprising in Europe before the French Revolution but it achieved nothing. Despite all its fervour and size, the Kingdom of God was not established on earth and the peasants were forced back into bitter subservience.

At the time it looked like Thomas's influence had finished, but the power of the Dark Heart Prophecy that he had unleashed had not yet come to an end.

Yamba's shaved head was inches away from the soldier's face as he screamed at him. It was the following morning and his new soldiers were having their first parade at the forward assembly area.

'And what is in your sleeping bag?'

Spittle sprayed out over the man, who was shaking with fear, his voice unnaturally high as he tried to shout his answer, 'Leaves, sir!'

Yamba brought his knee up into his groin; the soldier doubled up and fell onto the ground. The sergeant-major then brought his heavy swagger stick down on his back with a sickening whack.

'You are on your first inspection parade *with me* and you come with *leaves* in your kit!' he screamed. The soldier groaned at his feet; Yamba hit him again with the stick.

He moved on down the rank of troops standing to attention, rigid with fear, their webbing and rucksacks spread out on the ground in front of them. The next man knew his kit was not in order. He held out his hands, imploring forgiveness.

Yamba beat him repeatedly with the stick.

Alex, Kalil and Col blanched as they watched this calculated sadism. The troops were experienced African infantrymen that Yamba had recruited but he had not worked with them before and wanted to put his stamp of authority on them. After his experiences in the Angolan wars he was going to make very sure that they were more afraid of him than they were of the enemy. He knew it was the best way of turning them into an efficient fighting force and keeping as many of them alive as possible.

Yamba continued to work his way round the two ranks of men standing in a clearing in the bush.

Alex felt they had seen enough and gestured to lead Kalil away to continue their tour of the forward assembly area.

'Well, that's the first time I've been seen as the soft option in the regiment, I can tell you,' Col said, trying to lighten the mood.

It was Kalil's first morning on the base where Alex was putting the Battlegroup together. The tall cavalryman was on good form. He was back in camouflage gear, with a slouch bush hat and Oakley shades against the hot sun. He was feeling enlivened by the scale of the challenge that he faced, and was keen to show his employer what they had achieved so far.

The base had been set up on the site of an abandoned sisal plantation next to the Ubangi River. Alex had recced it on their way to the mine: it was far enough away from the airport to be secret but was near the river and had a jetty. Also the huge metal sheds, which had been used for storing the sword-shaped sisal leaves and the fibre that came from them, were still intact and served well as workshops, offices and barracks.

The plantation was a large site. Dotted in amongst the buildings, old sisal fields and surrounding jungle were over two hundred personnel of one sort or another. All the infantry were black: experienced Angolans and South Africans from Yamba's 32 Battalion connections.

The officers and NCOs were a mixture of South African—both black and white—alongside a few

Brits and Russians. These mercenaries were thuggish-looking men, mainly in their thirties and forties, dressed in camouflage fatigues. They were old Africa hands: heavily built and raw-boned, with moustaches, beards, crew cuts, and tattoos. They had the cold, quiet eyes of men used to dealing in extreme violence.

The atmosphere on the base was one of frenzied but purposeful activity. NCOs strutted around like starlings, pointing and shouting. The party toured the old plantation warehouses, which had been cleared and converted into workshops that were ringing to the sound of generators, compressors, grinders and welding equipment as vehicles were tested and fitted out to their commanders' spec.

Intermittent crackles of small-arms fire echoed across the base from the firing range as soldiers zeroed the sights of their weapons.

A brief rain squall passed over and they sheltered under the corrugated roof of a warehouse, watching the rain pour off the eaves. When they walked on they picked their way around the puddles in the red mud, which were already steaming as the sun came out again. To Kalil the whole place felt like being in an overheated sauna, the air and land were permanently damp and smelled of rotting vegetation.

'Right, let's head over there to the vehicle park.' Alex pointed them left to a stand of huge kapok trees. Strung out between them were cam nets, shielding the vehicles from any over-flying aircraft. Here were the Russian GAZ-66 trucks, snoutnosed brutes with huge wheels and high ground clearance to get over all but the toughest terrain. They would carry the troops, food, ammunition and other supplies the Battlegroup would need. Mixed in with them were water and petrol bowsers, an aviation fuel tanker and the radio truck.

On a large, cleared sisal field next to them, mechanised infantry were being exercised in the BMP 2 armoured fighting vehicles. Each had the hull of a tank but with only a very small turret on top with a 30mm cannon in it, and its main job was to carry a squad of eight infantry in the back. Two of the group's four BMPs were tearing around the training ground and then lurching to a halt to debus their troops as they practised defile drills, immediate counterambush measures and night laager techniques.

Alex began explaining these enthusiastically but sensed that Kalil had had enough when his eyes started drifting away into the middle distance.

'OK, right, let's go and see the airport then,' he said.

They retraced their steps to another large field on the other side of the plantation. In the middle of it under more cam netting were two helicopters being worked on by a gang of Russians.

'That's Arkady and the mechanics,' said Alex as they approached, and then stopped and looked quizzically at Col. 'Isn't that a band?'

'Er . . . no, that's *Mike* and the Mechanics, I think you'll find,' he said with a grin.

'Oh, yes.'

Kalil glanced from one to the other, unsure what to make of their joking around. He was trying to be hard-arsed and serious but the other two were enjoying themselves too much being back in the field, doing what they loved.

They stepped awkwardly over the large clumps of sisal that had been cut down to clear the field and approached the helicopters. Arkady saw them coming and waved. He was stripped to the waist and wearing a pair of faded blue shorts. His broad chin was covered in stubble and, as ever, he had a cigarette stuck in the corner of his mouth that waggled as he grinned and called out, 'Welcome to new Terminal Six, Heathrow Airport!'

Col replied with a hearty, 'Eh up, comrade!'

Arkady shook Kalil's hand enthusiastically and introduced him to Yevgeny, his co-pilot in the Mi-17, and the rest of the Russian ground crew.

'And here is star of show, Captain Pavel Karpovich, late of Russian Army Air Corps. I recruited him personally to fly the Shark. Best pilot they had!'

He put his arm around the shoulders of a slim, young Russian man with a mop of straw-coloured hair. He grinned at Kalil, slightly embarrassed by Arkady's praise.

'So, this must be the Shark that I have heard so much about, then?' said Kalil looking at the attack helicopter under the netting.

The Kamov Ka-50 was a spiky, angry-looking machine like a dark green scorpion. Its strangest feature was that the two main rotors were mounted one above the other. By rotating in different directions these cancelled out the normal need for a tail rotor and thus streamlined the airframe hugely. Midway along it were a pair of stubby wings with four hardpoints for weaponry, in this case four rocket pods. On the right of the armoured cockpit was the main armament of a 30mm cannon.

By contrast to its aggressive lines, the Mi-17 troopship looked like a dumpy depressed beetle. It had a bulbous design and its huge rotor blades drooped down around it.

Alex explained, 'The Shark is for combat and the Mil is for troops, casevac, supplies and reconnaissance.' He pointed out the alterations being made. 'We're fitting both with GPS, reconnaissance cameras and FLIR—that's forward-looking infrared—cameras, so that we can use them to scout ahead of the group when we are underway.'

He felt they had seen enough of the air wing and moved them on with a clap of his hands and a brisk, 'Right, let's head over to the ops room and I'll tell you the rest of the plan.'

EVENING, 20 OCTOBER 1525, BAHR EL GHAZAL REGION, THE KINGDOM OF SUDAN

Eberhardt had returned to his youthful habit of writing in his *The Quest for Glory* journals.

> Good progress today: thirty miles or more. Pilgrims happy enough in general but Diederich still struck by griping in the guts. Poor fellow looking very thin.
>
> Heat a problem but more shade now as we enter woodlands. No sign of bandits from the other day.
>
> Saw mighty deer off to the left, though. Hassan says we will see elephants soon. Tomorrow we start up into hills.

It was not as high-flown as it had been in his heyday as a writer but it reflected his better spirits. He always felt more alive when travelling; he loved the new experiences and the sense of entering the unknown. He slept with the book under his pillow every night and planned to donate it to his friend Ludwig Fritzler in Heidelberg University library when they returned from the expedition.

Now, though, he was too tired to write any more. He put his quill away in its case and sealed up the little inkpot. He peered at Albrecht, a vague shape in the candlelight over the other side of their tent.

'Time to do my blisters, please,' he said to his servant.

Albrecht grunted and heaved himself off the

floor. Dutifully he unwrapped the cloth puttees from Eberhardt's feet and began washing them. Mosquitoes whined in the tent around them.

'I'm worried about Diederich,' Albrecht muttered as he worked. 'Running a right fever, he is.'

'Hmm, Hassan says his herbs will do the trick,' said Eberhardt.

Albrecht made no reply but continuing washing.

'Is it the Devil, I wonder,' Eberhardt pondered, 'trying to stop us reaching the source of the Deathstone?'

Again Albrecht made no comment but continued with his task.

'We must press on as quickly as we can,' Eberhardt went on. 'I have a feeling of the Deathstone in my heart, calling me in to its home.' He stretched an arm out over Albrecht's bowed head. 'We must be quick, for the sake of Germany.' He made a dramatic upwards sweep. 'Tomorrow we will press into the final hills.' Though his eyes were failing they burned with febrile intensity; the glittering eyes of a saint and martyr.

Eberhardt called the men with him his twelve apostles. They were the ordinary German peasants who had survived the firing squad at the end of the Schlachtberg massacre. Eberhardt's typically charismatic explanation of it as a divine act had been enough to convince them to follow him. He explained that he was taking them on a pilgrimage. It was just that they were not going to a shrine in Germany or to Santiago de Compostela or to Rome, but to find the source of all danger to Germany in Africa.

Indeed, Eberhardt had come to see the whole of

the Knights' and Peasants' Wars as really just part of *his* Dark Heart Prophecy. It was the only thing that could make sense of the random collection of events that had occurred in his life. There *had* to be meaning in it somewhere, the ups and downs, the successes and failures. There *had* to be a purpose behind all his effort and suffering.

He had hired an Arab merchant in Cairo, Hassan Mohammed Khier, and twelve Nile soldiers to lead them into central Africa. Arab merchants had been going into the region for centuries to trade manufactured goods for slaves, gold and diamonds. Hassan said he had heard of the evil reputation of the volcano and for a fee he had agreed to guide the pilgrimage. Eberhardt had remembered the main details of the route he had sketched out as a young man in Constantinople. He had not been able to recover the map itself from Ludwig at Heidelberg University; after the war he was a hunted man and had had to flee the country.

The whole expedition had been financed by Eberhardt's treasure store from Mühlhausen. He had confiscated it from the rich and hidden it in the well in the back of his house in Brückenstrasse. After he had recovered from the battle at Frankenhausen he had sent a message to his washerwoman wife, via one of his new disciples, who had slipped back into the city. The master of the house had not yet returned after fleeing the revolution and so his woman was able to retrieve the chest and smuggle it out of the city in a rubbish cart.

They had reached Sudan by sailing up the Nile to Khartoum, where it split. They had taken the White Nile, south to Malakal.

146

In this dusty, forsaken town they had swung their small boats up a western tributary, the Bahr el Arab, and followed it through the town of Bentiu. There they had had to switch to smaller canoes as the river narrowed. They turned south again down the Bahr el Ghazal, which swung west following the grain of the land, through the village of Nyamlell.

The desert began to give way to grasslands, and then trees and sparse woods appeared. As the land became greener, the terrible glare of light reflected off sand lessened. The heat became less searing and more humid, but the fair-skinned peasants still suffered from sunburn and sweated terribly.

Eventually they could go no further up the river. They left the canoes at a trading station run by a friend of Hassan's and hired camels and bearers from him. A black African accompanied them as a guide. The peasants stared at him in horror. As he guided them southwest, isolated trees gradually merged into sparse forest and then the canopy closed in over their heads.

The first pilgrim died next morning. Diederich Weissmoller's body had been wrung dry by amoebic dysentery. After another day's travel on the camels their owner said he was going to turn back; he was afraid of the tribes that inhabited the land over the ridgeline, in the central African basin. They unloaded the baggage and divided it between the bearers.

The land was rising now and breaking up into hills and valleys. Their guide led them up winding tracks; they snaked in single file into the jungle, struggling up the slopes.

Eberhardt was affected by the heat and had to

lean on Albrecht to walk. Vegetation began to press in on them and they had to cut a path at times. The Egyptian soldiers split so that half were at the front and half at the back of the single file. The pilgrims clutched their swords and glanced around nervously at the strange plants and animal noises.

They were eight degrees north of the equator now, the heat was steamy, and heavy rainstorms soaked them regularly in the early afternoons.

Finally they came to the top of the line of hills. The guide summoned Hassan and Eberhardt to the front and stood with his black arm outstretched to show them a vista through a gap in the foliage. They stood puffing and sweating and looked into the land sweeping down in front of them.

A carpet of steaming green forest stretched out as far as the eye could see. Another river valley started beneath them, a fold in the land that gradually widened and dropped away to a large river flowing south.

This was the watershed. The dividing line between the rivers behind them, that had chosen to flow north into the Nile and towards the known world, and the rivers that turned their backs on all that was known and decided to run southwest into the interior of the continent. Introspective rivers, they had eschewed the outside world and were drawn by the magnetism of the Ubangi and eventually the mighty Congo itself.

Eberhardt stood on the edge. He leaned on Albrecht and looked down at the land in front of him. He had a sense of being pulled by a dark gravity into the heart of the continent. The guide,

148

the pilgrims, Hassan and the soldiers all stared at him.

After a pause, he looked at the guide and nodded.

They set off down.

30 MARCH 1941, HEIDELBERG UNIVERSITY LIBRARY, GERMANY

SS-Lieutenant Werner Fischer's hands shook as he held the large black telephone receiver to his ear. The crackling line to his headquarters eventually connected.

His voice was trembling with urgency: 'Eckart, it's Fischer. I need to speak to Sievers.'

'It's eight o'clock, he's having dinner with some brass,' came the response in a tone of dismissive authority. Eckart was always protective of his boss; Fischer had never got on with him. 'What's this about?' he continued suspiciously.

'Look, just get him, can you?'

'*I said*, what's this about?' Eckart was aggressive now.

Fischer realised he would have to offer some explanation.'It's big,' he gabbled in his excitement. 'It's, it's the big one, the one we've been looking for. He'll be pissed off if he doesn't hear straight away. I can't tell you any more than that.' In his excitement he swore, despite his usually reserved nature.

There was silence on the line as Eckart weighed up his annoyance at Fischer against any possible reprimand from his boss.

149

'What's your number there?' came the icy response. He wrote it down. 'Wait by the phone. He'll call you if he wants to speak to you.' The line went dead.

Fischer put the phone back in its cradle and stared down at the desk in the librarian's office, wondering how to explain his discovery to his boss.

After ten minutes the phone rang. He had lapsed into a daze, staring at the blackout curtains opposite him, and the jangling set his heart going again.

'Fischer, what is this all about? I've got the local Gauleiter and some Gestapo people upstairs; I don't want to keep them waiting.' Sievers sounded guarded.

Fischer released the pent-up outburst that he had been rehearsing in his head. He spoke for five minutes, during which he got up from the desk and began pacing back and forth, waving his free hand animatedly and sometimes picking up books on the desk to emphasise his points.

When he had finished, Fischer put the phone down, switched off the desk light, walked to the window, opened the blackout curtains and stared hard into the darkness as if he were trying to understand it.

10 APRIL 1941, LESKOVAC, MONTENEGRO, THE BALKANS

Bullets pranged off the sloped armour in front of him and SS-Major Otto Hofheim ducked his head back into the turret of his armoured car.

'Reverse!' he shouted to his two drivers. Between them they worked the two sets of complicated gearing and the eight-wheeled SdKfz 232 armoured car jerked back down the rise in the road. They had driven up it gingerly to scout the village ahead of them.

'Stop!' Otto called when they were shielded by the slope. 'Gunter, take her up into that olive grove on the right. I'll go out and see where the fire is coming from.'

The SdKfz 232 was the ugliest armoured car ever created. It looked like an upturned grey bathtub to which had been added a large V-shaped metal plate, like a snout, on the front as additional armour, bulging mudguards and a turret covered in radio antennae and anti-grenade grilles with a 20mm cannon and coaxial machine gun.

The forward-facing driver nodded and peered through the small vision slit to his right. He had been with Otto through the Polish and French campaigns and this sort of probing, using every feature of the land as cover, was standard practice for a recce squadron.

He watched as his commander jumped down from the hatch in the side of the large vehicle. Otto wore baggy combat trousers and smock in the new SS mottled camouflage pattern, with a stormtrooper helmet, and a Schmeisser machine pistol slung over his back.

Although he was only twenty-three he inspired great trust as well as affection in his men. Gunter wasn't sure how he did it; he wasn't a loud or aggressive officer, if anything he was quite understanding. He just got on and did things and people felt confident in him. His calm, cornflower-blue eyes gave you all the attention in the world when he looked at you. His appearance also helped: six foot two with a lean, rangy build, blond hair cropped in a savage short back and sides, skin freckly, with blond hair on the backs of his large hands.

But the main reason for the admiration was because he had guts.

'Nutter,' Gunter muttered to himself as he watched him head up the slope towards the enemy. He moved quickly and smoothly for a big man.

Gunter reversed the car away from him and then the fourteen-litre diesel growled as it blundered its way forward across the roadside ditch and into the olive grove.

Otto crouched down and crept up the final slope to the brow of the hill. Then, in full view of the enemy, he stood up and walked calmly across the road, looking towards the village. Halfway across he threw himself down just as the hail of metal ripped the air over his head. He rolled back down the rise as machine-gun rounds tore up the stones behind him. In the second before he went down he had spotted the muzzle flashes and now he ran back down the line of armoured cars in his squadron, issuing orders.

The six main fighting vehicles fanned out either

side of the road to advance up the valley towards the small hill town; the road was probably mined and he didn't want to walk onto one of them. His mortar team debussed and Otto remained with them on the rise in the road, directing the vehicles through his radio signaller. The other 232 heavy armoured car moved off to the left along with a half-track mounting a 37mm anti-tank gun. One infantry half-track went either side of the road and debussed their squads. The mottled green and brown of the soldiers' camouflage smocks and helmet covers blended in well with the bushes around them. They fanned out behind the vehicles; carbines, machine pistols and stick grenades at the ready to follow them into the town.

He kept his two light SdKfz 222, four-wheeled scout cars back down the road. The supply trucks, fuel bowser and the radio half-track with the unit's Enigma code machine remained out of sight further down the valley.

Otto took his radioman and walked and then crawled through a field on the left, up to the top of the rise again. Lying on his belly, he wriggled forward under a bramble bush and peered down through his small Zeiss field glasses at the tatty collection of buildings strung out along the road.

Being at the front of a reconnaissance unit on campaign was what Otto loved. He had the sense of daring that was needed to push on into unknown enemy territory. It was what he was good at and it had earned him a Knight's Cross and rapid promotion during the Polish and French campaigns from ensign to his current position as major.

He was now commander of the armoured reconnaissance unit of the élite First SS Division: Leibstandarte Adolf Hitler—the Adolf Hitler Bodyguard—spearheading the advance into the Balkans. The Führer had decided to secure the southern flank of his imminent Russian offensive and had thrown his mechanised SS division against the poorly equipped and divided Balkan forces.

As usual their blitzkrieg combination of heavy armoured punch, dive-bombing and sheer speed had thrown the enemy into confusion. They had already swept through Belgrade and were pushing on south towards Skopje in Macedonia. Resistance was slight and the roads in the mountainous terrain appalling, so light armoured units like Otto's were being used. They had encountered some resistance from police and local guard units armed with rifles and a few First World War-vintage machine guns. Otto suspected that this would be another such obstacle that could be brushed aside.

From his vantage point he watched the ugly field-grey vehicles lumber through the green countryside on either side of him. They crushed rickety wooden fences and snouted their way through old dry-stone walls. Once they were in position and the mortar team had dug in, he called over the radio net: 'All vehicles advance!'

Rifle and machine-gun fire cracked out from the positions half a mile up the valley, the sound echoing around them. He could see the muzzle flashes coming from a roadside café, the first building on the way into town, and a barn on the left. Otto directed fire from the mortar and the anti-tank gun onto them. Flashes of orange burst

154

on and around the buildings, followed by billowing clouds of dust and smoke. The enemy fire slackened off and figures began running back into the town.

Both buildings caught fire and smoke drifted across the view. His vehicles were nosing their way into the town now with the infantry scuttling between bits of cover around them. They were firing at targets in windows and on rooftops, and lobbing grenades; the flat cracks and shouted orders drifted back to him. The 20mm cannon in one car stabbed orange flashes at a building and then the vehicle disappeared out of sight behind it.

He was losing touch with his men and hurriedly called up the two light SdKfz 222 cars behind him. Once they drew level he hopped onto the back of the lead car with his signaller. Holding on to the equipment racks on the back of the vehicle, they roared off.

They followed a cross-country route into the town and pushed aside a barrier of carts as they entered. Smoke drifted around them as terrified civilians were herded out of houses and lined up facing walls with their hands on their heads. Harsh German commands rang out.

'They've mostly scarpered!' Sergeant Schenk shouted up to Otto from the roadside, jerking a thumb towards the other end of town.

'Secure the buildings. I'll form a perimeter at the far end!' Otto shouted, and then banged on the turret to drive on.

The village was quickly captured with no SS casualties. Prisoners were secured and shot along with the wounded. Slavs were *Untermensch* and Otto had been indoctrinated to take racial purity very seriously.

After the skirmishes died down he returned to the small square with an ancient olive tree in the centre to debrief his troop commanders and prepare a report for Brigade HQ. He was sitting by the door at the back of one of the half-tracks. He took off his helmet and scratched his shock of blond hair; it was stiff with grease after two weeks on campaign. His six junior officers were relaxing; sitting on the benches down each side of the half-track with their feet up on the opposite bench. They were laughing and joking and passing a bottle of retsina around.

The radio half-track roared into the square and jerked to a halt, its long antennae whipping back and forth. Rudolf Winkler, Otto's young signaller, jumped out of it and ran over to them with a piece of paper in his hand and an urgent look on his face.

'Hey, Winkler, what's the matter? We won the battle, didn't we?' Otto held his hands out in mock surprise at his worried appearance. The officers in the half-track were glad of the release of tension after the firefight. Tired, smoke-blackened faces cracked into smiles and they guffawed at the hapless radio operator. He reddened and twitched his hands at his sides.

'Signal come through direct for you, sir.' He paused.

'Ye-es?' Otto smiled and leaned his head on one side in a display of good-natured patience.

'Group signal number is from Wewelsburg, sir.'

'Wewelsburg?' Otto's smile became a frown.

The officers' attention cut from Winkler to Otto, their grins dying away.

156

'You dead back there?' the voice shouted in his headphones over the roar of the engines.

'No—I'm fine thanks. Can you turn up the heating?'

'It's already on full blast. We'll be over the mountains soon and I'll take her down then, so it should warm up a bit.'

Otto Hofheim grunted into his oxygen mask and went back to shivering quietly as he sat on a bucket seat in the back of a Messerschmitt 110. The big twin-engined fighter-bomber had taken off from a Luftwaffe forward airfield near Belgrade the day after the signal had come through. They headed northwest over Croatia and Slovenia. The lone pilot in the front had taken them up to 20,000 feet to clear the Alps as they roared towards Paderborn airfield in west central Germany.

Otto was sitting hunched in the rear gunner's seat facing the tail; the pistol grip of the 7.62mm machine gun was sticking in his face. He couldn't see anything outside; it was a dark night and ice had formed on the glass canopy around him. The noise and vibration at 320 m.p.h., close to maximum speed, was tremendous. All he was conscious of was the howling wind, the sound of his breath sucking in oxygen from the facemask and the biting cold. He had got into the plane still in his light cotton combat smock and trousers and, even with the addition of a Luftwaffe sheepskin jacket, he could not stop shivering.

When he had read the signal in the back of the half-track there was absolute silence from his brother officers as they looked at him. He had

157

read and reread the order:

To: SS-Panzer Aufklarung-Abteilung,
    Leibstandarte Adolf Hitler.
Major Otto Hofheim report Wewelsburg
immediately.
Transport waiting Belgrade airfield.
Message ends.

He was taken aback. He could not think why he had been recalled. And then there was that word: Wewelsburg. The order could not be argued with: he had to leave.

He turned to the officers, and forced his face to be expressionless and professional. 'I have to return to Wewelsburg immediately.' He held a hand up to still their protests. 'It doesn't say why.

'Heinz will take over command,' he looked at Captain Heinz Jahnke, his second in command, 'and will have rank of Acting Major in my absence. The campaign objective remains the same as before. You know what to do!'

The usual smooth and concise delivery of his orders pressured them into acceptance. They looked down at the floor of the half-track. They didn't like it but they didn't have any choice.

'Good luck!' Otto shook hands with them and left to grab his personal kitbag out of the armoured car.

Despite his outward calm he was battling against two contrary winds that had begun to blow inside him as soon as he had read the message. One was a hot angry indignation at having to return to Germany and leave his troops in the middle of the battle. He had trained up and melded the unit over two years of war—he was right in the thick of a campaign. How could he just pull out and leave them to it? What would his boys do without him?

Secondly, though, the cold wind of fear froze his soul. Wewelsburg Castle was the centre of the SS religion that Heinrich Himmler was in the process of establishing. It was associated with the occult and darkness. No one really knew what went on there and it was spoken about in hushed tones, even in the Waffen SS.

Otto and his fellow officers were zealous German nationalists and had been indoctrinated into accepting the racism of National Socialism, but even they balked at the lunatic notions that the Reichsführer dreamed of.

Himmler was a vegetarian teetotaller who thought he was the reincarnation of the Dark Ages German king, Heinrich I, and hoped to create an SS religion based on paganism. As part of Fascism's rejection of the Enlightenment, he wanted to turn out its light and move back into darkness, to create a consciously irrational myth to found a new society on. He had rebuilt the ruined castle at Wewelsburg to serve as a base for the unit that would create the soul of that Nazi nation, the Ahnenerbe—the Ancestral Heritage Research and Teaching Unit. So when Otto found out that he had been summoned to the castle he was deeply troubled.

What have I done wrong? was the thought that kept running through his mind. He could not believe that he had been summoned back for anything good. He had won the Knight's Cross for valour in the French campaign, and the citation and resulting publicity had been handled by his commander and the Waffen SS chain of command. He had fought well recently, but nothing spectacular that would merit such an urgent request. What would the Ahnenerbe have to do with combat issues anyway?

He also knew full well that the SS was not an organisation that played games. The death's-head units ran the concentration camps and dark jokes circulated among the troops about what happened in them. Otto had been a success in the system so far but he had seen its brutalities: the torture and execution of enemies, the beatings and suicides of comrades during his own training at the SS officer school at Bad Tölz.

Alone, in the dark and cold, his mind began playing venomous games with him, imagining actions that could have been interpreted as wrongdoings and awful punishments that could be inflicted on him. Who might he have offended in the high command?

He was so shaken up that a thought occurred to him in a distant way, as one might drive past an advert by the roadside; he could open the canopy over his head and jump out into the night to end it all. The mood of depression crushed his usual cheerfulness and kept him quiet throughout the whole flight.

At times like this he thought back to his parents. His father, Ernst Hofheim, ran a provincial solicitors firm in Gmund in rural Bavaria, and his mother, Traudl, was a devoted housewife and loving mother to her three sons. Even through the hardships of the twenties and thirties in Germany they had remained stolid and positive. They were a wealthy family with a large farmhouse and land around it.

Otto saw them now sitting in their armchairs either side of the fire, listening to the wireless in the sitting room as the bad news poured in. His mother would sometimes brush imagined dust off the lace collar she wore over her dress; his father, with his pipe clamped between his teeth, would remain set firm and unperturbed. After the news, his mother would simply make a little 'Hmm,' noise, switch off the radio and then go off to get on with things around the house.

As the dark plane dropped down through the night over the mountains, Otto gritted his teeth against the shivering cold. He had made contact again with the positive rock in his heart and resolved to keep his nerve.

*   *   *

The Messerschmitt nosed through the clouds and rain until the pilot picked up the flarepath of Paderborn airfield.

The plane touched down and hurtled through the night, dragging clouds of spray behind it like the billowing black folds of a witch's skirts.

Otto clung to his seat as they were buffeted from side to side and eventually taxied back round to the hangars. His long legs were cramped and stiff from the flight and he moved slowly and painfully down the steps in the aircraft side. The rain poured down, plastering his hair over his face.

He stood swaying on the tarmac, trying to get his balance back.

'They're waiting for you.' The pilot touched him

161

on the shoulder and pointed over to a large black Mercedes-Benz staff car that was driving up towards them.

'I don't know what they want you for but good luck, eh?' He smiled, took the leather flight jacket back from Otto, swung his parachute on his shoulder and set off at a run to the hangars.

Otto nodded blankly, the rain dripping off his face, wishing that he could be so carefree. He watched as the car drew up.

The SS driver wound down his window and poked his head out; he wore a black peaked cap with a death's-head badge. He shouted over the noise of the wind, 'Major Hofheim?'

'Yes.'

'Get in.' He jerked a thumb at the door behind him.

Otto dumped his small personal kitbag in the back seat and got in. He was glad to be out of the cold, but the smell and feel of plush leather in the staff car suddenly made him conscious of his appearance. The signal to report had said 'immediately', and you did not argue with an order from Wewelsburg.

He had not been able to wash much over the past two weeks. He was still in his combats, not his dress uniform; he stank of sweat and smoke, had a few days' growth of beard and was soaked to the skin. His hair was matted over to one side from the rain. Hurriedly, he tried to scrape it back into order with his fingers.

The driver was not inclined to talk so Otto sat in the back and tried to straighten his uniform up. The road from Paderborn wound through thick pinewoods, and then went briefly through Boddeken village, before going into a series of tight corners up and down hills. The driver knew the route and was in a hurry, throwing the big car around.

The headlights shone through the swirling black rain. At one point they glared over a chain-gang of concentration camp prisoners in striped uniforms doing work on the road. Guards in rain capes with dogs and machine guns oversaw them. One of the prisoners was bending down and looked up in surprise as they passed; his starved face, with a scrappy beard, sunken cheeks and dark eye sockets, stared open-mouthed into the bright light.

'Fucking Yids,' muttered the driver irritably as he slowed to pass them.

Eventually, on the approach to the castle, they came to a striped road barrier next to a sentry post painted in black and white chevrons. Otto could see the faint outline of the castle towers behind it, a darker black against the night sky.

Machine guns pointed at them from sandbagged positions on either side of the road, Alsatians on leashes barked furiously. Black, double lightning flash SS flags flapped in the wind above the sentry hut. Two helmeted guards in rain capes stepped out, one with his rifle pointed at them. The other nodded to the driver and shone a torch in Otto's face.

'Don't worry, he's all right. They want him in there,' said the driver.

Otto squinted into the bright light, and then the guard nodded and called back to the sentry post: 'Special transport arriving.'

Otto saw the duty sergeant pick up a phone, then the barrier was raised and they swept round to the left to a bridge over a deep moat. They drove across it and up to the huge wooden double doors of the castle.

It had been built in the Middle Ages on an outcrop looking north over the valley of the river Alme. After it had fallen into disrepair, the Prince Bishop of Paderborn had rebuilt it in a triangular design, unique in Germany. It then fell into ruin again but was taken over by the SS in 1936; Himmler felt that the weirdly shaped wreck had the necessary air of mystery that he wanted for his new cult. He had the castle rebuilt using concentration camp prisoners, thirteen hundred of whom had died in the process.

After another check by guards at the gate, the huge doors swung open and the long bonnet of the staff car nosed through a tunnel and into the dimly lit triangular cobbled courtyard. They parked along the shortest side. It was still raining, and Otto turned up his combat smock collar as he got out and glanced around him. Grey stone walls and Gothic windows rose up on all three sides, with steep-pitched roofs on top. Doorways were spaced along all sides with names and numbers stencilled above them for different departments and units. The triangle narrowed down in front of him into a great round tower at its apex.

The main gates crashed shut and an officer bellowed from a door behind him, 'Squad!'

A squad of four SS troopers in black helmets and greatcoats doubled out of the guardroom by the gate. Their Schmeisser submachine guns were held across their chests, their jackboots clattered on the stone.

An SS major in a black uniform stepped out of a

doorway and stood in front of Otto. The squad formed up behind him.

'Arms up!'

Otto lifted his arms and the officer removed his Luger pistol from his holster and went through his pockets. There wasn't much: a sodden packet of cigarettes and a box of matches, a compass, penknife and some crumpled chocolate.

Otto stared ahead of him with his arms stretched out either side; he rocked back and forward slightly as the man tugged at his pockets. Fear gripped him and he had to struggle to keep his composure.

Was this standard practice?

He didn't know. His worries began to resurface; images of interrogation and execution played in his mind. This couldn't be a hero's welcome.

Ahead of him the large double door at the base of the main tower opened, light spilled out and a figure beckoned them towards it.

'Fall in! March!' the officer shouted at the squad, and pushed Otto in front of them towards the door.

The stormtroopers marched him into the gloomy entrance hall of the main castle tower.

It was decorated like an old country hotel with one significant exception. Along the stone walls were suits of armour, crossbows and swords, heavy oak furniture and deer heads. But in the centre between two staircases was a large stone carving of Christ on a cross with his head knocked off.

Otto, though, was too tense to take in such details. He could not believe that his abrupt handling presaged anything positive. This feeling increased as they approached the two big stone staircases, one curved up and one down. Instead of heading up, as one would expect, to an audience chamber, the guards veered left and they clattered down the steps. Visions of dungeons and beatings lurched into his mind.

PRESENT DAY, 24 JANUARY, CENTRAL AFRICAN REPUBLIC

Alex stood at the bow of the ship and looked out over the Ubangi River.

It was seven o'clock in the morning and wraiths of white fog twisted themselves over the water around him. The thud of the ship's engine was muffled and merely exacerbated the great silence that they were pressing forward into.

He shivered and hugged his combat jacket tighter around him; he was cold after a night sleeping on the metal deckplates.

He turned his head to the left and watched the jungle on the north bank loom over the low fog.

The trees were packed tight as if they wanted to shut the viewer off from any knowledge of the interior. The green wall was so impenetrable that he felt scrutinised by it; like having a permanently suspicious travelling companion staring back at you.

It was a week after Kalil had arrived and the trucks, armoured fighting vehicles and troops of the Battlegroup were embarked on four flat-bottomed river ferries and a small river tanker. The ferries had driven right up onto the beach at the plantation to load the vehicles and troops the day before. Patrice had bought and fitted the ships in

Bangui and then crewed them with mercenaries and sailed them upriver.

Alex turned and looked ahead of him. The river was half a mile wide, a great brown snake, coiling down at him under the swirls of fog. He felt like Marlow in *Heart of Darkness*, on his old steamer, thumping upriver into the unknown. He could smell the low odour of the mud banks they passed, dotted with sleeping crocodiles. Occasional large mats of river hyacinths drifted downstream with storks on stilty legs staring imperiously at him from their floating thrones.

On their last night on the training base there had been an impromptu piss-up in the ops room warehouse. Alex couldn't work out if the thumping in his head was from the ship's engine or his hangover.

The Russians had led the charge. Yuri, the commander of a BMP, who had welded speakers to the top of his vehicle, had driven it into the open side of the shed and played 'We are the Red Cavalry' at full volume. It was an old Russian Civil War anthem with blaring fanfares of trumpets and the Red Army Choir thundering away. It had all the Russians instantly standing to attention, bellowing out the blood-curdling lyrics. Yuri said he liked to play it when going into battle to rouse the infantry.

Once they had started drinking, Arkady had lurched over, thrown an arm around Col's shoulders and taught him to say, '*Ni shagu nazad!*'

'Not one step back!'

It was Stalin's famous motto of defiance for the defenders of Stalingrad—the sort of simple absolutism that Russians responded to. The phrase had been picked up by the rest of the command element and taken to heart.

Alex noticed a solitary black figure standing in a pirogue near the bank. The old man was leaning on a pole and staring at the five ships in the convoy. Alex had seen very few people so far on the river and, to shield the military equipment from view, had had the ferries fitted out with metal frames along their sides. Heavy green tarpaulins were then strung between them.

To provide a cover story for what they were doing, large signs had been hung on the covers with the name of an invented logging company on it: Compagnie Forestière de Mbomou. A large tree in the midst of being felled had been added for the sake of the illiterate. There were numerous heavy trucks in CAR thundering around hauling logs out of the forest, so it was not an implausible explanation for onlookers.

The tanker at the rear of the convoy had been bought as a forward refuelling base. It had ten separate tanks now filled with aviation fuel, diesel and fresh water. Patrice had built a helicopter-landing pad on the long front deck so that they could use the ship's pumps to refuel the helicopters quickly. It would give them a halfway refuelling point on the way to the mine; other resupply would be done by airdrops from an Antonov AN-12 flying out of Gbadolite.

At this pace Alex had calculated that it would take a couple of days until they turned off north up a tributary of the Ubangi called the Chinko. He planned to disembark about fifty miles south of the mine and then overland it to the target from there. The river provided a covert way of getting close with a large fleet of vehicles, much less visible than just crossing it and then driving halfway across the country on normal roads. He knew that the army at the mine would be warned of the Battlegroup's approach by their outlying roadblocks, but he wanted to give them as little time to prepare as possible by disembarking and then driving hard and fast for the target.

This time alone also allowed some of his greatest fears to rise in his mind. Probably everyone's secret nightmare, on an irregular operation like this, was being captured. There was no Geneva Convention out here and prisoners of war were routinely tortured to death. In his time in Africa Alex had seen corpses that had been hacked to death over a period of days.

He turned away from such thoughts and scratched the stubble under his chin. The bristles had got long enough that they felt soft but it was beginning to get into the itchy phase of growth. He never shaved when on ops: it was too much hassle and the shaving nicks just got infected in the poisonously humid climate.

He thought about his ancestral home so far away in the milder climes of Herefordshire. He had had to call his father from the training base on the satellite phone and arrange for another lump of money to be sent through to him to stave off the bailiffs. One symptom of feeling more in charge of his life was the fact that he hadn't got riled by the old man this time, despite his alternate wheedling and haranguing. Instead, Alex just felt sorry for him. When the op was over and his bonus was paid, he wondered if he might be able to save Akerley. They had better get the assault done fast, though, because the creditors were closing in.

He looked away from the view of the river; the monotony of it was like watching a loop of a film play over and over. The rest of the troops were rousing themselves, rolling out from under the vehicles, where they slept to avoid the drenching dew. They shrugged out of their green sleeping bags like strange pupae emerging reluctantly to new life.

Kalil was just standing up, hugging his leather jacket around him and shivering, his normally neat hair sticking up on one side. 'Jeez it's cold in this goddam country! I need a coffee.'

Alex grinned. 'Come on, we'll get one.' He nodded at the small superstructure aft. 'Not long till we get to the mine now.'

Otto was marched by the guards down the curving stone steps. It became dark and the air grew chill. At the bottom, two dim lights flanked a heavy wooden double door studded with metal bolts. The major banged on it loudly with his fist; the sound boomed in the confined stone space.

A shout came from within and the officer hauled open one side of the door. He walked through and beckoned Otto after him; the guards remained outside. They stepped into a dimly lit circular chamber cut out of the living rock, thirty feet in diameter, with a high, domed roof. Around the rough walls were twelve flaming torches, each one over a stone seat made of a single block.

In the centre of the room was a circular pit, fifteen feet in diameter and two feet deep. Evenly spaced around it were three stone seats and, directly in line with the doorway where they stood, some steps going down into the pit. In the centre of it was a large circular mosaic: a rune symbol of twelve black lightning flashes emanating out from a black centre: the dark star or black sun—the dark heart of SS mythology.

This was the 'Realm of the Dead' where the twelve most senior SS officers met. Himmler liked to think of them as his modern-day Teutonic Knights. If they died in battle their ashes were to be placed in an urn on their empty seat.

Now, though, just three men were sitting on the stone seats facing into the centre of the pit. Otto could not at first make out who they were, the room was so dark. The major pushed him in the small of the back as a signal to walk down into the pit and then withdrew, closing the door with a heavy thud.

As Otto stepped down into the circle he was conscious of his baggy combat clothing and his dirty, unshaven appearance. This self-consciousness was overridden as he recognised the figure in the middle seat opposite him. His chest contracted painfully.

Reichsführer Heinrich Himmler was sitting with his legs neatly crossed and one hand pressed against his mouth, staring intently at Otto. He wore black jackboots, SS breeches and tunic.

Most observers agreed that he had the appearance of a nervous clerk. He was short and portly in stature. His dark hair was shaved painfully close at the sides and greased down flat on top; he wore round glasses over his narrow-set eyes and had a podgy, white face.

However, Himmler's lack of physical prowess had merely served to increase his viciousness once he was in power. He had already sent hundreds of thousands of people to cruel deaths.

Otto was a product of the organisation designed by this man to serve his every whim; 'Obedient unto death' was the SS motto. In his training Otto had been subjected to the most intensive physical and psychological regime ever devised. Faced for the first time by the leader of this organisation, Otto's doubts and fears were overridden by the training designed to turn him into an automaton. He threw back his head, clicked his heels together, flung out a rigid right arm and shouted, *'Heil Hitler!'*

Himmler acknowledged the salute with a small nod. Otto slapped his arm back at his side and stood rigidly at attention, eyes staring up at the wall opposite; fear made his body as tense as steel.

'So, you're a Bavarian lad, then?' Himmler smiled; the expression had an awkward look on him. He was ill at ease with other people and covered it up with an overly friendly manner.

'Yes, sir!' barked Otto. They were both Bavarians and had the marked regional accent.

'Where are you from?'

'Gmund, sir!'

'Oh, yes, I know it. By the Tegernsee, just along the lake there by the crossroads? Yes, lovely, lovely,' he smiled and nodded.

Before joining the Nazi party Himmler had been a farmer in the region, an occupation that had given him a strong belief in ideas of *'Blut und Boden'*— blood and soil—German nationalism. He often liked to talk about the 'sanctity of the soil' and its link to the distinctiveness of the German character.

'Did you sail there?'

'Yes, sir, as a boy, sir!' Otto saw a picture of the white sail of the family dinghy against a blue summer sky and the deep green of the hills around the lake.

'Good, good . . .' Himmler smiled again and seemed to be unsure how to proceed.

He jumped up and walked over to Otto across the rune mosaic. The top of his head came up to Otto's outthrust chin.

'So, you are a brave reconnaissance commander with a Knight's Cross?' Himmler reached out awkwardly and smoothed the lapel of Otto's combat jacket.

'Yes, sir.' He didn't need to shout now.

'Colonels Hauser and Steiner speak very well of

173

you.' The two men had run the Bad Tölz SS officer training school when Otto was there.

Otto didn't feel it his place to respond.

'So . . . the Volk have an important mission for you then,' Himmler smiled up at him.

Otto's brain slowly began to come out of his terrified automaton mode and function again. This did not sound like the lead-up to an execution.

'These men,' he gestured to the two officers seated either side of the circle, 'will explain all to you.'

Now that he had been given permission, Otto finally allowed his eyes to glance either side of him.

'Colonel Sievers?' Himmler smiled at the officer on his right and then turned and sat back down in his stone chair.

The thin-faced, grey-haired colonel looked up at him thoughtfully. Wolfram Sievers was the *Reichsgeschäftsführer*, the head of the Ahnenerbe.

'At ease, Hofheim.' He flicked a hand. Otto stamped his legs apart and stood rigidly with his chest pushed out and hands clasped behind his back.

'Stand easy.' Otto finally let his shoulders drop and looked down at the colonel.

'Now, Lieutenant Fischer here,' he gestured across the circle at the young, bookish-looking officer sitting opposite him, 'has been doing some reading in Heidelberg University and has come up with an interesting discovery.'

Otto looked at the gangly lieutenant; he had pallid skin, mousy hair and wore round glasses. He looked up at Otto with an enthusiastic smile.

'I think it is probably better if you sit down. This

174

may take a while.' Sievers gestured to the step. Otto sat down so that the four men were now facing each other over the rune symbol.

'Fischer, explain, will you?'

Fischer could hardly contain his excitement.

'We ...' he glanced nervously at Himmler, who nodded, '... have discovered,' his voice dropped to a whisper, 'the Dark Heart Prophecy.'

He picked up one of the pile of old brown leather-bound books that were stacked at his feet and flourished it triumphantly.

Otto looked at him attentively.

Fischer dropped the book back on the pile, sat forwards quickly, waved his hands and spoke in disconnected bursts. 'A threat to the Volk that we must defeat! The fifth battle looms! This is the final struggle against evil! We must find the source of the Deathstone!'

Sievers could see that none of this made any sense to Otto, so he interrupted Fischer's rambling.

'Major Hofheim, what we are getting at is that you will lead an armoured reconnaissance expedition across the Sahara. Rommel has pushed the British back far enough that we are now in sufficient command of the theatre for an expedition to be launched in safety.'

He picked a map tube off the floor at his feet, tipped the large sheet out, unrolled it and spread it out over the dark star.

'Can you weight it down?' he asked Fischer, who positioned volumes of *The Quest for Glory* on the corners. The three men then moved in and crouched round the map of north and central Africa. Himmler remained in his chair with his

175

chin in his hand watching Otto closely as Sievers began pointing things out.

'Tripoli is here, where you will be based. There aren't any SS units in the Afrika Korps so we will have to send the whole of your unit over from the Balkans. The campaign there is already pretty much over.'

Otto breathed a silent sigh of relief; he would be with his boys again.

'This is an SS operation and top secret.' Sievers flicked a quick warning glance at Otto, who nodded. It sounded interesting. His adventurous nature had perked up at the mention of the Sahara.

'The mission objective is . . .' Sievers' index finger paused in midair as he looked south on the map to find the location, '. . . here.' His finger stabbed at French Equatorial Africa.

Otto frowned; it looked a long way from Tripoli.

'Yes, it is a long way,' Sievers had interpreted his look, 'about two and a half thousand kilometres.'

'Why not paratroopers?' Otto's quick mind was already grappling with operation realities.

'We did consider it, but it's too far and we couldn't pick them up afterwards; the terrain is too forested for any aircraft to land near the objective. Also, our French friends are somewhat *divided* over where their loyalties lie.' Sievers raised his eyebrows mockingly. 'The Free French are not strong militarily and there aren't any forces in the immediate vicinity of the objective but they do operate forts and patrols in the Sahara in collaboration with the British. Any land force will have to be armoured to have some punch in case it runs into them.'

'What about fuel and water?'

'The Luftwaffe will establish a series of supply dumps along the route where its planes can land in the desert. It will also be able to drop supplies by parachute nearer the objective, once you get into the jungle.'

'And what do we do when we get there?'

'Well,' Sievers paused, 'that's a good question. That's why we are sending you there,' he smiled. 'Lieutenant Fischer is an archaeologist and will travel with you as the representative of the Ahnenerbe. He will oversee any surveying and digging on the site that needs to be done. You will assist him in all ways possible.'

He looked at Otto sternly to see that he got the point that he had to take Fischer seriously.

Otto nodded in understanding so Sievers continued, 'It will be tough getting across the Sahara but we think that it can be done. However, we have only just arrived in the region and have no experience of long-range desert travel. The Italians are really the experts in this area; it's been their colony for decades, after all. They have pioneered the skills, so you'll have to work closely with them and use a lot of their experience.'

Otto frowned at the thought of working with the Italians. Like many German soldiers he doubted their military efficiency. It had been their disastrous rout by a small British force that had forced the Germans to send the Afrika Korps into the region in the first place.

'I know, I know. They're not good at fighting but their old saharianos have been operating in the desert for twenty years now and know a lot more about long-range travel in it than we do, so you will just have to put up with it.

'You'll have a few weeks to work with them whilst you're waiting for your men to be shipped over from the Balkans. SS high command will make sure that you're given all possible assistance and the unit will be designated "Kampfgruppe Hofheim".'

Otto nodded appreciatively—he had his own taskforce!

'When do I leave?'

Sievers paused before explaining, 'You'll fly out from Paderborn tomorrow; we want you in there as soon as possible. Lieutenant Fischer will brief you on what we know of the historical background to the Dark Heart Prophecy.'

Fischer beamed enthusiastically. Since he had discovered *The Quest for Glory* two weeks ago he had worked hard on a summary of it. He had presented this to Himmler, who found the combination of Eberhardt's strong German nationalism and the occult mystery surrounding the Deathstone irresistible. Since then he had thrown his whole weight behind an expedition to find the source of the Deathstone and save Germany from its great but unspecified threat.

They had then launched a thorough trawl of all possible reconnaissance unit commanders, which had led to Otto being selected as the most able. SS and Luftwaffe logistics and cartographic staff were already hard at work plotting routes to the objective and calculating supply requirements.

Having finished his briefing, Sievers sat back on his seat and the other two men did likewise. Sievers looked at Himmler. He was smiling quietly; enjoying the spectacle of his modern-day knights planning war over the rune symbol. Otto's battle-stained appearance added the touch of adventure that he relished.

'Major Hofheim, you have been given a great commission by the Volk.' For once he spoke quietly and seemed content. He beckoned Otto to him, so the major got up, crossed the SS rune and stood at attention in front of him.

'A lot rests on your young shoulders and as a symbol of this I am going to give you something that I want you to keep and to remember this by.' He reached into his tunic side pocket and drew out a ring.

Otto stiffened at the sight of it. SS rings were steel and engraved on the outside with the skull and crossbones death's-head emblem and rune symbols. Around the inside was the signature of Adolf Hitler. They were usually given only to senior SS officers and were regarded as sacred objects.

Himmler looked up at the tall, blond soldier in front of him and handed him the ring. Otto received it awkwardly and fumbled it onto his left ring finger.

He was overcome by the whole occasion: being spirited away to Wewelsburg, the fear of interrogation and execution, meeting the great Reichsführer himself and the responsibility that had been placed on him.

All he could do was respond with a spontaneous outburst of passionate loyalty. He threw out his right arm, clicked his heels and shouted, *'Heil Hitler!'*

Otto touched the heavy brown cover of the book; it was stained and warped with age. His hand rested there for a moment, sensing its venerability, before he slowly opened it and laid the edge carefully down on the desk.

He was sitting in a hushed, oak-panelled library in the castle the morning after his briefing. Rested, fed, washed and shaved, he had been kitted out in a major's dress uniform. He was still puzzled by the nature of the expedition he had to lead but he was feeling excited by it as well: in command of his own unit again, a mission from Himmler himself and the prospect of Africa, all made him feel alive and alert.

He looked at the heavy Gothic script printed on the frontispiece:

The Quest for Glory

A True Account of the Life and Works of Eberhardt von Steltzenberg, a Knight and Hero of the German Nation, of his Labours and Struggles in the Wars of the Knights and the Peasants for the German People, and of his Expedition, called the Dark Heart Prophecy Expedition, wherein are recounted his Right Worthy and Valorous Actions unto parts most Outlandish, whereupon he did Struggle to find the Origins of a most Terrible Deathstone, Worthy to be Feared.

As told in His own Words and set to Rights by the Labours of his Friend and Admirer, Ludwig Fritzler, Librarian of Heidelberg University.
August 1527

Otto got lost in the middle of the enormous title and had to start reading it again.

By the time he had got the gist of it he had been put off from detailed reading of the book by the wordy style of the sixteenth century, a time when writing in German, as opposed to Latin, was an almost sacred activity to be indulged to the utmost.

Fischer had explained the outline of the prophecy and the mission, but Otto's curiosity was aroused by the highly unusual nature of the book and he had requested an hour alone to read it himself. He had never seen anything like it; it was all the more intriguing for its cumbersome but authentic touches. He ignored Fischer's neatly written notes stuck in the pages, directing him as to what to read, and began exploring the tome in his usual independent way.

The book was a typeset résumé of Eberhardt's journals. It started with a highly partisan account of Eberhardt's life, presenting him as a model Renaissance man: a scholar and soldier who exhibited conspicuous morality in all his deeds. He was learned and yet athletic, attractive to women but respectful of their virtue. He was from an ancient and famous German noble house.

It didn't sound very plausible, and Otto flicked

on. He began to pay more attention as the book switched to the diary sections actually written by Eberhardt. These had been edited by Ludwig to remove all bawdy references to his sexual conquests but were still full of vivid accounts of action in the Italian Wars, the Knights' War and at the Schlachtberg. Otto was intrigued, both as a soldier and because he was surprised that such currently civil parts of Germany could have been scenes of such violence.

Also, in the vigour of the writing he began to feel something of the character of the man in whose footsteps he was supposed to follow. Otto was surprised by the violence of his religious imagery but he was used to such passion from National Socialist speeches and put it down to Eberhardt being of good German character. He thought he was mad but he half admired him as well.

He flicked on and began to take a detailed interest where he came across a crude woodcut of Eberhardt's sketch of the route taken into Africa. Otto had spent an hour earlier that morning staring at maps of Libya, Egypt and the Sahel, slowly absorbing the names, bearings and distances of the space that he was to operate in. This map was to the south and east of that area he had looked at but he was at least familiar with its path through Egypt, Sudan and French Equatorial Africa.

He turned over and read through the diary's account of travelling through Cairo: the frustrations of finding a guide into the area, the problems with disease and morale. Then there was the account of the journey up the Nile and across the Sudan. Otto found himself sympathising with the numerous problems that Eberhardt had experienced in organising the expedition.

There was a brief mention of the death of one of the pilgrims, Diederich Weissmoller, but then the narrative moved swiftly on. Occasionally someone called Albrecht was mentioned, and the writer seemed increasingly obsessed with his own health.

The expedition had got a long way into Africa with only one casualty from disease. Otto was amazed that they could do it; he had no concept of what travel in the area was like at the time. Once they crossed the watershed into central Africa, though, things seemed to get much worse.

In the jungle they were shadowed by hostile tribes, or 'devils', as Eberhardt called them. They were rarely seen clearly through the dense vegetation but appeared to be naked or body painted when they were. They carried bows and spears, and one night a lot of the baggage was stolen by them.

The group arrived at a tributary of the main river, the Chinko, and boarded some dugout canoes. They drifted downstream, nervously glancing up at the strange tree canopy over them.

More and more tributaries flowed into their river, its volume swelling as they entered the tropical lowlands. Eberhardt described it as getting fat and lazy, losing its sense of direction, swinging them back and forth.

The tribes returned to harry them, hating and fearing outsiders as slavers come to take more of their people away to misery. Archers began taking pot shots at them from the bank. Kaspar Funcke died from an arrow in the throat.

At a certain point, the Arab trader, Hassan, had the boats pull into the bank and they climbed a particularly large tree with a rope ladder. From a platform high up they were able to look out over the flat landscape and see the volcano on the plain in the far distance, shoved up over the surrounding forest.

Eberhardt wrote: 'An alien outcrop, thrust up over the land by the Devil, a mile or more across. Starting gentle and then sloping up almost to the vertical around a circular rim. A most strange occurrence, dominating all around. I am fearful but excited at the thought of approaching it.'

Soon after this, Hassan split from the pilgrims and carried on down the river with his soldiers to trade his goods in the interior for slaves. The remaining eleven pilgrims were left to make their way unaccompanied, west from the river, overland to the mountain.

On their first night in the jungle they were attacked by the devils. Klaus Kreuter and Kersten Voyll were killed with spears; Klaus was dragged screaming off into the dark, never to be seen again. Their porters all deserted them and the expedition was in danger of collapsing as it neared its goal. Only Eberhardt's strength of will and conviction forced them to drag themselves on the next day.

His health was deteriorating and the diary entries got shorter. The tribes killed three more pilgrims in hit-and-run attacks over the next two days as they struggled through the dense bush. Eberhardt gave instructions to Albrecht that if he did not live his steward was to ensure that *The Quest for Glory* was to be taken back to Ludwig in

Heidelberg. Albrecht now carried his baggage and supported him as he walked.

Finally they reached the slopes of the sacred mountain and slept the night in a tall tree for safety. In the morning they scouted round the base of the outcrop. Through a gap in the trees they saw a gully that ran up the south side of the mountain to a split in the vertical wall of the volcano's rim. Eberhardt wrote that it was the best route to get up into the crater and see what was in the heart of the mountain. They piled their remaining baggage at the foot of the gully and set off straight away.

The next entry was made two months later by Albrecht. He wrote that they had made good progress up the mountainside and were nearing the narrow gap in the crater rim that would give them access to their goal. But in mid-afternoon they had been attacked by more tribesmen, who seemed to be intent on defending the entry to their sacred ground. There had been a desperate mêlée in the jungle on the steep slope, swords striking out against spears and shields. He had seen Eberhardt clumsily swinging against an attacker when he was stabbed in the back with a spear. Albrecht had rushed to defend him but had slipped and tumbled downhill. He heard screaming and then shouting from the tribesmen as they came after him. He fled down the hillside.

Terrified, he had hidden all night in a tree at the bottom of the gully waiting to see if anyone else had escaped. In the morning he had given up hope and forced himself to turn away. He retrieved what he could from their baggage pile, including the diary. Then, stumbling and weary, he retraced their steps back to the river and followed it out of the region.

Starved, disease ridden and ragged, Albrecht was the only survivor to make it back to Cairo. He threw himself on the mercy of a German merchant, who took pity on him and allowed him to convalesce in his house.

Eventually Albrecht recovered and, following his master's instructions to the last, made his way back to Ludwig Fritzler at Heidelberg where he handed over the battered volume of *The Quest for Glory*.

Otto sat back in his plush leather chair. He breathed out and felt his shoulders relax. He looked out of the large picture window at the green spring landscape and the cloudy day outside. It was all so long ago and so far away; what did all this have to do with the Nazi struggle for the German nation now?

He didn't know, and in the end it didn't matter. All he did know was that he had been given a clear order and an exciting mission; he confined himself to that for now.

He checked his watch. He had to see the cartographers in five minutes to get all the up-to-date maps that they had of the theatre of operations.

He closed the heavy leather cover, picked the book up and walked slowly out of the library, thinking about the dangers that lay ahead of him in Africa.

'All stations halt and close up! Kilo One ford river on my left. Kilo Two, ford on my right!'

As he was barking the orders into his helmet mike, Alex was simultaneously sliding down into his commander's seat in the tank and pulling the heavy hatch closed over his head.

He switched from the command radio to the internal tank intercom. 'Tshombe, ford at speed.' If there were any enemy in the vicinity he wanted to be on to them quickly.

As he banged the hatch closed there was a hiss as the aircon system pressured up. His tall, rangy body squeezed into the tiny metal seat. Packed close around him, inches away from his head, was a mass of electronics: range finders, fire-control systems, fuse boxes, dials, connections, plasma screen and LCD readouts.

His gunner, John Chiwale, sat right up against his left elbow, and Tshombe, the driver, was between them down at his feet. The cramped space smelled of grease, diesel and stale sweat.

Tshombe accelerated down the slope into the shallow river. Inside, they were thrown from side to side as the tracks flowed over boulders. Then, as they hit the steep bank opposite, Alex was thrown back in his seat, banging his helmet on the hatch rim.

The two BMP troop carriers roared out of line behind them and plunged across the river on either side: Yuri commanding Kilo 1, and a South African, Renier 'Rennie' du Toit, in charge of Kilo 2. Alex's tank was Kilo 5. Yamba and Col were in the other two BMPs at the rear of the column.

Up until that point the overland journey had been an uneventful one. They had made slow progress, only fifteen miles since they had disembarked from the ferries early that morning.

So much for my blitzkrieg dash to the mine, Alex had thought as he looked around from his commander's hatch at the front of the column, and drummed his fingers impatiently on the breech of the heavy machine gun mounted beside him.

He knew that jungle was not ideal terrain for armour. The benefits of tanks were firepower, protection and mobility, but trees cut down their visibility and the poor roads reduced speed.

During the morning, when Alex had looked back along the vehicles weaving through the bush, it was like watching a line of ships rising and falling on a heavy sea as they drove over undulations in the muddy ground. The troops in the trucks sat on benches along the midline with their rifles pointing outwards, fingers on triggers and eyes darting warily at the forest as it passed them. The green camouflage paint of all the vehicles was stained to halfway up with red dust.

To try to continue some sort of deception about the force, Alex had had the bright, vivid colours of Central African Republic flag painted on the sides of the vehicles to pretend that they were government troops. His tank and the BMPs had similar flags proudly streaming from poles on the front of them. Looking down from his hatch on top of the turret he felt like some sort of medieval knight advancing into battle on his armoured warhorse.

However, Alex was disappointed that his ruse didn't seem to have had a chance to work. They either hadn't seen any local inhabitants or they had fled as soon as they had been sighted. Soldiers in these parts were synonymous with rape and murder, so the mere sight of the convoy, government or not, was enough to induce panic.

As the tank had driven out of the trees towards the ford, some women washing their clothes looked up from their labour and stared at it. They were wearing pagne—brightly coloured print wraps—with children tucked into the back of them. Their hair was spiked up from little squares all over their heads like old naval mines.

It had taken a second for them to register what they were seeing and then they had run off screaming. Alex had guessed that the women must be near a village and therefore that there might be troops from the mine there, hence his rapid order to close up and sweep into the attack.

The three armoured vehicles snorted up the riverbank with water streaming off their tracks. The trees on the other side were sparse and they stormed through them. The jungle fell back as they neared the village.

'Kilo One and Two, encircle the village. I will take the centre!' ordered Alex.

The forty-five-tonne, high-tech monster blundered into the centre of the village and then stopped, its radio aerials waving back and forth. Silence descended over it.

Alex used the camera on the turret to scan 360 degrees. He watched the images on the screen right in front of his face: a pathetic circle of red mud huts with thatched roofs, greying and drooping down over their eaves, on his left a huge kapok tree and next to it a church—a corrugated-

189

iron roof on metal poles with a crude painted sign on one side: *'La Voix de Dieu'*.

Everyone had run off. He could see cooking fires still smoking and chickens scratching around the hard-packed earth.

Kilo 1 and 2 drove up from opposite sides and their radio reports crackled in to his headset.

'We see nothing,' from Yuri.

'Ja, bru, they fucked off pretty quick, eh?' from Rennie.

Alex thought for a second. There was no point wasting precious time trying to find people to interrogate for local intelligence.

'Village is clear. All stations reform and advance.'

15 APRIL 1941, TRIPOLI, LIBYA

The big green Luftwaffe, Blohm & Voss 138 seaplane swung over the harbour; its three turbo-props roared as it banked.

Otto leaned over to his left to watch the docks and shipping slip by under him. The port was busy with Italian and German vessels crowded around the wharfs unloading tanks, trucks and guns to supply the Axis forces fighting the British, hundreds of miles east, along the coast towards Egypt.

'The harbour master says he wants us to wait for that Italian destroyer to get out of the way,' the pilot leaned back and shouted over the noise of the engines in the cockpit. He pointed at the slim warship nosing its way across the seaplane landing lane.

Otto and Lieutenant Werner Fischer were the only passengers, and had come up to the cockpit to watch the landing. It was a sunny but breezy spring day; the sea was navy blue, offset by whitecaps whipped up across it.

The pilot increased the power and the Junkers engines powered them round again.

Having never landed in a seaplane, Otto was alarmed by the huge spray of water that shot up either side of the cockpit as the hull touched down. They had been flown out of Paderborn to Genoa, and then made their way in stages down the east coast of Italy to Messina in Sicily before boarding the seaplane to cross the Mediterranean to Africa.

The plane gradually sank down into the water

and taxied over to moor on a buoy. A Kriegsmarine motorboat was waiting by it to collect them.

Otto and Werner jumped down into the launch and caught the luggage thrown down to them. The sailor at the wheel of the launch was a grumpy man from Hamburg, who looked askance at Otto's SS uniform. He had not had the chance to get the sand-coloured tropical kit that the sailor wore but had instead been quickly fitted out from the stores at Wewelsburg in neat grey trousers and tunic with a black belt, black jackboots and a peaked cap with the standard death's-head emblem on it. The sailor took in the black Knight's Cross hanging at his neck and the two collar tabs: the SS double lightning flash and his major's four-diamonds rank badge.

He made no comment, but the SS were not popular with the regular military because of their privileged status. He accepted the passengers grudgingly into his launch and then pointed east across the harbour. 'Welcoming party waiting for you over there, sir. Italians,' he added in his dour Hamburg accent.

With that he revved the engine, spun the launch east and tore across the choppy harbour; away from the main port and towards the Al-Madinah— the Old City. They wove in and out of the busy shipping: E-boats, flak-ships, cutters, minesweepers, lighters, dhows.

A south wind blew off the land to greet them. Despite the buffeting and spray, Otto stood up and held on to the launch's windshield to steady himself. He stared eagerly ahead at the packed shoreline of the old harbour. A line of tall palms ran along the seafront. Behind them he could see the outlines of minarets and mosque domes above the white stucco buildings. He took a deep sniff of the strange mix of sea salt and desert dust; he was eager to explore the new world in front of him.

'Looks fascinating,' he shouted down to Fischer, who was sitting in the cover of the windshield.

'Hmm,' Fischer nodded and smiled, squinting through his glasses and the spray, 'a lot of history there.'

The launch curved and drew level with a stone jetty next to the Al Sarayah al Hamra. It was crammed with brightly painted fishing boats tied up alongside. Close up they could see that the harbour edge was crowded with stalls and people: Moorish merchants wearing flowing jellaba robes and red fez were selling dates and oranges under striped yellow awnings. Off-duty Italian soldiers mooched around looking out of place.

The launch slowed to an ambling pace along the wharf as the sailor scanned the crowds for their reception committee. 'That's him there, the officer with the chicken on his head,' the sailor pointed.

Otto saw a tall Italian officer waving to them from up on the edge of the harbour wall. He was from the Bersaglieri regiment, dressed in sand-coloured breeches and tunic, brown jackboots, Sam Browne belt and a pith helmet with the unit's distinctive plume of black cockerel feathers blowing around on the top of it. His face was lean and tanned, with a neat beard. A small, stocky sergeant stood behind him.

'That's your welcoming committee, sir,' said the sailor, nodding up towards them as he manoeuvred the boat in against the slimy green side of an old dhow. 'They'll get your quarters sorted out—Italians've got all the best digs in town—and then take you over to the Afrika Korps command.'

Otto nodded, looked up at the officer, smiled and then waved.

'How's your Italian?' he muttered out of the side of his mouth to Fischer.

'Well, my Latin is good but unless we are going to be discussing Cicero I will be a bit stuck,' said the young lieutenant, pushing his spectacles up onto the bridge of his nose.

The two SS men scrambled across the low deck of the dhow with their bags. A confused scene then took place as they simultaneously passed their kitbags up to the sergeant, clambered up the wall and tried to greet the Italian colonel in the middle of a crowd.

He in turn was painfully conscious of the appalling performance of the Italian army that had necessitated the arrival of the Germans and tried to make up for it by repeating effusive greetings in heavily accented German.

'Our honour guests! Yes, welcome, welcome!'

Otto nodded and smiled, relieved that the officer had been sent to greet them because he spoke German. Everything had happened in such a rush over the last two days he had not been able to anticipate such crucial details.

'Welcome at Tripoli!' the colonel continued to gush as he pumped first Werner's and then Otto's hand.

'Thank you, Colonel. We are very glad to be here and to have the chance to work with our honoured Fascist allies.' Otto had heard that sort of phrasing on propaganda broadcasts and hoped that it would strike the right note.

The colonel's smile faltered and he suddenly looked embarrassed and uncomfortable. Otto realised he had not understood a word that he had said and his heart sank. His calm smile did not alter but inside he thought, 'How the hell is this going to work?'

The colonel glanced behind him nervously and gestured to someone to come forward. A petite young woman had been standing behind him, unnoticed by Otto. She slipped through the crowd, stood in front of him and thrust her hand out.

She spoke clearly in German but in quick snatches and only came up to his shoulder height so he did not catch all she said amid the hubbub around them.

'Miss Aisha Hmidi, official interpreter for the Fascist' something 'Council of the,' something 'Tripoli.'

He slowly bent his head down as she said this and shook her hand; it felt small and delicate, like a bird, in his big rough palm.

In the second that their heads were close he took in a very striking, fine-boned face: high cheekbones and huge, dark brown, doe-shaped eyes with perfectly plucked arched black eyebrows, all offset by subtle lipstick, and pearls. Her thick, jet-black hair was carefully swept up and coiffured in a glamorous style. They looked at each other a split second longer than was necessary.

He clicked his heels and as he bowed his head respectfully he couldn't help catching a glimpse of a plunging cleavage and a trim figure. She wore a clingy, cotton frock in a subtle but stylish lime print that, with a string of pearls, set off her dusky skin perfectly. A crocodile-skin handbag was hooked over her elbow.

The colonel pushed forward and returned to his effusive original manner but this time in Italian. Aisha stood next to him and dipped her head to this side, listening carefully.

When he had finished she looked Otto in the eye with a serious expression and gave her translation in a clear, confident tone: 'Colonel Pavone welcomes you to the Fourth Shore of Italy and is sure that the co-operation of the Fascist glorious allies will result in the victory.'

Her German had a heavy Arab accent but was comprehensible. Otto took it in but found that he was actually staring at her face as she spoke rather than listening to what she was saying. He was struck by the duskiness of her skin; it was so unlike anything that he was used to back home. His eyes were hooked on her sharp cheekbones and then the tiny frown that wrinkled her smooth forehead when she concentrated as the colonel gave another speech.

'You will be staying in the most beautiful house in Maqbara quarter. We drive there now. Please we come now.'

The Italian sergeant picked up Otto's bags and pushed a way through the crowd to a large open-topped Maserati staff car, parked on the kerb of the Lungomare.

There were some polite 'After you's before the colonel and the driver got in the front, with Otto, Werner and Aisha in the back seat. Werner was overawed by Aisha's beauty and confident manner, and responded to it by treating her with fussy formality as a defence. He was wary of sitting next to her on the back seat so they ended up with Otto in the middle.

The car pulled out into the busy stream of trucks, carts, camels and donkeys on the wide boulevard and headed through the narrow streets of the Old City. Honking the horn, the driver barged his way ahead through the mêlée. The colonel turned around occasionally and shouted about the different sights they passed. Aisha's head was close at Otto's side as she spoke the translations into his ear.

Outwardly as calm as ever, Otto found himself excited by a torrent of sensory stimuli. His head turned left and right continuously as they drove along, seeking out new sights, sounds, smells.

Hook-nosed Touaregs with indigo turbans, the defensive glances of veiled women, a streak of red blood curling through the dust outside a slaughterhouse. Everywhere the bleating of goats, camels and donkeys and the smell of their dung. He glimpsed a man standing outside a butcher's with a camel's head on a table next to him; its eyes were closed and its long curved lashes gave it a curiously beatific expression.

All these sensations went straight into his bloodstream without the usual filter of familiarity. In the midst of them he was also conscious of another feeling—his leg was pressed against Aisha's soft, warm thigh. As he dipped his head to her translation of the colonel's tourist commentary, he also took in her soaring perfume. Unbeknownst to him this new sensory river was lifting him gently up and floating him downstream, gradually detaching him from the person he normally was.

They finally emerged on the other side of the Old City and into the Italian quarter, with its modern,

197

wide boulevards shaded by palm trees. The red oleander trees were in flower and the neat grass verges were a joyous green. The German officers' villa was a fine, colonnaded, white building set back from the road behind a shady garden, and overlooking the Maqbara Park of macchia trees and lawns.

Otto and Werner were shown around and then the colonel made his excuses.

'My driver will collect you in an hour's time here. We will then be planning the start of the campaign of our victory,' Aisha said, tossing her head back and flashing her eyes to sign off her last translation with a flourish. The colonel saluted gallantly and drove off with her.

Otto and Werner stood on the drive and waved them off. Both of them stared rather too long at the small dark head in the back seat.

'She's a cracker, sir,' said Werner wistfully.

Otto nodded, expressionless, still looking after the car.

He paused and then broke into a big smile and looked at Werner. 'Yes, she certainly is,' he laughed, and turned back into the house.

*　　　*　　　*

'What's the matter?'

Otto frowned at the lieutenant sitting opposite him.

Werner's face suddenly twisted in alarm; his eyes widened behind his round spectacles.

'Um,' Werner looked down and mumbled, 'our translator is here.'

The SS men were on the veranda of their villa,

smoking and enjoying a cocktail in the warm evening as they waited to go out.

It was the end of a hectic working week planning the operation and Otto's unit had arrived from the Balkans, so Colonel Pavone had invited them all out to dine in the Old City with some Italian officers.

Attempting nonchalance, Otto twisted round in his chair, but even he couldn't help but twitch as he locked on to Aisha sauntering along under the lanterns strung above the garden path.

She walked with her eyes down and her hands modestly crossed in front of her; a silk shawl hooked over her elbows. The pose spoke of someone who knew that she was attractive and had no need to prove it.

She was wearing a long, pale yellow silk Cassini evening dress; backless but with a sculpted front that was coutured to show her curves. The colour set off her dusky skin perfectly; with the matching handbag, heels, pearl necklace and black hair elegantly swept back, she radiated sex appeal barely restrained by extreme good taste.

Both Otto and Werner stood up too quickly as she walked up the steps onto the veranda.

'*Fräulein.*' Otto paused for a moment with his hands spread wide, honest enough to admit that he was speechless, rather than blathering to cover it up.

She batted her long black eyelashes, dipped her head and smiled graciously, happy to acknowledge the compliment.

'*Fräulein*, yes, marvellous,' agreed Werner, fidgeting nervously. 'I fear we must be late. We must not let our allies down, hmm . . .' he coughed humorously.

'Oh, don't worry, they're Italians,' Aisha smiled, and flapped one end of her shawl casually. She didn't seem too bothered about them. 'Anyway,' she continued, 'we're in Tripoli now, not Berlin!' She poked Werner jokingly in the chest. 'We can afford to be a bit late.'

He blanched at her familiarity; she was in a much more relaxed mood than the severe office persona that they had been used to over the last week. She was always very neatly dressed and exact in her translation; quickly irritated with herself if she could not find the right words.

Otto stood back and watched the display contentedly. 'So you're going to take us through the parks?'

'The *giardinettos*,' she looked him in the eye as she corrected him. 'Yes, I love the Italian way of doing things. The *corso* is one of my favourites.'

'Why's that?' he frowned.

'The clothes—it's all about the clothes,' she laughed. 'You walk and you talk and look at what everyone is wearing. I love it!'

'Um, yes, well, I don't think we add too much there?' he smiled, and indicated his black dress uniform and the peaked cap on the table with its death's-head badge.

She cocked her head on one side and looked him up and own.

'Well, it looks good on you,' she said charitably, and adjusted the black Knight's Cross at his throat.

'National Socialism has much to recommend it, but tailoring . . . ?' he smiled.

'Well . . .' she shrugged and pouted at him. 'Shall we walk?' She turned and led them off. Otto fell in at her side and Werner trailed behind, relieved not to have to try to make conversation.

'. . . Well, I am an admirer of Fascism at least,' she continued her thoughts. 'The Italians have done so much to modernise our country: electricity, roads, hospitals.' She turned to look at Otto beside her. 'My father always said we were such a backward country before they came—so medieval. Now we have this,' she gestured around her at the wide boulevard lined with rows of soaring palms as they walked across it and into the park.

'He's a businessman—he does lots of deals with the colonial government. He wanted me to have all the benefits of the modern world.'

She had always been the princess of the family. Doted on by her father, she had regarded herself as too good for the local boys, whom she drove mad with her haughty Western sophistication.

She counted her achievements off on her fingers. 'So I went to an Italian school, I play piano, I learned Italian, I learned German, I learned English,' she dipped her head in acknowledgement towards him, 'and I always wanted to work for Mussolini.'

'Why?' Otto never had much time for him personally.

'Well, the Fascists are so dynamic!' She turned to him enthusiastically. 'They get things done! They're not like all the men here, sitting around all day drinking coffee, muttering and worrying over their beads.' She tossed her head in irritation at them. 'And anyway, look at the style!'

They were walking along a marble path through the park between topiaried orange trees hung with lanterns. All around them was a hubbub of excited chatter as beautifully attired Italian men and women came out for their evening stroll.

In wartime the custom of the *corso* faced an unusual regulation. It could only take place before the moon rose—as soon as it came up people knew that the nightly RAF bombing raids would start. The danger heightened the atmosphere: high-pitched laughter drifted over from groups around them.

'If the old mullahs had their way I'd be locked up at home now.' She smiled and waved at some Italian officers, who called out to her as she passed them.

'Come on, let's get a carriage!' she said as they came out the other side of the park and onto the wide Gargaresh Road that ran along the seashore before twisting back into the Old City. She gave a sudden skip and dashed into the road to flag down an open horse-drawn carriage as it clipped past.

The old driver pulled in to the kerb and they got in, with Werner sitting facing the other two in the back seat. It was beautiful to ride into town with the warm sea breeze blowing over them; Otto took off his SS cap and let it ruffle his hair. He watched a stream of traffic flowing past them on the other side of the road.

'Look—it's the Exodus.' Aisha pointed at it and laughed.

Otto glanced at her, not understanding the joke.

Carriages, taxis, trucks and donkey carts were piled up with people, and passed in a river of noise: belching engines, squeaking carts and chattering people. They looked like normal Tripolitanians; the swarthy men wearing scruffy jackets over thick roll-neck sweaters.

'They're Jews,' she said, and pointed at them again. 'When the Tommies come over to bomb they go for the harbour, but the flak puts them off and they always overshoot and drop their bombs on the Jewish quarter. So every night now they run away to the countryside. You know, the Exodus?'

With two fingers she mimicked a little figure running away, and laughed again.

Otto's face suddenly hardened and he stared at the people streaming past him. He had never seen Jews close up. There weren't any in rural Bavaria and he had only seen them on Nazi propaganda posters and in SS films, where they were presented as the embodiment of evil.

To be unexpectedly this close to so many of them was a shock for him. He stared at the race he had been indoctrinated to hate, looking for the telltale signs as outward signifiers of their wickedness. Instead they just looked like tired human beings worn down by their nightly trudge.

Aisha saw the look on his face and stopped smiling. The Italian Fascists had never made an issue of the Jews and she had forgotten that they were such an object of hatred for the SS.

Otto continued to stare at them in hateful silence.

*   *   *

Everyone was drunk.

They had dined on camel steaks and full-bodied red Cyrenaican wine. The officers were flush-faced and had loosened off their ties and uniform jackets.

The air was thick with cigarette smoke being

203

stirred gently like soup by the ceiling fan. The restaurant, the Grand Albergo D'Italia, was on the upper floor of an old Moorish palace by the souk.

The Italian swing band broke into '*Il Valzer di ogni Bambina*', the jaunty tenor and trumpet belting it out.

Pavone's officers at one end of the table joined in the chorus. Otto's men at the other end banged the table in time to the beat but could only make out the last word of the title and so bellowed it all the more: '*Bam-bina!*'

Aisha maintained her poise in the midst of this mayhem. With her bare shoulders, sculpted hair and yellow silk dress she was a little oasis of elegance in a sea of uniforms.

She was smoking a long French cigarette and watching Otto through the smoke. He sat at the German end of the long table, tipped back on his chair, glass of wine in hand, listening to his men.

His second in command, Captain Heinz Jahnke, recently arrived with the unit, walked up behind him, put a hand on his shoulder and shouted something in his ear over the noise of the band. For a second Otto seemed not to have understood and stared drunkenly ahead. Then a retort came to him and he shouted it over his shoulder. The crew around him laughed and he turned back to laugh with them. As he turned he saw her staring at him and grinned.

A feeling ran through her like a shot of hard liquor.

Aisha's poise slipped off like her silk shawl and she looked momentarily lost. As she stared at him, the question occurred to her, for the first time in her life: Could I love this person?

For Aisha the war was the most exciting thing that had ever happened to her. She was twenty-two years old, intelligent, bored and frustrated by the feeling of living in a dusty backwater. Suddenly she was pitched into a job fighting in the great global crusade against communism, surrounded by hearty men in glamorous uniforms, pretty much every one of whom was making varying degrees of effort to sleep with her. She liked to think she had impossibly high standards and fended them all off with casual disdain. This drove them to acts of desperation and reinforced her certainty that they were beneath her.

Then Otto had appeared in her world and she was no longer so sure of herself. She saw now how striking he was in his black SS uniform as he leaned back in his chair: the strong bones of his face, the blond hair slicked back, his confidence and easy grin. In her imagination he fitted into the Nazi propaganda images of invincible SS stormtroopers.

Otto was enjoying himself too much to realise how fascinated she was by him. He had spent most of the last week working long hours with her as they sorted out the logistics for the expedition. He was so effective as a commander because of his single-minded attention to his military duties, and had kept his mind on the job; the intensity of the work had suppressed any personal feelings. However, now that he had time to relax he felt an alternative centre of consciousness rising up alongside his usual professionalism.

Visually, Aisha tantalised him. She was so different from the pale-skinned, straw-haired Bavarian girls he was used to. *Mauerblümchen,* they called them: wallflowers. Safe, sensible, little Miss Average.

To him the intense black of Aisha's glossy hair was like an elixir, and the dusky sheen of her skin mesmeric. The quick, highly strung movements of her trim figure contrasted to his calmness: the rapid flick of her head when she walked into a room, the jaunty little swing of her handbag when she started up some steps, the intensity of her frown, with her mouth pressed tight and brow furrowed, when she concentrated on getting a translation perfect.

By blood she was an Arab and therefore *verboten* for an SS man, but all the more enticing because of it. The allure of the unknown to him was what had made him such a good reconnaissance commander in the first place. He was really just a small-town boy looking for adventure. Aisha was that adventure—more exotic and sophisticated than he could have imagined, and hence she bypassed all rational constraints on his behaviour. He didn't believe a word of the ridiculous Dark Heart Prophecy that had sent him on this mission but as long as it provided opportunities for adventures like this, he wasn't complaining.

The Italian band finished their song and bowed out for a break to the accompaniment of noisy applause. The Germans felt it was their turn to contribute some *Kultur*. Sergeant Schenk, a beefy, balding mechanic, burst into the newly written Afrika Korps anthem and the others joined him bellowing out the words and ending in a ragged finale with:

Es rasseln die Ketten,
Es dröhnt der Motor,
Panzer rollen in Afrika vor!

'To Rommel!' shouted Otto, and held up his wineglass to their stunningly successful commander-in-chief. Since he had launched the Afrika Korps campaign he had reversed the Italian disasters and pushed the Allies back a thousand kilometres into British-owned Egypt.

They all clinked, and Colonel Pavone came over to accept the toast. Aisha followed him to translate.

The suave colonel had been trying it on with her for months now, but to no avail. He had seen the look she had given Otto, ruefully scratched his ear, given her a calculating look and then written off a long-imagined night in bed with her.

Otto stood up to clink glasses and they then stood rather awkwardly, unsure what to say and so turned to talking shop.

Speaking through Aisha, the colonel said, 'I got a call from Pietro Gallina this evening at last. He's the desert expert you'll need for navigating. He finally managed to make it to a phone. His house has been behind enemy lines for ages until Rommel pushed them back.'

Otto was aware of the secrecy of the mission and wanted to keep it SS only, and so politely tried to refuse the suggestion. 'That's very good of you but I don't think we will need him. I have led reconnaissance units across Poland, France and the Balkans. My crews are the finest men in the SS.'

The colonel was not fazed by this Teutonic

arrogance. He smiled and shrugged. He nodded in appreciation of the point; he was nothing if not generous in defeat.

'Well, that's all good . . . but the Sahara is not France. If you don't know what you're doing you can't just stop off and ask the way. No matter how good your men are, it will fry you pretty quick if you get lost. We used to lose a lot of guys in there when we first took Libya, and you are going further than we ever did.'

He closed one eye and squinted as he did the calculation.

'It's a good twelve hundred kilometres of deep desert *and* the Tibesti mountains that you've got to get through before you even hit the semi-arid lands in the Lake Chad region.

'You see, the thing is, on the coast the desert is hot but you're always near the main road to get your bearings and resupply. Out there the easiest thing is simply to get lost—it all looks the same and the maps are useless.' He held up his hands in despair. 'They have big patches that are just blank. You have to be an expert in solar and stellar navigation. How long is it since you used a solar compass?'

Otto didn't reply because he didn't want to lose face, but inside he knew it was a long time since he had even seen one and he wouldn't know how to use it. He had been trained for European land campaigns, not sailing across an ocean of sand where naval navigation techniques were more important because of the lack of landmarks.

'No!' the colonel warmed to his theme and held up his hand with an air of finality. Italian pride was also coming through here; he wanted to show that the Italians could actually do some things well. 'Doing it without expert help would be suicide, but,' an index finger was held up for emphasis, 'Pietro Gallina is your solution! He's an old friend of mine; he was head of our desert survey group until he retired a few years back. He must be seventy by now but he's as fit as a snake—spent years in the desert with the tribes. They call him "Abu Ramla", father of the sands. He knows *everything* you'll need to know about desert travel: navigation, finding the wells, where the stocks of food are that we buried out there. He'll show you how to use a solar compass.

'Unfortunately he's retired so I can't just order him to accompany you. He lives in Cyrenaica, up on the Jabal al Akhdar—he likes his solitude. I told him you would be setting off to see him tomorrow so he's expecting you and,' he gave a graceful smile, 'you'll need to take an interpreter.' He glanced at Aisha.

'Also—as a final gesture to our Fascist allies I insist that you take my car—the finest Italian engineering! An Alfa Corto Spyder. It's a thousand kilometres to Cyrenaica and you'll need a fast car to overtake all those damned supply trucks.' He hung his head in a display of boredom. 'Fifty k.p.h., urgh! It's a long way to Benghazi at that speed—believe me, I have done it enough times!'

Otto and Aisha both looked down at the ground as the implications of this new development sunk in. They would be going on a long journey together.

PRESENT DAY, WEDNESDAY 28 JANUARY, MBOMOU PROVINCE, CENTRAL AFRICAN REPUBLIC

Alex looked down at Yamba from his vantage point in the commander's hatch of the tank as they waited under the trees.

The black sergeant-major was sitting on the ground and reached out to pick a blade of long grass. He held it by both ends and used it to scrape off the beads of sweat that had been squeezed out of his shaved head by the pressure-cooker heat. He flicked the drips of moisture away.

It was midday and the thunderheads hung motionless in the blue sky, stupefied by the heat.

They had advanced twenty miles in total from their landing point on the banks of the Chinko and had laagered up in a bai—a clearing burned out of the trees years ago by a lightning strike. It was three hundred yards wide, and the task force had dispersed around the perimeter, keeping under cover in the trees with weapons trained outwards.

They were waiting for Pavel to land in the Shark. He was scouting ahead along their intended route, using the powerful cameras and infrared optics that they had fitted under the nose of his aerial beast.

The digital information was being beamed back to the signals truck where it could be viewed on a TV screen or printed out as aerial photographs to be distributed to troop commanders on the ground.

On the road half a mile ahead lay their first

major obstacle. Alex had called a quick conference with his commanders to discuss how to handle it and they were waiting for Pavel to complete the recce and then land in the bai so that he could give them first-hand details. They had marked out an LZ for the chopper with orange dayglo panels in the middle of the clearing.

Thirty miles south of the mine, they were approaching a line of small hills; only gentle slopes a couple of hundred feet high but still enough to dominate the road and an obvious place to build a sentry outpost. It was at roughly this distance from the mine that Alex had hit the Muti Boys' roadblock on the initial recce mission so he was doubly wary.

The heat made everyone slightly lethargic. The soldiers not on sentry duty picked blood oranges from the bushes or chewed the pink stalks of wild sugarcane that grew in the open area of the bai.

They looked up as they heard the loud whirr of the Shark overhead. Pavel circled the LZ, checking it for obstacles.

'I think I have infrared contact on first hill to right of road. Over,' came the excited Russian voice over the radio to Alex. He glanced up at the black flight helmet in the cockpit as it set down in a cloud of dust and grass.

'What did you see? Over.'

'Three infrared signatures close to themselves. Can't think it is animals. Over.'

Alex thought about what it might be. He knew that there were forest antelopes that gave out the same heat level as a human and travelled in small groups. But it was suspicious that they happened to be on that particular hill.

Pavel shut off the engines, their note lowered gradually as they wound down. The cockpit door popped open as he hurriedly unbuckled himself.

The heavy crack of the first mortar bomb exploded over on the far side of the bai. It was a ranging shot and buried itself in the earth so the shrapnel burst upwards ineffectually, but it stunned everyone for a second.

Then experienced reactions set in and the Battlegroup was galvanised out of its torpor. Troops scuttled about, bent double: grabbing weapons and buckling on helmets and body armour with quick, practised movements.

'Pavel! Take off again!' shouted Alex over the radio. The figure hesitated with one leg out of the cockpit and then rapidly pulled it back in, slammed the door shut and hit the starter for the engines. The rotors hadn't stopped moving and began to pick up speed again. Alex urged them on in his head: 'Come on! Get off the ground!'

He could not afford to lose his gunship. The enemy must have seen it drop down into the bai and then opened up, trying to hit it when it was a sitting duck.

'What's happening?' Kalil poked his head out of the back door of the signals truck and shouted across to Alex.

'We've got a contact. Don't worry; just get back inside the truck!'

The Lebanese was adept at being a playboy in Mayfair but Alex didn't want him getting in the way out here.

'Kilo Two! Kilo Three! Advance on first hill to right of road. Encircle and try to take prisoners.'

He wanted them for intelligence on the mine.

'Kilo Three. Roger that: advance on first hill to right of road,' Col's broad Lancashire tones sounded calm and in control. His BMP reversed out of the bush and tore across the bai, followed by Rennie's.

Another mortar exploded, this time on the near side of the clearing. They were bracketing the target—the next one would be on the button.

Come on, Pavel! Come on!

The engine note was high now. The twin rotors were whirring in different directions. The body of the aircraft shifted slightly as the weight came off the wheels.

Get off the ground!

Pavel pulled power and went through the fastest transition Alex had ever seen. The Shark was so powerful and agile that it simply flipped on one side, shot across the clearing and out over the trees. The next mortar was an airburst right over where it had been.

Alex breathed a sigh of relief and keyed the mike. 'Pavel, stay clear until I need an airstrike. I'm sending Col in to clear the hill.'

The next day was the Führer's birthday.

Otto and his men, tired and dishevelled, had to drag themselves out of their beds early and try not to be sick as they stood on the parade ground in the sun.

Finally they were dismissed and retreated to a restaurant terrace overlooking the harbour for a celebratory lunch. Aisha appeared wearing her trademark clingy cotton frock, her hair perfect. She was looking a lot fresher and happier than the men were. She had a small crocodile-skin valise with her; she was leaving with Otto straight after the lunch for Cyrenaica.

Tagines of lamb and bowls of couscous were demolished by the hungry Germans but the bottles of wine on the table remained untouched.

'I don't even want to look at it—take it away,' muttered Werner, shielding his eyes from the bottle in front of him. The others laughed; the academic was beginning to be more accepted by the SS soldiers.

A sustained hubbub of conversation replaced the pained silence at the beginning of the meal. The soldiers undid their tunics, chewed on watermelons and sat back to smoke. Even Werner perked up and got out his cine camera. He panned around the table and the men waved tiredly at him.

'Sir,' he called to Otto, 'I need something to film in front of the view.' He pointed at the harbour.

Otto looked up from his conversation with Aisha and stared at the lieutenant for a moment. Then he shrugged and nodded. 'I think you need someone a bit more photogenic than me.' He stood up and made an inviting gesture to Aisha. 'Shall we?'

She laughed and they walked up to the rail; the men clapped and cheered.

'Right, so what do we have here then?' Otto blew smoke out of his mouth and gestured to the harbour with the cigarette in his hand.

Werner was not an expert cameraman, and swung back and forth between him and the view.

'So, over there,' he pointed down at an Italian freighter unloading tanks onto the wharf, 'we see the arrival of the latest generation of Italian tanks. They will be sent to take on the massed Allied forces in the desert—just as soon as they wind up the elastic bands.'

The Germans laughed raucously and applauded; Italian tanks were notoriously useless. Aisha clapped her hands and laughed, flashing a look at the camera.

The spool ran out and Werner gave it to Aisha: 'A present from the Ahnenerbe, *Fräulein*.'

She was delighted—'Thank you, Werner,' and gave him a kiss. He reddened, prompting another round of applause and whistles from the soldiers.

Otto went to discuss timings and arrangements with Heinz Jahnke, his second in command. When they finished lunch he brought the Alfa round to the front of the restaurant. The Corto Spyder was the height of technology and elegance. Painted in Italian racing red, it was a soft-topped two-seater with curved mudguards and a long bonnet with the famous Alfa badge perched on it. Spare tyres, water and a rack of twenty-litre jerry cans of fuel were strapped on the back for their long trek.

Otto and Aisha piled their bags into the tiny

boot. It was mid-afternoon and he wanted to get as far as he could before morning. Colonel Pavone had warned him that driving in daylight was safe near to Tripoli but that as they approached Pietro Gallina's house near the frontline, they risked attack by British fighter-bombers coming in off their aircraft carriers out to sea. Otto was therefore going to drive all night to see if he could make it through the danger zone under cover of darkness.

The coastline of Libya ran east to west for fifteen hundred kilometres with the large indent of the Gulf of Sirte in the middle of it. They were at the western end of this. At the other end the coast bulged out into the Mediterranean in the Jabal al Akhdar plateau where Gallina lived.

The men stood around the car admiring its lines. Otto put the roof down, Aisha tied on a polka dot headscarf and the red sports car roared off along the Via Balbi coast road.

As they drove, the green farmland gave way to the Sidran desert of stunted camel thorn, rocks and clay. On their left the brilliant aquamarine sea sparkled; sometimes the road swerved right up onto the cliffs overlooking it.

They passed through the oasis villages of Suk el Giuma and Tagiura, with endless rows of date palms. Seeing Otto's German uniform the children came rushing out from the roadsides shouting *'Eier! Eier!'* and holding out eggs. They had been quick to learn German sales patter. He smiled and waved but sped on.

The road was packed with military convoys; every bullet and drop of water and fuel used by the 200,000 men at the front had to be transported from

Tripoli to where the front had stabilised around Sollum. Huge grey Italian trucks, red diesel tractors towing spare vehicles, sand-coloured German light trucks and armoured vehicles lumbered back and forth along both sides of the road, as the colonel had warned them. They hugged the right-hand verge to allow the red Alfa to flash through the gap down the middle.

Otto and Aisha made good time and soon began to pass the debris of war from the recent German offensive. The roadsides were littered with ammunition boxes, British four-gallon Shell cans, bullet-riddled vehicles and the burned-out hulks of trucks. Italian and British tanks had been blasted onto their sides or had their turrets ripped off by explosions. Sometimes they had to slow down to drive over bits of road where a burning vehicle had melted the tarmac.

They snacked on German army ration packs. Aisha made a face as she tried the Scho-Ka-Kola chocolate. Otto shrugged and smiled. 'OK, it's ersatz. We can't get everything right!'

After the walled town of Misratah, the sun set behind them and they put the roof up. The bright V of the headlights forged past the endless columns of trucks that they passed with a monotonous *whum, whum, whum.*

Otto began to feel the effects of the night before, coupled with the long drive. He and Aisha had chatted amicably at the start of the drive and then lapsed into companionable silence. Both were happy to enjoy the other's company but did so from the safety of their official positions. Now, though, he needed a more sustained conversation to keep himself awake through the night.

217

'So, tell me your life story then,' he said suddenly.

She looked at him perplexed. 'What do you mean?'

'Well, you know, start at the beginning and keep going. We've got a long way to go.'

'Um?'

'Where were you born?'

'Tripoli.'

'What happened then?'

She laughed, trying to think where to start.

'Well, my father always said I was born bossy—but I just told him to keep quiet.'

Otto grinned and settled back to listen.

'My mother was very Western. She always had the latest copies of Italian *Vogue*. I used to lie around all day flicking through them.'

So she began to talk about things that she had known but never realised she knew. Otto nodded, said, 'Uh-huh,' and sometimes asked a question but otherwise was blissfully happy to let the silk stream of her voice pour into his ear.

A strange interaction developed where she talked and Otto drove; each excelling in his or her own way. He had both hands on the wheel, holding it firm and narrowing his eyes slightly as he steered them round the corners, leaning into them. He was totally focused; his hands traced the curves of the road as gently, accurately and meaningfully as he would trace the curves of a lover. The sensation of smooth acceleration slipped through them both.

The gravitational pull of it was taking over her body as the road curved, swinging it this way and that, taking her out of her ordinary orbit. She let her head roll as she talked; she was not herself.

She drifted from side to side, let go and slept, and when she woke briefly, he was there again by her side, as hard and intense as he had been before.

*　　*　　*

Dawn came up fast in front of them.

It seeped into the black-and-white shapes of night and then overwhelmed them in a rush. Colour, shape and texture bloomed all around: brilliant blue sea broke out on their left, emerald-green macchia bushes and the red slopes of the Jabal al Akhdar on their right.

Aisha stirred in the seat next to him; the feeling of discomfort pulled her back from sleep. She felt horrible: tired, unwashed and hungry. Her neck and back ached from sleeping upright and her head was fuzzy. She opened one eye reluctantly and rubbed her face, trying to wake up.

Otto noticed her stir.

'We'd better find somewhere to get off the road. Dawn is when the Hurricanes come in off the carriers.' He inclined his head left to indicate the British ships out to sea over the horizon.

She nodded mutely, not feeling capable of speech. He flicked his eyes from side to side, looking at the odd track or farm gate that they passed.

She trusted him to find somewhere but felt she ought to look like she was making some effort to help so she stared groggily out of her window and then turned idly to look back behind them.

'Aye!' the yelp of fear came from her involuntarily. 'There!' She pointed out to sea.

The two Sea Hurricanes flashed sharp against the blue sky and then disappeared behind a cliff. The single-engined fighters were right down at sea level, hugging the coastline, using every contour to shield them from view, waiting for the opportunity to leap out onto a convoy.

Again they shot into view. They were moving so fast that the whole landscape became clumsy by comparison. Aisha saw their yellow desert camouflage, the red, white and blue RAF roundel on the fuselage and how one fresh-faced pilot had pushed back his canopy to enjoy the rush of cool air.

Otto immediately braked hard and swung the car onto the dirt verge.

'Out, out, out!' he shouted.

He had been strafed by Hurricanes in France and knew how dangerous it was to be in a vehicle.

Aisha scampered round to him on bare feet, having kicked off her heels. He picked her up and hurried up the verge, across some shingle and into a stand of macchia bushes away from the road.

He put her down and they both peered anxiously out of the foliage. The road was straight and flat for a mile and they could see a convoy of ten grey Italian trucks lumbering along it towards them.

They tensed, wanting to rush out and warn the drivers but fearful of leaving cover. The moments dragged by but eventually the convoy drew level.

'I think they've missed them,' Otto whispered cautiously as the trucks trundled past their hiding place. The drivers turned idly to stare at the red Alfa skewed on the verge with the driver's door hanging open.

Otto and Aisha stepped out from the bushes

and watched the end truck lumber half a mile on from their spot. He began to feel slightly foolish and grinned at her sheepishly. She snorted in relief and smiled at him.

The Hurricanes sprang over the cliff edge and roared right over them at two hundred miles an hour. They had seen the convoy and wheeled back out to sea to come at them from behind.

Twenty feet overhead, the slipstream made the dust jump under their feet and ripped leaves from the bush behind them. The deep roar of their engines was split by the barking of their 20mm cannons.

The last truck disappeared in a storm of red tracer fire. The fuel tank exploded in an orange sheet. Three more trucks detonated as the Hurricanes swept along the line hammering them with their guns. Lorries slewed, crashed and scattered to the verges, drivers jumping from their cabs and running. The Hurricanes overshot them and then flicked their wings in a display of triumphant agility. They banked and swept back out to their seaborne lair.

Otto and Aisha stepped out of the bush and stared at the plumes of black smoke pouring up into the fresh blue sky; their brute ugliness defiled its early morning purity.

Aisha felt weak from her tiredness, the sudden shock and the appalling scene in front of her.

She covered her eyes with her hand and turned her face away. Involuntarily she pressed her forehead into his chest.

Otto stood staring over her at the whorls billowing up into the sky. His face was dark and firm. He was thinking what he should do.

221

A long moment passed.

'Come on,' he said tenderly, taking her hand and then sweeping her up again to carry her back to the car. As he carried her he spoke quietly over the dark mane of her hair nestled into his chest.

'They will deal with their casualties. We don't have any medicine so we can't help them. If we stop we could be hours, we must press on.'

She didn't listen to the meaning of his words; she only sensed the deep timbre of them rumbling through her from his chest. She leaned her head against him and surrendered to the childlike feeling of being carried.

He put her back into her seat, started the car and drove on again in silence. She curled up with her head in her hands, suffering in silence. He knew they needed to get into shelter.

A couple of miles further on he saw a group of buildings out on a headland to their left and turned down the dirt track to it. It was an Italian settler farmstead: a two-storey white stucco house with a large veranda and balcony looking out north to the sea to catch the cooling breezes. The house was surrounded by twenty-foot-high, red oleander trees that were in the full flood of their spring colour, gushing flowers from every bough.

White outbuildings formed a courtyard behind the house, and Otto drove in through an arch and parked. The settlers must have left in a hurry to escape the British as the door into the house was ajar and items of clothing were scattered across the large steps leading up to it.

'Come on,' he said to Aisha gently. She was numb from the shock and staring out of her window. She nodded mutely and began to move again; slowly opening the door and stepping out.

Otto pulled their bags out of the boot whilst Aisha cautiously walked up the steps and pushed the door open. She picked up a coat-stand that had fallen across the hallway and walked into the high-ceilinged room, looking up and around her with the feeling of a trespasser.

The house was silent. She crept through the hall and on up the broad stairway in front of her, looking for a place to sleep. She walked along a wooden-floored landing and turned right into the master bedroom. The French windows were ajar and the winds of dawn blew softly through the white muslin curtains. She pushed them aside and walked out onto the balcony. She pulled out her hairpins and shook her heavy locks so that they fell down her back. She leaned against the stone balustrade—it was cold against her stomach—and looked out at the whitecaps ruffling the fresh blue sea. She felt the wind cool on her face and let it run its hands through her hair.

Otto came to the top of the big staircase, holding the bags in each hand. He paused for a moment.

He put the bags down, walked along the landing, through the open door into the bedroom and out onto the balcony. He stood behind her, not looking at the sea as she was but staring down at the dark spill of hair that fell around her shoulders. He could see the grain of it; each filament special to him.

He reached out his hands with a feeling of reverence and touched her shoulders. Slowly he turned her round to face him and kissed her softly.

*   *   *

They slept until the afternoon.

The white muslin curtains stirred occasionally in the wind but they lay still on the wide bed, curled up together. Eventually he rolled on his back and she rested her head on his chest.

A great calm existed between them; they had both arrived somewhere and did not want to leave it. They entered this new place as if they were walking into a cathedral; it felt vast, silent and awe-inspiring. They explored it slowly, taking in one glorious sensation at a time. He drew in the smell of her perfume and then savoured the texture of her thick hair as he ran his hands through it. She sensed the hairs on the back of his hand as he stroked her cheek and then, as she looked at him lying on his back next to her, she took in the strong set of the bones of his face.

They sat on the balcony, ate some oranges and drank some clear water from the house cistern. Then they lay on the bed and slept again. Both were surprised and shocked by what was happening to them: here they were in the middle of a war zone, with people being shot and killed nearby, and they were lazing in a villa, lying in a big white bed all day, sleeping, eating and kissing. They had urgent work to do. It felt illegal but beautiful to stay where they were, so they remained, paralysed by the pleasure.

They had each been brought up strictly. But for all their outward support of these belief systems, all they really wanted to do was escape them. Here was their chance. From then on, the rest of their world was black-and-white, with this one spot of colour. It was all silent but for this one sound. Everything was bland but for this one taste.

Otto had initially regarded Aisha as fascinating but his dedication to the Party, the Fatherland, his men and his mission had all been much more important. But now, this alternative emotion had somehow risen up stealthily within him and eclipsed his professionalism.

Where had his usual, single-minded zeal gone? He could still see it, but it was a long way off and looked so small and insignificant, like some childhood toy that had once meant everything to him but that, when rediscovered as an adult, seemed pointless.

When he sat on the balcony with her, overlooking the sea, she was too beautiful to look at directly, as if he were trying to look straight at the sun. So he just held her hands and looked at them instead as if they had just become the two most sacred objects in the universe. They were as individual as her face and he memorised their shape.

For Aisha the coast journey marked the dividing line between the two halves of her life. She had got into the car Aisha Hmidi and she got out of it Aisha Hofheim. She had been brought up to value meaning, to respect absolutes. All her life she knew she had a great well of talent and love to give to someone and had created a wall around it to guard it jealously from lesser mortals.

However, all she was really looking to do was to find an altar to lay these gifts on. Otto had involuntarily charmed his way through her wall and from then on he was her cause.

Eventually, as it drew near to evening, he looked down at her nestled against his side.

'We ought to get going,' he muttered.

She didn't respond for a while but then just hugged him tighter; she stuck her nose into the gap where he had undone his shirt and breathed in deeply. He stroked her back.

'Hmm,' she agreed.

It took three such muttered reminders over half an hour for them finally to sit up and get going.

Gradually they sped up. They washed quickly and she fixed her hair and make-up. He followed her down the stairs, carrying the cases.

In the big hallway she suddenly stopped and laughed.

'What?' He put the cases down.

She waltzed around the large hall with her arms out, her head back, laughing.

'What?' He started laughing as well.

She came back to him, her hand over her mouth, giggling. 'I feel like I should say thank you but I don't even know whose house this is!'

She nestled against his chest and he put his arms around her and rocked gently from foot to foot, swaying her with him.

Col's mean eyes narrowed as his BMP troop carrier crashed through the bush to attack the hill. He was hunched low, peering out round the grenade launcher mounted in front of his commander's hatch. He wanted to see as much as he could going into the contact, but equally, he didn't want to get shot.

He had ordered them off the road and they were tearing along, weaving between trees. He was an old hand at this game and enjoyed the anticipation of a firefight, trying to guess where the enemy were and how to come at them.

As they approached the foot of the hill, he called over the radio, 'Right, Kilo Two, Kilo Three. Halt and debus! Rennie, take right flank. I'll take left.'

'Ja, bru,' came the terse Afrikaans response.

The vehicle plunged forwards as it braked hard. The two armoured doors at the back swung open on their hydraulics and the infantry squads ran out on their respective sides, immediately finding cover and then looking for targets over the sights of their AK-74s.

Col got his squads of infantrymen lined up on either side of him with rapid hand movements. Visibility was about twenty feet. He could just make out the men nearest him in their camouflage amidst the dense bush. It was a clutter of vines, ferns and dead leaves, gloomy from the high tree canopy overhead, but lit by an occasional shaft of sunlight coming down through it.

'Advance!' He jabbed his left hand forwards, the other clutching the grip on his assault rifle.

They moved off, all senses switched forwards, over the muzzles of their rifles, scanning ahead for the enemy.

Sweat ran into Col's eyes and his breathing sounded incredibly loud in his ears. They waded forward through a small stream. Cool water ran over the tops of his boots and trickled down so that he could feel it running over the instep of his feet.

An innocent popping sound came from up the hill and then the sharp crack of rounds going over his head.

The mantra of pairs fire and manoeuvre basic infantry drills took over.

Dash forwards, down on the ground, crawl to one side so you don't put your head up where you went down. Sights—look for the enemy.

Shouting to his buddy: 'Prepare to move!'

Pause.

'Move!'

Col rose and loosed quick-aimed bursts of suppressive fire towards where the enemy were as the soldier next to him repeated the same manoeuvre as he had done: dashing forwards and then going down as Col covered him.

They began a good rhythm, moving forwards steadily.

The BMPs advanced with them, their 30mm cannon stabbing flashes into the gloom.

'Magazine!' Col shouted to his partner and they paused.

Roll on his side. Pull off the old mag. Exchange it for a new one from his chest bandolier. Slap it home with the palm of his hand. Cock weapon. Roll back into position.

'Prepare to move!'

And they were off again.

A shadow detached itself from a tree ahead and ran towards another. Muzzle sight onto it quickly; swinging with the movement of the target until slightly ahead. Quick five-round burst. The man was thrown sideways, flinging his rifle up into the air.

Col turned to each side to check the line of his men moving forwards, and glimpsed one soldier cowering behind a tree after a near miss from incoming fire.

'*Ssstop wanking!*' he bellowed with such ferocity that the man snapped his terrified eyes round towards him. All the training they had put in at the base paid off as he saw his sergeant-major and instantly obeyed: gathered his wits, checked his weapon and rejoined the attack.

Through the mayhem of shots and shouting around him, Col sensed an upsurge in the incoming fire. The deeper note of a heavy machine gun began barking at them. A burst cut through the air above him, shredding chunks of wood off a tree and showering him in white splinters.

A mortar burst in the tree canopy overhead. Airburst shrapnel fizzed around him and leaves and branches tumbled down. Someone was hit along the line to his left and started screaming.

An RPG fired and the grenade streaked towards one of the BMPs, exploding against a tree.

Resistance was stiffening. They must have brought up reinforcements from somewhere. At this rate they weren't going to be able to take any prisoners without sustaining significant casualties. Col knew Alex wouldn't think that was worthwhile.

He got into cover, rolled on his side and pulled the radio handset out of his backpack. He got through to Alex.

'Kilo Five, this is Kilo Two. Situation is we're getting malleted here wi' mortars from hill to right of axis of advance. Request air support!'

Alex agreed to his request for an airstrike and he pulled his men back, marking their position with an orange smoke grenade to show Pavel where not to fire.

The Shark had been loitering in a holding pattern away from the firefight. Pavel was furious at having been nearly blown up on the ground, the most humiliating end for a pilot.

When Alex's order came through with the fire mission co-ordinates, he rogered it calmly and then yanked the machine out of its circle, relishing the fierce Gs that pressed his body against the side of the tight cockpit.

The Shark was a murderous machine, coming in low and fast over the trees. Pavel dropped the nose slightly and fired off a pod of twenty 80mm rockets into the top of the hill. The rapid puffs of smoke whipped away in the slipstream as they left the pod. The trees on the hilltop exploded in orange flame.

Pavel whipped the aircraft round and out of range again and then circled in behind the hill. He rolled in and loosed off another pod of rockets.

A maroon Toyota pickup truck broke cover along a track running up to the back of the hill. Looking down, he could see it flitting underneath the tall tree canopies; the driver racing for his life. He switched on his main armament targeting system and zeroed it. He banked and opened fire, letting the machine hang in the turn just long enough to obliterate the target with a clattering burst of 30mm fire.

He felt the aircraft buck as the petrol tank exploded underneath him and a quiet smile of revenge spread over his face.

'What it looks like is that this was an outpost that was initially manned with only three men and a mortar, but that they had a mobile reserve nearby that they brought up during the contact.'

Alex was giving his debrief to his commanders in the back of the signals truck later that afternoon.

Kalil, Col, Yamba, Rennie, Yuri, Arkady and Pavel were all squeezed into the enclosed lorry between the banks of radios, satellite communication equipment and photo reconnaissance analysis displays lining each side.

'That's when we started taking heavy machine-gun hits, and then they got their mortar going again,' Col chipped in.

'So these guys must be pretty pissed about the Shark,' said Kalil with a grin towards Pavel, who smiled and nodded.

Alex was relieved that his boss was in a confident mood.

'Whadda we know about that guy you found up there?'

They had recovered the bodies of twelve boy soldiers as well as one man in his forties. Alex nodded thoughtfully and rubbed the stubble on his chin.

'Well, he's definitely Arab or North African of some kind. Has anyone seen that kind of cam pattern before?'

Heads shook around the room. The combat fatigues were old and faded, and no one could place the distinctive mottled pattern.

'Whoever these guys are they seem to be running the show and are professional soldiers. They know

232

what they're doing, so watch out for them.'

After a brief discussion of the route ahead Alex decided they needed to get going again.

'OK. So, gentlemen, usual drills and actions apply. Let's crack on!'

They spilled out of the door at the rear of the truck and hurried to their vehicles.

Pavel and Arkady flew their helicopters back to land on the ferries moored in mid-river to await call-up from their secure base.

Engines coughed into life and the column set off again. They progressed through the line of hills without further incident.

As they came down onto the flat again, shells started screeching over them and exploding off to the right, their bangs muffled slighty by the heavy foliage. It was only speculative fire and not accurate, but it was enough to cause concern. Radios crackled back and forth along the line.

'It's not mortars, no.' Col ducked as a shell went horizontally over his head and exploded in the bush.

'It's those 106mm recoilless they've mounted on Unimogs. Coming in from the west,' Yamba said as he watched the shells streak across the column from his BMP at the back of the line. 'They know we are coming now and they have the co-ordinates of the road.'

Alex listened to the reports in his tank.

He decided to call in the Shark and radioed the fire mission to Pavel. They needed the helicopter to spot the enemy. Trying to do it from the ground in this terrain would be impossible. It would take him minutes to lift off from the ferry and cover the thirty miles to where they were.

233

Pavel was sitting in his cockpit waiting for call-up. He started the engines, pulled power, and his two turbofans, each pushing out 2,200 h.p., sent him skimming back across the treetops.

He followed the road and then broke off west from where the column had dispersed into the trees to avoid the incoming fire. He slowed to seek out the target; his eyes flicked from the jungle to the infrared monitor on his heads-up display, searching for any sign of the enemy.

In the end it was too easy.

'I have him!' he radioed in. 'Narrow lake to west of axis of advance. Vehicle at northern end.'

Alex sat in his cramped seat and checked the maps and aerial photographs folded up on his knees.

The lake was half a mile west of the road. They must have parked the recoilless there because it was one of the few places where the line of fire would be uninterrupted by trees.

'Roger. Proceed to attack target. Be careful!'

Pavel dropped down to a hover between two high treetops. He was sure they hadn't seen him; he was going to enjoy this. He pushed the Shark up from cover and accelerated in towards the target, flicking the arming switches on his rocket pods. Then he swept in low along the line of the ribbon lake.

'Target acquired.' His thumb hovered over the red launch button.

There was a sound like sheets of metal being ripped.

'I'm taking hits!'

The aircraft lurched right as 23mm rounds slammed into the titanium armour along his left side.

Red lights lit up across his instrument displays.

'Port engine out!'

The smooth whirr of the engines behind him was replaced by a horrible grinding sound. The main rotors began to judder and the airframe shook violently.

'Landing on east of lake!'

There was an explosion of Russian shouting from Arkady, who was listening in from his helicopter on the ferry.

'Arkady! You stay put! I will go and get him!' Alex did not want two helicopters shot down.

He looked at the maps and photographs on his knees again, guessed a route to the lake and barked, 'Kilo Five will proceed to lake to recover Shark. Kilo One and Two, follow to support.'

The one thing they all feared was being captured. From what he had seen of the way the Muti Boys treated human beings he wouldn't wish it on his worst enemy. He had to get Pavel back.

He reached over his head and clanged the hatch shut. Locked down like this he was trapped in a metal coffin, unable to see through the armour around him, straining his neck to look through the ring of periscopes around his hatch or watch the TV monitor in front of him. The roar of the 1200 h.p. diesel reverberated inside the metal box as they accelerated down the road.

A main battle tank at full tilt was a fearsome sight: forty-five tonnes of metal moving at 50 k.p.h. on suspension so smooth that it seemed to flow over the rough ground.

'Half left,' Alex barked out to Tshombe as they neared a stream that led off to the lake. The tank skewed round the corner, clods of mud spewing up in high arcs behind each track.

There was a muddy pond ahead. The front of the tank hit it, sending a huge curtain of red mud up into the air. As this happened, Alex swung the turret to the side and then back again to avoid getting his optics covered. The whole movement was so fluid: splash, swing and then back on track as they roared through.

'Half right!'

They had reached the lake and swung right to run north along its eastern shore. Charging along the narrow fringe of gravel beach under the trees, the left track threw up a fantail of bright water whilst the right sprayed stones.

Pavel had said that his port engine had been hit so Alex swung the gun round to the left, seeking a target on the western shore. He saw something on the monitor sticking out from the jungle on the beach opposite, and locked onto it.

Here the laser guidance system came into its own. The main gun became intelligent. No matter how much the body of the tank bucked and plunged along the shoreline, the barrel stayed locked on target like an evil eye. Its baleful blank stare twitched up and down as it followed the target, indifferent to any interference.

With incredible fluidity, the turret moved independent of the hull of the tank, as if the two bodies were intelligent entities working together. The barrel swung left as the target became more visible.

Alex could now see the back of a DAF truck, with a twin 23mm anti-aircraft gun mounted on it, sticking out of the jungle. The whole thing had been an ambush.

The gunners heard him approaching and the twin barrels swung round to line up on the tank.

'Fire!'

There was a heavy punch and reverberation in his head as a tonne of metal rammed back into the tank next to his left elbow.

John, his gunner, flinched away from the tremendous noise. Then the clank of the automatic loader opening the breech and shoving another round in, and the stink of exhaust gases and cordite; blinking his eyes to clear them.

From the outside there was a burst of white propellant smoke from the end of the long barrel as they fired and then the tank flowed remorselessly on through it.

Alex stared at the plasma screen in front of him, watching the target: a bright flash on the truck body and the instant distortion of the air around the impact by the shockwave as the round exploded on target. Then a slower billowing as black smoke and brown dust expanded outwards. Pieces of truck and bodies rising up into the air, filtered by gravity, the lighter pieces flying higher and the heavier slamming back to earth.

'Enemy anti-aircraft gun destroyed,' he reported to the BMPs following in his wake. The gun swung back in line seeking new targets.

He heard the thuds of machine-gun rounds hitting the front of the tank: enemy infantry firing from the end of the lake. A heavy bang made him wince as an RPG hit the reactive armour on the hull and it exploded, blowing the projectile out and away from the tank. Now he was relying on old-fashioned cavalry shock—sheer terror caused by

237

the speed of the charge. All of Alex's senses were sharpened.

Soldiers ahead were jumping up from shell scrapes and running into the bush.

Machine guns onto them: John with the 7.62mm coaxial and Alex with his commander's 12.7mm on the top of the turret. Both guns looking out of the hull eagerly, seeking their prey and chattering death at them.

Enemy positions overrun, the tank roaring over the bodies of the injured, tracks tearing them up and flinging them behind; terrifying and scattering any resistance.

Heading towards a Unimog truck parked at the end of the lake, already raked with machine-gun fire, a huge barrel of a 106mm recoilless rifle mounted on the back of it. Another punch and clang from the main gun and it exploded into pieces.

Alex already scanning around with the camera; smoking body of the Shark crashed into the treeline behind the truck.

Tank rammed through the burning debris of the truck, bouncing pieces ahead and the tracks flowing over the jagged remains.

Cockpit door had been forced open and bloodtrails led out of it and into the bush.

The tank stopped.

Its gun traversed back and forth along the impenetrable tree line, the eye of the barrel blindly seeking Pavel.

14 JUNE 1941, IDEHAN UBARI. SAHARA

Otto and his *Kampfgruppe* roared across the flat sand of the desert at 70 k.p.h.

It felt good to stand up, stick his head out of the hatch and feel the wind on his face rather than the stifling heat inside the armoured car.

After their six-week, two-thousand-kilometre journey, he and his men looked like savages. His face, arms and legs were caked in yellow-red dust; he hadn't washed for three weeks since they had left the water sources in the tropical jungle. They had six weeks' worth of beards, the sweat and dust in them had matted into mud so that, along with their hair, they stuck out at odd angles. Their desert camouflage uniforms were sweat-wrinkled and torn.

Otto wore sand goggles and an Arab headdress. When he took his goggles off, the gaps in the coating of dust made him look like a skull. The men were all in bad shape: underfed, suffering constant headaches from dehydration, the buffeting of travel over rough terrain and sleep deprivation. They were covered in ugly tropical ulcers. Otto's left hand was still bandaged from where he had accidentally leaned his palm against the side of an armoured car at midday and burned it on the sun-heated metal; the raw pain had been with him for weeks.

At least the painful sunburn of the first days had given way to a deep brown tan, which meant he no longer feared even the faintest feel of sunlight. He found that he got used to most things: the constant dust in his throat and the taste of petrol in the water they drank from refilled petrol cans. Pietro Gallina had taught him a huge amount about the art of desert travel: how to navigate with a sun-compass, how to wrap an Arab headdress to keep the dust out of eyes, mouth and ears, how to eke out every drop of water and fuel, how to find buried supply dumps.

But the ferocity of the heat had been something that none of them could prepare for. It had been fifty-two degrees in the shade yesterday during their midday halt. They stretched canvas awnings on poles out from the sides of their vehicles and lay in their shadow, gasping like landed fish. He had been sure that he was going to die, his brain boiling in his skull. The effort of moving air in and out of his body was too much; it was like trying to breathe hot cotton wool.

Otto was navigating at the head of the convoy in an SdKfz 232 heavy armoured car. Behind him was their artillery, a Mercedes three-ton truck with a Flakvierling-38 quad-mounted 20mm anti-aircraft gun capable of pouring out 800 rounds a minute in case they encountered the enemy. So far, in six weeks they had managed to avoid all contact. He hoped that this would continue; they were now on the home straight, the last five hundred kilometres back into Tripoli. He was hoping for air resupply soon by the Luftwaffe. However, this was also the most dangerous area; they were within range of Allied aircraft.

The six trucks and armoured cars stretched out in a line behind him were all that were left out of the original eleven. The rest had suffered mechanical failures: broken petrol-pumps, coolant systems,

240

axles, springs and punctures, and been abandoned where they broke down.

The remaining vehicles were covered in kitbags: personal packs, bedding rolls, food and ammunition boxes, spare wheels, digging tools, and mats and water cans. Bringing up the rear was his ever-reliable second in command, Heinz Jahnke, in their precious petrol truck.

They were heading north across a flat, burning waste. The sand here had dried into a hard crust of reddish-yellow dust and they could drive at full speed. It was a joy after weeks of crawling over rubble and boulder fields. They had suffered frequent punctures and broken springs when loose boulders forced up one side of a truck and then dropped it down with a sickening crash.

The wind was from the southeast, and blew a great brown dust cloud out to their left-hand side. The vehicles behind him were staggered off to his right so that they didn't drive in either his dust cloud or his tracks, which would mean they would break the hard crust and bottom out.

Otto's eyes were fixed on the prismatic compass in front of him. They burned from watching the dancing needle all day; he dreamed about it at night. With no objects to take a fix on in the last two hundred kilometres he had had to keep a constant watch on their heading. His mind was wearied by calculations of bearing, speed, distance travelled, and water and petrol consumption rates.

He had guided his men across the Sahara to the volcano in the tropical jungle and back again. They had suffered sandstorms, thirst, breakdowns, intense heat and freezing cold at night. And what had they found?

Nothing.

After they had struggled through the dense bush trails to the volcano, Werner Fischer had surveyed the site, measured it, made excavations, taken photos, scratched his head and finally had to admit he could not find anything of archaeological significance.

Otto never thought they would find anything. He had always found the whole idea of the Dark Heart Prophecy ridiculous, so he was not disappointed. But he was infuriated by the waste of effort.

The only good thing to come out if it was that the crews had performed so well. He was proud of them. They had been stoic in the face of hardship; knuckling down and getting on with it, faces set in grim determination. Heinz Jahnke had, as ever, been his great support with his willingness to listen and his understated humour.

Whenever his mind wasn't taken up with work, it automatically defaulted back to thinking about Aisha. First thing in the morning and last thing at night he wondered what she was doing and relived their experiences on the coast road journey. Just a few more days and he could see her again.

'Aircraft, sir!'

Sergeant Schenk grabbed Otto's shoulder and pointed over to their right. He had been standing in the hatch behind him, looking around enjoying the breeze, and had spotted them.

Against the cloudless blue sky he could see two dark dots circling them. He quickly brought his field glasses up. He squinted his sore eyes and could see that they were twin-engined and flying in tight formation.

Messerschmitt 110s? Like the one that had flown him back from the Balkans to start this whole escapade?

At this range he couldn't tell. It would be reassuring to make contact with friendly forces and get some air cover for this last dangerous run back into home.

He keyed the mike on the radio to his vehicles.

'Aircraft at three o'clock high, two miles. Check weapons. I will fire flare.'

The gunners in the vehicles behind him swung their machine guns and cannons out to the right, fired off brief test bursts and zeroed the aircraft in their sights.

Otto pulled the flare gun from its clip on the armour plate inside the car. Even if they were enemy, he had nothing to lose by sending the signal—they would have been able to spot the convoy's dust cloud from miles away.

Green was today's colour, according to the codebook, so he slotted the cartridge in and clicked the hinged breech shut. He raised the pistol and fired over his head. The bright green dart soared off into the sky, trailing green smoke. He waited for the return flare to spout from the cockpit of the lead aircraft.

None came.

The planes dipped their wings and swung in towards the racing convoy.

'They're Beaufighters!' he shouted over the RT. He felt Gunter give the armoured car an additional spurt of speed.

Great, Otto thought, the most heavily armed fighter-bombers the Allies have got. Four 20mm cannon and six .303 Browning machine guns packed into the nose, with a mixture of underwing rockets or bombs.

'Turn left into the dust cloud!' It was their only hope of cover on this featureless plain. 'Open fire when in range!'

'They're coming in!'

The two dots grew larger and then separated; one was heading for him at the front of the convoy, one for Heinz Jahnke at the rear.

The seven vehicles swerved left. He gripped the side of the turret as Gunter spun the wheel and they lurched away from the aircraft and into the swirling fog of brown dust churned up from the desert. They couldn't see much in it at ground level but he couldn't tell how well hidden they would be from the air.

The vehicles broke their tight formation and spread out. The drivers started weaving to make themselves harder targets to hit.

'Watch it left!' Otto shouted to Gunter. The Mercedes truck had suddenly veered out of the fog. They swerved away. Its quad gun was pointing backwards and opened fire. He heard the hammering of the four cannon and saw the storm of red tracer blast back at the aircraft.

He ducked back inside the turret; it was dark and stifling inside. He swung it round to bring the long black barrel of his own 20mm cannon to bear. He peered through the narrow sighting slit in the armour plate; his head constantly bashed around by the hectic motion of the car.

He had lost sight of the aircraft in the dust. The tiny view jiggled around but then he saw a constant dark blob in the sky, coming in low and fast at thirty feet. He closed one eye, gripped the weapon's pistol grips and squeezed the trigger.

The enclosed space of the metal turret resounded to the clatter of the gun. He raked the sky in front of the aircraft with bursts of coloured tracer, trying to gauge the deflection between the two moving objects.

He saw the nose of the Beaufighter sparkle and then, after a split second, gouts of dirt were blasted off the ground as the impacts of the ten guns raced in towards him. There was a roaring as a storm of cannon fire exploded around him. Machine-gun bullets banged and whined off armour plate, and cannon shells exploded in the rear-mounted engine of the armoured car.

Steel splinters zipped around him. The engine gave a scream and tore itself to pieces in a cloud of metal debris. Power drained from the vehicle, a loud moan came from the driveshaft as the friction overcame it and they lost speed.

The aircraft roared overhead. Otto glimpsed its sky-blue underbelly flash over the open turret hatch. They had come two thousand kilometres to be shot to pieces in the home stretch. It had got them and was getting away. Bloody-minded anger seized him.

'No you don't!' he shouted, and swung the turret back round after it. He kept up a sustained stream of fire through the dust.

The car ground to a halt with a screeching noise; broke through the crust and sank lopsidedly into the sand. Silence rose up from the noise that had surrounded him. The protective dust cloud began to drift away; he could see blue sky breaking through over him. The Tommy would be coming back in for a second run and they were sitting ducks on a flat plain.

He stood up out of the hatch and searched after the plane. He glimpsed it through the murk.

'Got him!' he shouted exuberantly.

He'd hit him. The big fighter-bomber was trailing a line of white coolant back from its starboard engine.

'He's breaking east, back to base!' he laughed, and the crew cheered from inside the vehicle.

He looked to his left, and saw the second plane dive back into the dust cloud as it billowed away from him.

A tree burst up out of the desert, ragged brown branches forked out as the debris from the explosion of the 250-pound bomb rained back down to earth. There was a deep thump and a blast wave hit his exposed face. Light flashed through the fog, turning it orange for a second.

'The fuel truck! They've hit the fuel truck!'

The other Beaufighter must have seen it stacked with oil drums full of petrol and hunted it down. The hideous black hand of burning gasoline reached up into the sky.

'Heinz!'

Otto struggled into Tripoli four days later, sent Lieutenant Fischer to wire his report back to Wewelsburg and then returned to his villa by the Maqbara Park.

Aisha had heard of his return at army headquarters and was waiting for him on the veranda in the hot evening.

The six weeks that he had been away had been torment for her; not knowing where he was and if he was even alive.

Afterwards they lay still and she listened to his heartbeat slowing.

'What happened out there?' She had never known the true reason for the expedition but she sensed that he was angry about it.

He was somewhere a long way away and did not want to return to such details; he lay still for a long time.

'A total waste of time in pursuit of a ridiculous prophecy dreamed up by idiots.'

'A prophecy?'

'A waste of time. Some idea from a bunch of cranks that cost four good men their lives. I don't want to talk about it.'

There was nothing she could say so she kissed him again.

In the morning they were both unsure how to face the world.

On what terms did they proceed? What were the new rules?

Aisha was at a loss. She had become a woman and felt unnerved by it as she stood clutching her handbag and waiting to return to her parents'

247

house.

They had each other for only a week in the baking nights of Tripoli. It meant everything to them but the war rolled on regardless. The very week that they had come together the world had been rent apart by the biggest ever armed struggle in its history. Hitler launched his crusade against the Soviet Union. Five million men rolled over a frontline that stretched over a thousand miles from Finland to the Black Sea.

The Reich had need of Otto and he was flown out with his unit. He was in turmoil—devastated to be leaving his love but eager to be in the main battle rather than this African sideshow. He was committed to this war of racial purity against the Jews and the Salvic *Untermensch* that was going to make a perfect world. His SS regiment, Leibstandarte Adolf Hitler, was flung straight into the southern sector of the Russian campaign in the battles for Kiev, Uman, the Crimea and Rostov.

Only after he had gone did Aisha discover the enormity of what had happened to her. Another human being had been created.

'So, you're sure it was an ambush?'

Kalil looked at Alex, his face grim.

It was late that same afternoon and the commanders were meeting in the back of the signals truck again. They were a tense, silent circle, sitting around the map table.

The background crackle of the command radio net was the only sound until Alex replied after a thoughtful pause, 'Must have been. After the Shark rocketed the hill they knew they had to get rid of it. Our using it was the only way that we could have spotted and stopped the speculative fire on the convoy.'

Alex's dark brows furrowed as he thought the situation through from the enemy commander's viewpoint.

'Set up the Unimog at one end of the lake with the 23mm hidden in the trees waiting for the chopper to make its run past it. Very neat. They know what they're doing.'

It was a simple trap and he had fallen right into it. Some commander he was. He could hear a replay of his voice giving the fire mission orders to Pavel. The overconfident tone made him wince.

They had followed up the bloodtrail from the helicopter with troops from the two BMPs that had charged after Alex. The trees were too dense to take the vehicles in and the soldiers had to proceed cautiously for fear of ambush. Eventually they pushed through onto a track where tyre marks showed a vehicle leaving at speed. They had lost Pavel.

Alex rubbed his hand ruefully over his black hair;

it was sticky from the heat and flattened down by his helmet. He was grimy and tired after the adrenalin buzz of the action died away. He was the Battlegroup commander, and the lives of two hundred men hung on his shoulders; they felt very heavy now.

The old feeling of failure began to circle him again, like a hyena in the night scenting blood. It barked his father's voice at him: 'Fucking failure!'

Col, Yamba, Arkady and the others all nodded and looked down; supporting their chief in silence.

The radio gave a loud crackle as someone tuned into their frequency.

'*Est-ce que ça marches?*' a coarse African voice blurted out to someone next to him.

There was a murmured assent.

'*Ah! Bonjour mes amis!*' The voice was now filled with drunken triumph. '*Vous écoutez à moi?*'

Everyone in the truck turned and stared at the radio in shock. It was no one from the Battlegroup. The mine troops must have been searching frequencies and tuned into their general comms net.

Colonel Ninja continued his drunken raging. '*Votre copain avez un message pour vous!*'

A scream cut through the air. It was Pavel.

More hysterical laughter from a number of people.

'*Mais qu'est-ce que c'est le problème avec ton doigt, mon petit? Tu as neuf autres.*'

Pavel sobbing with pain from his missing finger.

Alex lunged across the room and switched the radio off. They all knew that torture was the usual lot for prisoners captured in these wars but they didn't have to hand the enemy a propaganda coup on top of it.

The whole lot of them felt sick. Kalil went white and covered his face with his hands. Even the hardened Afrikaner, Rennie, looked shocked. Each tried not to think what was happening to their comrade.

The fight had gone out of them. The hyena saw its chance and lunged in at Alex, biting into his heart. His face betrayed his thoughts.

Arkady saw his expression. He was the most wounded by the screams of the young man that he was responsible for recruiting but a Russian instinct in him cut off any further self-doubt.

He looked around the group in the room, raised a warning index finger and said quietly: '*Ni shagu nazad!*'

Eyes flicked over to him.

They remembered the meaning of the words.

The simple logic had worked at Stalingrad and they could feel why now. There was no other way out of this except forwards.

Arkady repeated the words slowly in a menacing tone, making eye contact with each of them.

There was a gradual nodding of heads as they assented. They knew what they had to do.

Alex looked at the implacable resolve of Arkady's face. He nodded and murmured, '*Ni shagu nazad.*'

He forced his heart to expand out against the fangs of self-doubt that were sunk into it.

He was the commander. What did he expect—a joy ride?

Each man muttered the expression as the group broke up, heading back out to their vehicles with hearts darkened but resolved.

Aisha's pregnancy was shocking. Her parents were Western by Libyan standards but even in Europe such behaviour was unacceptable. The society of the day could not countenance such fecklessness. Her father fiddled with his worry beads and cried pitifully as her mother stood next to him and glared at Aisha. Her family were outraged by her behaviour and disowned her. She was forced to leave the family home and moved in with some secretaries from work.

Aisha was wounded to the core but her combative nature took up the struggle and coped somehow. Otto's love would sustain her. She hoped.

The boy was born in March 1942; in the absence of his father Aisha called him Amir.

She was well liked by the Italian high command and continued to work as a translator and secretary for them. The war was going well and she was posted forward to Benghazi, five hundred miles to the east, to help with staff work there. By September Rommel had pushed the British back even further into Egypt.

Then things began to go wrong. In November Montgomery launched an attack on the overstretched Axis forces at El-Alamein and inflicted the first major defeat on them. In the same month, more Allied forces successfully completed the Torch landings in Morocco and the war in North Africa was effectively over. Caught between two fronts, Rommel could only fight a rearguard action until the inevitable happened and 240,000 Axis troops surrendered in March 1943.

Aisha was evacuated with the Italian high command to southern Italy. She was still committed to the Fascist cause and was terrified of capture by the Allies. The war continued to get worse. Between August 1942 and February 1943 the fate of the world hung on the city of Stalingrad. Soldiers fought each other with sharpened spades in the sewers until, after a combined total of one and a half million casualties, von Paulus's starving Sixth Army surrendered. From then on, the war was over.

Aisha was slowly going out of her mind with worry about Otto. She had had only three letters from him in nearly two years and she did not know if he was now amongst the dead.

What he had said in his first letter was even more wounding. He was cautious in response to the birth of their son and begged her to keep the identity of the father secret. Race was the ideology behind the war that he was engaged in, and Gestapo racial purists hunted down deviants. Men in his unit had been sent to the dreaded penal battalions—a form of protracted death sentence— for relationships with Slav women. It would take only some zealous back-office bureaucrat to put two and two together and he would quietly disappear from his unit—excellent commander or not.

Aisha was stunned by this. The Italian Fascist ideology that she followed was different from Nazi ideas. It was based on obedience to the state and had never taken on the 'blood and soil' racial politics that Hitler put forward. She had never fully appreciated how much racial hatred was the basis of the whole SS mission; only now did she remember the way that Otto had stared so hatefully at the exodus of Jews in Tripoli. At the time she was so carried away with the romance of her handsome Aryan hero that she didn't think about what motivated him. The slur that he had now cast on her and her child was searing: that the blood in their veins, the very fabric of their being, was impure and shameful.

With this stinging instruction Aisha retreated north with the Italian Army HQ as the Allies landed in Sicily and then on the mainland. Her job was to liaise with the German command and so, when the Italians surrendered in September 1943, it was easy for her to transfer her services over to the Wehrmacht. She felt it was her only hope of staying in contact with Otto. Her languages and efficiency were still in demand by the Germans, but she sensed the way the war was going and began improving her English by secretly listening to the BBC at night on the radio.

The retreat north over the Alps continued. She struggled to bring up the baby in the middle of a war. She was helped by the other secretaries but trying to get baby food and clothes was a constant battle. The Alpine winters were freezing and the child was sickly and racked by coughs.

The winter of 1945 was the worst. She had not heard from Otto for over a year. The news from the Eastern Front was unremittingly bad; defeat followed defeat. The Russians were pushing on mercilessly and the Americans and British were forcing their way in from the west. So many soldiers had died that old men and boys were being forced to serve. The country would have sued for peace in 1943 but the will of the Führer expressed through the fanatics in the Nazi party organisation drove them on.

She was stationed in Munich with Southern Command Army HQ. She remembered how bright the huge red swastika banners looked in the sunshine, draped down the front of the building. Sometimes they hung the bodies of 'defeatists' there as well, with signs round their necks saying: 'I betrayed the Fatherland' or 'I am a coward and ran away from the enemy of the people.' Three hundred thousand Germans were executed for resistance to the Nazis; as their hold on power slipped, so the fanatics amongst them became more vicious.

The whole of society was breaking down: water and power were cut, people were starving, the sawdust content in their grey bread ration kept increasing and gangs of feral orphans roamed the streets threatening passers-by for food.

There was little water to wash in and Aisha felt disgusted with herself at how dirty she was. She tried desperately to maintain appearances, covering her greasy hair with a headscarf at work.

Both the army and Nazi officials were becoming increasingly hysterical as the Allies closed in on them from two sides. Parties were held at HQ where they got drunk and sprayed around bottles of vintage French champagne, captured in the glory days of 1940. She remembered the sour stink of it in the morning in the offices. Nobody bothered to clear up.

There was no coal to heat her tiny flat and frost formed on the walls at night. She piled her coat, a rug and as many blankets as she could scavenge onto the bed, and laid her clothes out under the top layer so they weren't freezing when she put them on in the morning. She lay in bed with the child at night, her legs drawn up around the boy and her head wrapped in a towel against the cold. She never got warm, though, and would wake up in the morning with her muscles stiff and tired from shivering all night.

Heavy Allied bombers droned to and fro overhead in waves that rattled the windowpanes and made the glasses in the kitchen tinkle against each other. She was on the outskirts of town, so escaped the terrible bombing and firestorms, but she lay there thinking: God, how many of them are there? Will they never stop? She put her hands over her ears to try to shut out the noise but the bass droned through.

The noise, the cold and the coughing of the sickly child kept her awake until she was so tired that she blacked out.

She dreamed of meeting Otto again.

PRESENT DAY, THURSDAY 29 JANUARY, MBOMOU PROVINCE, CENTRAL AFRICAN REPUBLIC

'Right, Alpha Fireteam will go here and exit right. Bravo will go in the centre here and exit straight ahead. Charlie is on this side and exit left.'

Yamba made emphatic stabs with his hand to indicate where they should go from the back of the big helicopter.

The clam-shell doors under the tail boom had been taken off to clear the exit ramp completely; it was going to be only a short hop into the complex.

It was 05.00 hours and still dark but there was enough starlight for the men to see him.

H-hour was 05.15.

Yamba was going to lead Bravo Fireteam in the final assault on the refinery building. The plan was to use the BMPs and the tank to engage the pillboxes and knock out the remaining anti-aircraft guns: one on a truck and one in an embrasure near the main gate.

As soon as that happened they would signal for Arkady to lift off from the clearing two miles out from the mine and set the troops down inside the complex to attack the huge rectangular refinery shed on the southern shore of the lake. They were going to land on the clear area between the shed and the hangar where they had seen the helicopter land to collect the weekly diamond run.

There were three doors into the refinery, one on either end and one on the south side, away from the lake. One fireteam had been tasked to each door.

What lay inside the building they had no idea, but Kalil was very insistent on two things. One: that they take the shed intact, and two: that they kill the controller of the operation, the old man in the tie that they had seen walking along the shore of the lake.

After the loss of the Shark, Alex had pushed the Battlegroup on rapidly to this final assault phase, driving through the evening and the night to within striking distance of the mine. After routing the troops at the lake he didn't want to give them any time to regroup, plus—the thought in everyone's mind—he hoped to be able to reach Pavel in time.

As they had driven nearer the mine they could see, in the bright moonlight, the huge bulk of the volcano, a mile east of it, towering over the land. It was such an anomaly, so unnatural the way it swept up out of nothing, that it unnerved Yamba.

He could see Arkady now, stumping around next to the huge helicopter, the tip of his cigarette glowing brightly as he nervously sucked in nicotine. They had only had a few hours' sleep and wanted to get on with the assault.

'OK, final checks now,' Alex called to his men.

They spaced out with their buddies and began checking each other's kit: settling their webbing and bandoliers, strapping and restrapping body armour, nervously adjusting helmets. Then checking their weapons: AK-74s and PKM light machine guns, their bulky magazine boxes clipped on underneath. Designated men carried small fixed charges to blow the doors open and each had a supply of grenades.

When completed he signalled them into the

helicopter. The troops were good soldiers but, as they filed past him, Yamba could see the sweat gleaming on their tense faces, heads down and eyes darting from side to side. Assault rifles were hugged tight across their chests, rounds already chambered, safeties on and fingers on triggers.

There was no talking, just sharp nods as they entered the aircraft in the correct order and then turned round to face the exit at the rear. They were packed in tight next to each other; each man stared at the back of the helmet of the man in front, sequestered with his own thoughts.

They all knew the layout of the plant and what they had to do—all that mattered now was to have the courage to do it.

30 MAY 1945, OUTSIDE MUNICH, BAVARIA, GERMANY

'What is your relationship with Lieutenant-Colonel Hofheim?'

The American voice was businesslike and without malice, but Aisha still felt threatened by it.

She had left her son with a friend from work and travelled to a prisoner-of-war camp on the outskirts of Munich to find Otto.

It was three weeks since all German forces had surrendered unconditionally.

She hated the GI's calm and reasonable manner; sitting behind the desk opposite her, with his neat crew-cut hair, his podgy, corn-fed face and his round spectacles. He did not look like the starved, ragged people that she lived with, who existed on meagre rations in bombed-out cellars.

But what she really resented was that she was not in control.

She had been part of the people in command, the state, the ones who decided others' fate. But now she was one of the defeated, just another of the millions of displaced persons sloshing around Europe like flotsam after a shipwreck.

This clerk, this bureaucrat, could control her life with a simple tick in a box. De-Nazification was what it was called. It determined her access to ration cards, travel permits and housing, and thus the wellbeing of her child.

In her usual way she had dressed up when under pressure, to try to maintain some dignity. During the winter she had exchanged a bag of potatoes for a gorgeous fur coat; it belonged to the proud wife of a district judge who, crazed by hunger, was selling her possessions on the roadside. Now Aisha pulled the collar of her coat tighter around her throat and stared back at the clerk.

What could she say?

'My husband.'

No, that would be a lie; he wasn't.

'He was someone I fell madly in love with four years ago and haven't seen since. Who has written three letters in all that time and whom I haven't even heard from in over a year. Who I haven't known if he is alive until last week, and for whom I haven't had a single waking moment when he wasn't in my thoughts.'

'Miss Hmidi?' The GI looked at her, his pen poised.

'He is the father of my child,' she said slowly.

The clerk wrote something on his form.

Had he damned or absolved her?

More questions followed.

'Where was the child born?'

'Tripoli.'

'What is your nationality?'

'Libyan.'

'What is the child's nationality?'

A pause.

The GI looked up and stared at her again through his spectacles.

'I don't know!' she snapped.

The question went to the heart of her dilemma.

What she wanted to say was: 'I have held a torch for this man through the darkest hours this world has ever known. I have worn myself thin trying to keep alive the little scrap of life that we made

261

together. And the first letter I had from him about it was the most wounding thing I have ever received, because he tried to deny that our son was related to him and implied that together we are subhuman. So now I don't know if he is going to reject us.'

Paranoia had set in over the years. She did not trust Otto any more and the tension showed.

The clerk wrote something on the form and then looked at her sympathetically—how she hated that.

'Miss Hmidi, I think you should know that Lieutenant-Colonel Hofheim is,' he paused and tried to think how to put it most kindly, he flapped a hand on the desk, 'not perhaps what he was.'

Aisha tensed. What did that mean?

'You will be allowed ten minutes with him now but you must realise that as a colonel in the Waffen SS he will be subject to intense scrutiny by military intelligence and may well be put on trial.'

He looked up at the military policeman with a rifle slung on his shoulder, standing behind her. 'He's in the hospital complex.'

The MP led Aisha along a corridor of barbed wire separating two fields full of thousands of former German soldiers. The men were filthy and unshaven, looking tired and depressed in their tatty grey uniforms. They smoked or stared around them listlessly. Machine guns were trained on them from tanks and half-tracks parked outside the wire. Occasionally the bored GIs would fire bursts over their heads just to remind them who was boss.

The men crammed in on her from both sides and stared. She avoided looking at their dirty, bearded faces as she picked her way through the puddles with as much dignity as she could muster.

The 'hospital complex' proved to be an overstatement. What it turned out to be was a factory shed. It had been put up during the war to manufacture light arms and was one of the few large buildings in the area with a roof undamaged by bombing. The air was damp inside and men on stretchers were fitted in around the machinery on the floor, which in many places was just packed earth. Metal girders supported the high, corrugated-iron roof. It was dark and quiet apart from an occasional cry of pain that echoed around the large space. It smelled of machine oil, sweat and putrefaction.

The MP spoke to a tired-looking junior doctor sitting at a desk made of packing crates by the door. The young man looked at him resentfully, checked a clipboard and then pointed to the far corner of the building.

'He's over there; up against the wall. Ain't in good shape.' He shrugged.

Aisha stared numbly ahead and followed the guard. Her anger at being in this humiliating position had been overcome by fear of what she would find. What had happened to her love?

She hugged her arms around herself as she stepped over the bodies and puddles of urine on the floor.

'Konnen Sie, bitte, mich Wasser geben?'

A wounded man clutched at the leg of the MP as he walked past. He shook him off and continued on.

When they got over to the far wall he started checking the labels tied to the stretchers. He was a

263

farm boy from Mississippi and drawled at her.

'Yah, that'll be him, right down the end there. Guess I'll leave yah'll to it, but remember yah got ten minutes—*and I mean that.*' He pointed at her and then turned and walked off.

Aisha looked along the row of stretchers and hesitatingly walked on.

*   *   *

Otto lay on a stretcher on the floor; he could feel stones in the packed earth poking into his back.

His vision was restricted by a dressing over his right eye and the bandage that was wrapped around his head. If he focused hard he could look out under the cloth and see a piece of machinery on his left and a brick wall on his right. Otherwise he couldn't move or see anything.

His body had become a nexus that connected a series of pain centres. The stump of his amputated left foot hurt most. They told him they had cut it off but he hadn't been able to raise himself up to look at it. The NCO from his regiment who spoke some English had translated what the American doctor was saying: the shrapnel wound in his ankle from the Katyusha strike had gone septic so they'd had to amputate.

He could feel pain from the bullet wound in his side, his dislocated shoulder, perforated ear drum, the stitches across a gash in his scalp, countless bruises and the fiery itch of flea bites on his chest and hands. The smell of pus was in his nostrils and the rough army blanket itched his naked body.

Aisha looked down at him and wondered who he was. It had been four years since she had seen him.

Her memory was of a pristine, healthy hero; this invalid on the floor at her feet did not seem to be human. He had aged twenty years; his unshaven face was lined and drawn from malnutrition. His head had been shaved to stitch up his scalp; it was white, raw and covered in cuts. As she kneeled down she caught the smell of sweat and infection. She could not think of anything to say so she just stared at him.

Otto sensed someone next to him. He tilted his head slowly over to the right and focused his left eye up at her.

He knew the woman looking at him but he couldn't think who she was or what she was doing here.

Aisha. A great wave of joy swept through him; she saw the eye looking at her well up.

'What happened to you?' she managed to whisper. She bent closer to him.

Other things came back to him, things he had done she must not know about or she would be ashamed of him. Guilt diluted his joy.

'Otto,' she said more insistently. She reached out, found and squeezed his hand under the blanket. 'What happened?'

He tried to think how to tell her. How could he put all those things into words? Into those little noises.

He couldn't even face remembering them himself, let alone communicating them to someone else. They were two different elements, his memories and words: fire and ice, earth and air. How could the two things ever come together? He was too tired even to try.

She saw the light go from his eye, it closed and

he turned his head away from her. She squeezed his hand but he would not look at her.

'Otto, look at me!'

It was too shrill, she knew, but she was desperate. To have him so close now after four years, and then for him to turn away like that was too much.

As she kneeled next to him the suppressed pain of four long years, wound tight inside her, began to come loose; her composed mask cracked and she sobbed. She wanted to reach out to him but she could not think where to touch him. She stretched her hand out over the terrible, wounded head. The hand shook and fidgeted over him, wanting to help but uncertain how to.

The guard, standing at the end of the row of stretchers, hitched his rifle uncomfortably on his shoulder and looked away. He hated it when women cried so pitifully.

The other prisoners looked up from their stretchers at what was going on.

'Go on, talk to 'er!' shouted a chirpy soldier from Berlin with a broken leg in the stretcher next to Otto.

It was well-intentioned, but his crass intrusion into this most private moment was too much. Like all dignified women Aisha hated losing control in public, but her hurt and confusion was so great at that point that she shouted at him through her tears: 'Shut up!'

'Yeah, shut up, Weissy,' called his friend from further up the row.

'Piss off! I was only trying to help.'

'Hey, knock it off down there!' bawled the guard. He sensed the situation was getting out of hand and marched back down the line towards Aisha.

'OK, lady, your time is up. Come on, you can see ya fella again some other time. Come on.' He bent down and started to lift her up with his free hand under her arm.

'Get off me!' she shouted, and pushed him away.

She stood up on her own, trying to mop her tears with the back of her hand. She didn't want the guard to hear what she wanted to say so she quickly kneeled down again and whispered, 'I love you,' in Otto's ear. Then she stood up hurriedly and marched off before the guard dared to touch her again.

Otto lay still and made no response; he was an evil man who didn't deserve love.

At first the war on the Eastern Front had gone better than even in Hitler's wildest dreams.

The Russians were hopelessly unprepared when the blitzkrieg hammer fell on them. As Otto's unit pushed forwards over the steppes, he drove past huge columns of dazed Soviet prisoners.

Those were the heady days. Stalin had a nervous breakdown and was not heard of for weeks after the invasion. The Soviets reeled back and back, and the tanks, trucks, half-tracks and dive-bombers of the master race swept on; streaming past burning huts and sobbing peasants.

But after huge initial advances, the Germans became victims of their own success. The vast distances that they had covered stretched their supply lines. The Soviets regrouped after their disastrous start, learned their lessons the hard way and came out fighting. In December they finally halted the Germans after a battle that caused a million casualties in total. They were barely twenty miles from the centre of Moscow; Wehrmacht officers were able to see the city's buildings through their binoculars.

The war stalled and General Winter began to wear down the invaders. With less need for reconnaissance troops, Otto and his men were switched from their light vehicles into a heavy Panzer division.

During these times Otto's inner confidence was intact; that rock of certainty that he stood on when the whole world seemed to be swept away around him. The SS won a grudging reputation from the Wehrmacht for toughness through their devotion to Nazi beliefs. They attacked harder and were capable of taking much higher casualties and still operating as a fighting unit. Consequently they were always sent to the places where the fighting was fiercest. If a particular hill had to be taken or a sector of the line held, then Otto's unit would be sent there.

He remembered those grim briefings in freezing dugouts lit by the stump of a candle, when the officers crowded round a map on an upended oil drum. The bearded, exhausted faces of the men took in the operational details that the colonel put in front of them.

'Ivan has twelve T-34s on that ridge there. We have five Panzer IVs, three Tigers and an assault gun . . .'

Their experienced minds resolved the facts and figures into reality and calculated the odds against them.

At those times the men's eyes would flick around the group looking for each other's reaction. They would see Otto's calm stare and relax.

Well, at least Hofheim looks like he thinks we can do it. Maybe I will get out of this alive after all, the faint-hearted would think.

What kept him going were his devotion to Germany, the thought of his family, and Aisha. They became the triptych that he set up somewhere deep inside himself. His devotion to duty had been twisted into a corrupt racism but at least his desire to do well by his parents was pure. His brothers, Karl and Ernst, were in the army as well—he wasn't sure where—but he knew they would all strive to do a good job.

But the centrepiece of the altar had become Aisha. As he flogged across the frozen steppe in the iron-cold turret of his tank he would suddenly feel the warmth of her again in the hot Tripoli night. He would smell her perfume amidst the diesel and engine oil, the cordite and the sweat. It would be a memory so vivid that he would look around suddenly to see if she was there.

In his head he kept a recording of the sound of her laugh. When he heard a good joke he would think: I wish Aisha was here, she would have laughed at that, or: I must remember to tell Aisha that when I see her. He would talk his day through with her as he went off to sleep.

But every man has his limit. For four years Otto was in the middle of the most intense combat yet seen by man. The scale of the brutality that he encountered, and later committed, was unprecedented. The physical and nervous strain of it wore him down; gradually destroyed his confidence in himself and other people.

Over the years he found he couldn't remember what Aisha looked like. Her outline faded. She became indistinct and blurred—a longing in his soul rather than a clear entity in his mind.

Aisha wrote to him telling him about the birth of Amir. He found himself terribly confused. He was a young man caught up in a situation beyond his emotional maturity. She had become such an idealised force for him that to have her appear in reality was disturbing, especially with the news of such an additional burden as fatherhood.

The racial complications of the situation quickly asserted themselves in his mind. Aisha was an Arab and therefore a Semite, almost as bad as a Jew in the Gestapo's eyes, so he could not be known to be associated with her. For that reason he wrote a confused response that told her not to mention the child again.

He began to feel that he had made a young man's mistake with her. One that had saddled him with a responsibility that he had not asked for. The heat of the desert had gone to his head and he was now trapped by a moment of madness.

Meanwhile the war continued to take its toll on him. In the summer of 1943 Leibstandarte Adolf Hitler was involved in the recapture of Kharkov. The Russians had almost run out of troops and were using civilians, men and women, equipped with improvised weapons. When the German tanks were exposed at the front of the assault, ahead of their infantry, these ill-armed peasants leaped out of foxholes.

From inside the tank Otto heard the thud as someone jumped up onto his track covers.

He drew his Luger pistol and pushed open the metal visor to see who was attacking them. The face of an old man was right in front of him screaming with anger. At the same time that Otto shot him the man squirted battery acid through a rubber tube. Two memorials of the event stayed with him—the hideous scar across his forehead and the memory of that hateful face.

How could an old man be driven to do such a suicidal thing as to leap onto a Tiger tank? How could a human being want to kill him so much?

In July 1943 Otto fought in the Kursk offensive, the largest land battle ever. He remembered the hot sun shining down on the unending steppe, covered with a sea of waving green grass. A huge plume of dust was sent up as the army made its way across the land. There were trucks, staff cars, bowsers, radio wagons and then, nearer the front, tanks: the new Tigers and Panthers, Ferdinand self-propelled guns, old Mark III and IV Panzers. Thousands of vehicles were dotted like strange fungi across the grasslands.

He lived two weeks of his life in a man-made mechanised hell. The whole world shook when five thousand tanks rumbled across it and the sky vibrated like a drum-skin above their heads as waves of aircraft flew over. Squeezed between these two elements were tiny human beings caught in an environment not yet sensed by mankind.

Iron waves of tanks crashed into each other. Otto went headfirst into the mêlée. He could remember only blurred snapshots: glimpses of T-34s flashing across the narrow vision slits in front of him. The boom and clang of the massive 88mm gun by his side became so frequent that he could hardly hear it. He yelled instructions to his gunner.

'Tank at ninety degrees right. Armoured piercing. Fire!'

'Firing!'

'Hit! Destroyed!'

'Tank full ahead. Fire!'

'Firing!'

'Hit! Not destroyed—he's firing at us! Fire again!'

A twenty-five-pound lump of metal travelling at three thousand feet per second hit the front of their tank; Otto's brain jarred at the enormous clang that ran through the vehicle. The round had ricocheted off but his driver was dead, killed by the kinetic energy of the hit right by his position in the hull.

He saw hundreds of tanks hit and burning across

the steppe: men on fire, jumping out and waving their arms until they fell over. A Tiger tank magazine hit and exploding, sending the turret and gun, weighing ten tons, way up into the air before crashing back down.

Then there were the Russian winters. The howling blizzard from Siberia that numbed the bones of Otto's face and stung his eyes. At minus forty degrees oil froze in engines, and tanks and half-tracks could not move. Vehicles were left at the roadside and troops tramped across the white landscape with the wind whipping their greatcoats around their legs. His unit had hundreds of frostbite cases: fingers, faces and toes turned black and swollen when they thawed out. Otto lost the tops of his ears and the ends of his fingers.

After the German defeat at Stalingrad they all knew the war was over. Quietly, members of his unit would say that they should sue for peace now while they still had an army left. Retreat was not something that they were prepared for; they had been indoctrinated with the belief that they were the conquerors of the world and had no means to deal with the unease of failure.

He could not make sense of any of it. There was no sense to be made of it. Two great ideological giants were wrestling each other, tearing each other apart and dehumanising everyone involved in the process. After a while it became instinctive for him simply to fight and fight and fight. That was all that they could do: fight or be killed by the Russians; fight or be killed by the Gestapo field units who shot anyone at the mere suggestion of defeatism.

And then there was the guilt. The worst of it

came from when his unit was put on anti-partisan operations in the Ukraine; they had rounded up hundreds of Soviet activists. In 1941 the local population still saw the Nazis as liberators from the Soviet oppression of the 1930s, which had killed over a million people in the man-made famines. Ukrainian people came out in crowds to see the executions. Families cheered as they hanged the hated Russians—so many that they did it from the back of trucks, backing up to the gibbets and then pulling away.

He remembered one woman. She was in her twenties, attractive in her own way: a full figure, thick brown wavy hair, cheap print dress. Her arms were bound behind her back and a filthy rag was tied across her mouth. He shoved the noose over her neck as the truck drove away from the gallows. She could not scream but she tried desperately to reach her hands out from behind her and grab something, anything, to stop that terrible gravity, which she knew was coming, from seizing hold of her neck.

Her eyes reached out to him, trying to get hold of him. If they could have grasped him then they would have crushed him with their intensity but the rope jerked her back.

At the time he thought that he was just doing his duty but then he found himself enjoying it; carried away with the sheer brutality of his power. The shouting of the crowd, his comrades' grins around him, Leibstandarte Adolf Hitler's motto: 'Give death, take death', all turned him into a merciless, de-humanised automaton.

He began to drink. 'Anti-bomb medicine', he called it, to help him get over the shakes and actually sleep. Schnapps became his preferred prescription; the switch he reached for in order to turn off. At the beginning of the war he had despised those who drank for their nerves. He was proud of his independence and ability to cope with pressure, and he viewed those who drank as contemptible human beings. But now he was becoming all that he despised—an old soak.

In June 1944 the regiment was shifted west to face the D-Day invasion. Once again they took the brunt of the Allied attack and retreated during the winter through the Ardennes, then Belgium and into Bonn. In February 1945 they were switched east and thrown into action defending Budapest against the Russians again. After defeat there they retreated west through Austria and into southern Germany.

Finally they were back on home soil, but it was not the Bavaria Otto remembered: the shattered towns, with smashed roofs, their streets littered with rubble, glass and tangled telegraph wires. The smell of burned houses in the air, with people squatting on the streets brewing up scraps of cabbage in billycans.

Enemy Typhoons and Mustangs screeched overhead at roof level, strafing and rocketing anything that moved. Tanks lay knocked out at the side of the road, skewed at odd angles with their barrels still pointing at targets that had long since moved on.

His luck began to run out. He took a ricochet in his side that smashed two ribs. He was caught in a Katyusha strike, a massive fall of high-explosive rockets that blew out an eardrum. He tumbled into a shell-hole for cover but his foot stuck out and his

275

ankle was hit by a large chunk of shrapnel. The wound went septic.

He was lucky not to have been left with the other wounded, to be shot by the Russians at the side of the road. All the SS were trying to do now was flee to the west so that they could surrender to the Americans rather than catch the wrath of the Ivans.

He was given a precious space on top of the last Tiger tank; they were stripping down a tank each day for spare parts. Driving through a forest, he looked around and saw the top of the tank covered with injured men, their bandaged stumps flailing helplessly as the vehicle swayed over the rough ground.

On 8 May 1945 SS Leibstandarte Adolf Hitler surrendered to American forces at Steyr in Bavaria. In June 1944 the regiment had had a combat strength of 19,700 men. A year later there were 1,600 survivors.

So Lieutenant-Colonel Otto Hofheim was lucky to be alive, but in fact it was only the empty husk of him that was left on the floor of the POW camp. He was physically shattered but those wounds would heal in time. Psychologically, the light that had been inside him, the light that had shone on that evening in Tripoli in the Grand Albergo d'Italia, that had dazzled Aisha with its easy confidence and good humour, that had kept him going during the freezing darkness of Russia, that light had gone.

As he lay on the earth of the Germany that he had fought for, he thought of the idea of blood and soil that had driven him to this place. But all he could feel emanating up from the ground was a cold darkness filling a void.

'Preparations complete, out.'

The signal from Yamba told Alex that the troops were loaded on the Mi-17.

He was sitting in his commander's hatch; the tank was alone on a track with jungle all around it.

His breath smoked in the pre-dawn cold, illuminated by a patch of starlight coming down through a gap in the tree canopy. He could just make out the long black barrel elevated in front of him, pointing through the trees towards the mine, waiting quietly for H-hour. He flicked his wrist over and pressed the light on his watch: 05.14. One minute to go.

He had laagered the trucks and other soft-skinned vehicles with the helicopter two miles out from the mine. Kalil would remain there with the signals truck until the fighting was done.

The four BMPs were under Col's command, on the main road, a mile east of where Alex sat in the tank. The semicircle of the mine complex lay due north of them, stretched around the southern shore of the lake.

Col would drive north through the trees on either side of the road to avoid mines. They would then engage the defences around the main gate to create a diversionary attack that would allow Alex to put the tank with his secret weapon into action.

The troop carriers would have to be careful to avoid the D-30 howitzer in its bunker by the gate. It was a cumbersome weapon, but one 122mm shell would finish a BMP straight away. There would also be RPGs and possibly shoulder-launched anti-tank missiles, so he had briefed Col to be cautious.

He was feeling nervous but glad that the wait was almost over. The worst bit was sitting around wondering if he had thought of everything, feeling that crushing weight of command and fear of failure settle on his shoulders. He clenched his fists in front of him and squeezed his eyes shut for a second as he shouted at himself: Come on!

He looked at his watch again. Thirty seconds to H-hour.

It was a classic pre-dawn attack; using the cover of darkness to approach the target and then having the benefit of daylight to prevent confusion during the follow-up actions.

He slipped down inside and closed the hatch over his head.

'Stand by to fire,' he whispered to his gunner.

FEBRUARY 1951, BONN, WEST GERMANY

A loud bang and Amir Hofheim flinched.

He stared up at the sound of the front door crashing open. With his wide brown eyes the boy looked like a startled fawn.

He was yet to turn nine and was doing his maths homework on the kitchen table with Aisha. She was dressed as the model 1950s wife—pearls, chic red dress and a matching apron.

She also tensed up but tried to cover it by peering more closely at his books laid out in front of them.

'Well, darling, look, how did this equation work?' She pointed at a previous example they had done together, but it was an ineffectual distraction: neither of them could concentrate any more. They were listening to the sound of Otto's footsteps along the entrance hall, trying to decipher his mood from them.

Was he drunk again?

Would there be another row? One of those terrible scenes where he shouted at her and the boy; whose mixed race he now attacked as a symbol of his own imperfections.

The prosthetic limb below Otto's left knee always gave him a lopsided gait but now it had a dragging sound added to it that was the danger signal. He had been drinking.

The footsteps came down the long hall and stopped outside the kitchen door at the back of the large house. Neither Amir nor Aisha pretended to look at the homework now, both waiting, tensed,

279

for the shouting to start.

Otto pushed the door open with his foot and stood swaying in the doorway. His suit was crumpled and his tie was askew. He had been out drinking with an old SS comrade who was in town on business; the smell of schnapps and cigarettes carried into the kitchen.

The strong bones of his face were still there but his features had been distorted by guilt and drink; heavy lines were carved on them by the strain. The ugly acid scar was splashed red over his forehead and the tips of his ears were ragged from frostbite. His easy stride had cramped up, his shoulders hunched with tension.

The drink with his comrade had allowed him to let out some of his anger, calming his usual argument with the world, so for once he was not looking for a fight. Instead he stood swaying and stared at the two frightened people sitting at the kitchen table. They both stared back at him.

A long moment passed.

A large part of Otto wanted to say something friendly and make a joke as he had been doing with his old friend just half an hour ago. He could have said it. Aisha was the woman whom he had loved and still did. The boy was his son, and he did feel something for him, confused though it was by his racism.

But some black hand reached up from his heart and strangled the words in his throat. He was an evil, guilt-ridden person—what could he say to good people like them?

He looked away and allowed the door to close slowly. He turned and shuffled up the large staircase.

Aisha and the boy both breathed again and looked down at the table. The thread of their concentration was gone; she knew that they could not recover it again.

'You'd better go to bed, darling.' She hugged him tight, stroked his thick black wavy hair and kissed his forehead.

He packed his books neatly into his school bag, in the exact order that he would need them for his lessons the next day. He was a very orderly boy. He slung the rucksack on his shoulder, opened the kitchen door, paused to listen and check that his father had gone into his study, and then scurried up the stairs.

Aisha sighed and looked at the table. What a strange life they had fashioned for themselves.

Soon after the war, she and Otto married and she now worked as a senior civil servant with the West German government in its new capital in Bonn. Her career was the one thing she seemed to be able to get right and so she put everything into it. Relations between European nations were being reforged, and with her combination of charm, rigorous efficiency and languages she was much in demand.

Otto had spent a year in POW camps after the war, recuperating and being interrogated before he was finally released by the Americans. When he got out he searched after his family and found that his parents had been killed in a bombing raid and that both his bothers had died on the Eastern Front.

His father had converted the family wealth from the farm and the law firm into gold during the war. Otto was able to recover it and followed Aisha to

Bonn where he used the proceeds to buy a large nineteenth-century villa on the hills overlooking the Rhine; property was still cheap in Germany then.

The SS officers' network got him a job as an office manager in the huge Deutsche Bundespost headquarters building down the hill by the river. It was a secure, undemanding job that bored him to tears but it was all that he could cope with. He drank every night but was always ready and on parade in the morning; moody and withdrawn but an efficient enough manager. Germany was filled with scarred war veterans like him and people in the office just put up with it.

Aisha slowly set about cleaning the kitchen—it was pristine but she wiped the table anyway. As she worked she thought for the thousandth time—why do people make bad emotional decisions? What temporary insanity relieves them of their senses so that they commit to people that they are fundamentally unsuited to? What then drives them on against all the evidence to stick with this choice? Fatalism, a need for romantic self-sacrifice?

She didn't know.

Was it just a trick of time and place that had brought them together?

The intensity of that time in the desert had launched their relationship like a dove being thrown up into the sky. But then there had been the four terrible years of separation and uncertainty. The wings of her love for Otto had grown tired in the face of this and his ambivalence about their son.

Now she felt like a bird flapping around on the ground, trying to get airborne again but forever

282

weighed down by the memory of that beautiful, unrepeatable time.

She didn't understand the guilt and horrors that drove him. When they had still slept in the same bed, she would sometimes hear him shout in his sleep 'Reload!', then give a desperate sob, turn over and carry on sleeping.

They had both found a brief moment of freedom and love in the desert. But back in the real world they had somehow just created another disciplined system of their own to surround them. They were oppressed by its confines but afraid to leave it at the same time.

She stopped wiping the table and stood with one hand pressed to her forehead as if she had a terrible headache.

How could they go on like this?

'Open fire!'

Alex barked out the order. The crash of the report split the night around them and sent birds screeching up out of the trees. The tank rocked back on its tracks with the recoil. The gun snatched into the turret and then the auto-loader pushed it out again with another round ready in the breech.

Ten rounds of high explosive to soften up the defences.

He didn't want to give it any more as he feared that they might have locating radar that would allow the howitzer to bring down counterbattery fire on him. He wasn't going to get into an artillery duel so he pumped the rounds out as fast as possible. It wouldn't be highly accurate as they were working on bearings from satellite photos and he had no forward observer to call in corrections, but it would be a nasty wake-up call for the mine troops that would get the attack off to a good start.

His gunner, John, was sweating next to him under the dim interior lights as he worked the gun: checking the aim on each shot, counting them down.

'Rounds out!' he shouted after ten.

They were both part-deafened by the reports.

'OK, let's go!' Alex called down to Tshombe, who flicked on his night-vision goggles.

They tore away into the dark, west along the track, ready for their crucial role in the assault.

Otto slumped down at his desk in his dimly lit study upstairs.

This was his retreat from the domestic dystopia around him. When the nightmares kept him awake he would come here and doze in his big green leather chair with the light on. At times like this the weight of sadness that pressed down on his chest made it hard to breathe.

He had bought an old Luger; there were thousands of them on sale on the black market. Now he was about to begin his favourite relaxation activity of stripping the pistol down, laying the pieces out on his blotter, oiling them one by one and then putting them back together again. He would slide the mechanism back and forth, cocking and uncocking the gun with a satisfying click. He found the cohesion of its machined parts a soothing contrast to his family relations.

Otto was caught in a self-reliance trap. He had always been self-made and successful: never learning how to fail. Any capacity for introspection had been beaten out of him in the SS. After the war he knew that he was evil, and faced the problem of living in the same skin as that person. He felt that he had caused his guilt so only he could deal with it; no one else could absolve him.

The neat domestic boundaries that Aisha policed so vigilantly in her quest for perfection had become prison walls that hemmed him in, trapping and intensifying his brooding.

A floorboard creaked outside his study door.

The boy must have been eavesdropping. A flush of anger went through him and he quickly cocked the pistol.

'Amir! Come here!'

The door opened slowly and the terrified eyes of the boy peered round the gap to see his father pointing the gun at him.

The boy stared at the muzzle of the pistol.

He knew that the small black hole was filled with danger and he tensed in its merciless gaze.

The face above the outstretched arm was filled with dull loathing.

Otto sat behind the heavy wooden desk. His greying hair, normally swept back neatly off his forehead, was now askew, lit from behind by the standard-lamp.

He gazed at his own flesh and blood across the desk.

The boy was in brown paisley pyjamas, blue dressing gown and slippers; a toothbrush was clutched in one hand. He had his mother's birdlike build; his arms thin as matchsticks. He would never be a star sportsman.

He looked so pathetic that Otto could not maintain his anger against him.

'What were you doing outside my door!' he growled.

The boy was too scared to speak but raised his toothbrush to show that he had been on his way to the bathroom down the corridor. He was usually very good at moving silently round the house; he had perfected the art to avoid meeting his father.

'Hmm,' growled Otto, 'if you had been in the war I would have shot you.'

He lowered the gun.

As the black spot moved off him Amir breathed

again.

His father's mood changed as he realised that he had overreacted; shame made him try to gruffly compensate for it.

'You see, when you're fighting the Ivans, you don't give them a second chance. Kill them before they kill you. Look here,' he reversed the pistol and offered the butt to Amir. 'Here!' He waved it at the hesitant boy, demanding that he approach and take it.

'Hmm,' he grunted with satisfaction as the boy took the weapon.

To Amir it felt heavy; he held it in both hands. It seemed to have a deadly gravity all of its own.

'You see, every man should know how to take a gun apart and reassemble it with his eyes closed. If it's dark and it jams, you can't just light a candle to see what you're doing or Ivan will come and get you. So, now, press that catch there to release the magazine.'

The metal oblong slid out of the butt smoothly.

'Now, put the magazine back in.' Otto took Amir's hands and showed him how to slide the two pieces back together again.

'Good,' he said with satisfaction as it clicked home.

The gentle touch and the word of praise felt so strange to Amir.

Ever since the boy was four, when this damaged man had limped into the world of motherly love that he shared with Aisha, he had only ever radiated suppressed anger.

Amir was fascinated now by the gun, his fear overcome. With its weight, the hardness of its metal and the precision of its design, it seemed

287

intoxicatingly powerful. One minute he had been cowering in its stare and the next here he was holding it, controlling it.

His natural curiosity took over and he wanted to know more about this source of pleasure and paternal approval.

'Who are the Ivans?'

'The Russkies.'

'Why do they want to come and get you?'

'Because there was a war!'

'What would they do to you if they got you?'

Otto looked away from him as he remembered the fate of so many of his comrades.

'They'd shoot you, string you up or throw you in prison for years till you rotted.' No SS men had returned from the Russian POW camps.

'You see this?' He pointed to the liverish flesh on his forehead and down the side of his face.

Amir nodded. He had always wondered where it came from but had never spoken to his father about the war.

'Well, when I was in Kharkov, we went into the Ivans' wire and they stormed my tank. They were climbing around on it. So I opened the visor,' he mimicked pushing open the armoured flap, and peered out. 'And what did I see? An old Ivan granddad with a tube of acid, which he squirts at me.'

Amir looked horrified. 'What did you do?'

'I shot him with this.' He tapped the gun in Amir's hands.

Otto had never talked to Amir about his role in the war but the man-to-man good mood from his drinking with his old comrade earlier was carrying over. He began to take a perverse enjoyment from confessing what he normally hid.

'You see, I was in the SS.'

Amir's eyes widened.

After the war the full extent of SS brutality had been exposed. At school they had all gone through rigorous de-Nazification lessons with pictures of the camps and the gas chambers. The teachers derided the organisation as the embodiment of evil and taught him that Germany must be ashamed of itself because of men like that.

'I was in Leibstandarte Adolf Hitler,' he pronounced the last four syllables carefully. 'The Führer was a great man—he knew how to solve problems.'

Amir stared at him in shock. It was as if his father had said: 'I was in the bodyguard of Satan incarnate.'

Because of the indulgence his father had just shown to him, Amir tried to bypass this awkwardness by changing the subject.

'Is that where you met Mummy? In Russia?' he whispered.

'Eh?' Otto looked at him irritated. 'No, you idiot, what would your mother be doing in Russia?'

Amir looked down.

'No, I met her in Tripoli. That's where your lot come from.'

'What were you doing there?'

Otto looked at him calculatingly, trying to think how much he wanted to be drawn on this subject.

'Wasting my time.'

'What do you mean?'

Again a long pause.

'I was sent there to look for a thing called the Dark Heart Prophecy.' He pronounced the words contemptuously.

Amir gawped at him. It sounded fascinating.

Otto decided he might as well continue, having come this far.

'Don't get excited. It was a complete waste of time. It said that there were going to be five great battles and then some great threat to Germany that we had to stop. The war was supposed to be the last great battle but I don't think it was . . .' He drifted off and then realised that his words might be misconstrued as a belief that they just hadn't reached the last battle. 'No, I mean I think the whole thing was a load of shit from the start.'

Amir was shocked to hear his father swear.

'There was some idiot called Eberhardt von Steltzenberg, from the Knights' War, and he had this vision—wrote it down in his diaries that the Ahnenerbe found in Heidelberg library. So they sent poor bastards like me out to Africa chasing after it. I lost some very good men proving that there was nothing in it.'

He felt again the shockwave on his face from the exploding petrol truck that had killed Heinz Jahnke.

'But I met your mother.' He sounded wistful. 'And I suppose you wouldn't have been around if I hadn't been sent there.

'Maybe you will be the great threat to Germany, eh?' He looked at the weedy boy next to him and laughed at him.

Amir held the gun and looked down; he always seemed to disappoint his father.

'Otto! What are you doing in there?' Aisha's shrill question sounded from down the corridor. She marched up and stood in the doorway, not daring to enter Otto's territory.

'What are you doing?' she demanded.

'Just talking!' replied Otto angrily. He knew he would be in trouble for having the gun out in front of the boy, and he sounded angry to defend himself from the coming onslaught.

'What is that?' She saw the gun. 'How can you let a child play with guns? *Otto!*' For her the word was no longer his name but a sound that encapsulated all that was contemptible in the world.

'Amir, put the gun down and get out of there!'

Amir did as he was told and slunk away down the corridor.

Aisha swung the door shut, turned and walked wearily back to her bedroom.

Yet another battle in our relationship. How many more?

Col waited with the four BMPs in the dark.

Kilo 1 under Yuri, Kilo 2 under Rennie, Kilo 3 under his command and Kilo 4 under Josiah, a black South African.

He watched the seconds tick away to H-hour and then tensed.

The heavy crack of a tank round came from the west to his left. Seconds later he heard the deeper boom as it hit the mine ahead of him.

He counted off the ten reports and then muttered a terse, 'Let's go!' into his radio mike. The troop carriers moved off through the bush, the drivers weaving as fast as they could between the huge black tree trunks.

They spread out with fifty yards between them in a semicircle around the main gate, Col and Yuri to the west of the road and Rennie and Josiah to the east.

The trees thinned out as they neared the hundred-yard zone that had been completely cleared of vegetation around the perimeter of the complex. Behind that lay the strip of mines next to the wall of razor wire. In the greenish glow of his NVGs Col could see the fires of buildings burning inside the complex from the tank shells, smoke drifting across it.

A good start but a lot more work to do yet, he thought.

Col radioed to the others: 'Kilo Three going in.' He always led from the front.

They accelerated out of cover and into the open, fifty yards west of the squat outline of the bunker with the howitzer by the main gate.

That was the thing he was really worried about.

None of the BMPs had armament heavy enough to bust open reinforced concrete and take it out cleanly. Their main job was to be a diversionary attack so they were going to operate like a ring of four dogs baiting a bear, darting in and out before the heavy gun or an RPG could hit them.

The eight infantry behind him all opened the hatches above their heads and stood up out of the back; two had RPG launchers and the rest machine guns. With the 30mm cannon in the turret and an AGS-17 30mm grenade launcher in front of Col they packed quite a punch.

'Open fire!' he called, and the vehicle erupted as they gave it everything they had. The cannon and machine-gun muzzles stabbed out bright flashes, streams of tracer cut the dark and the two RPGs scorched off at the bunker. Col trained the AGS on it as well and coughed out a slow stream of grenades. He watched the end of the howitzer barrel carefully; it was swinging round towards them.

'OK, reverse!' he shouted, and punched the switch next to him for the smoke-grenade launcher. The three tubes on each side of the turret coughed and the grenades landed in a fan shape in front and began spewing out a screen of red smoke.

Machine-gun rounds smacked into the armour on the front of the BMP as gunners in trenches behind the perimeter wire opened up on them. The vehicle quickly reversed and they were hidden in the smoke and bush again. A roar came from the bunker and the huge howitzer shell tore through the smoke to their left and exploded in the trees behind them.

'Kilo Four!' Col shouted over the radio. It was Josiah's turn, out on the far east of the semicircle. Col wanted to keep varying the direction of attack as much as possible to give the howitzer the maximum arc to have to swing back through.

When they lurched to a halt in safety, Col was sweating heavily. He heard an explosion of firing from his right as Josiah's men opened up and a storm of return fire hit them. This was a dangerous game they were playing and the defenders weren't going to be foxed by his manoeuvres for ever.

He found himself clenching the grip on the grenade launcher in front of him and muttering, 'Come on, Alex! Come on, lad!'

*   *   *

The tank crashed through the bushes on the edge of the lake and stopped on the water's edge.

Alex and John scrambled out of their hatches and began to assemble the metal tubes attached to the back of the turret. They prised open a vent on the left of it behind the gunner's hatch, assembled a series of tubes into a long pipe, slotted one end of it into the hole and bolted it securely in place.

They were on the northern shore of the lake: Five hundred metres across it to the south lay the curved beach and the dim lights of the bungalows and the refinery on the shore. Behind that they could see the explosions as the battle raged around the main gate, streams of red tracer arced up into the night.

As they drove round to the lake they had been listening to the increasingly desperate shouts over the RT from Col and the others as their comrades struggled against a rising storm of gunfire.

Alex was feverish with haste. He shook the wide tube with both hands to check it was secure. John slammed and locked covers over the normal engine air intakes. Alex pressed the stopwatch on his wrist and then the two of them scrambled back down through their hatches and slammed them shut over their heads. The aircon hissed as the seals pressured up.

The tank drove straight into the water.

Alex watched the green view on his night-vision periscopes and screens; he could still see the glare of the building lights across the water, the angle lowered as they got nearer to the lake surface.

The water rose over the front of the tank as they drove down the shallow beach. He could hear the gurgle and slosh of it as it filled air cavities on the tank exterior. It came up to the bottom of the turret. Now it was sloshing over his vision sensors, the lights on the screens in front of him blurred.

They drove deeper into the lake; the water was over the top of the turret. The camera above his head submerged. The screen in front of him dimmed.

Some light.

No light.

Darkness.

They were underwater.

They had five minutes of air.

Engine noise louder now, throbbing inside the sealed metal box. Tank continuing to go deeper; he felt the incline leaning him forwards in his seat. He had stuck a tiny spirit level on the wall next to his right eye as an objective measure. Now he flicked his gaze across at it—the little bubble was wedged at the back of the tube.

The metal snorkel stuck out above them, sucking air down into the engine. He checked the stopwatch on his wrist, watching the seconds run down on their air supply.

Traction was becoming more soggy.

This was the crucial bit—would they get bogged down in mud, the tracks churning aimlessly in deep silt at the bottom, the whole of his bizarre military adventure coming to an ignominious end with him and his crew drowning in an unknown African lake whilst his comrades were shot to bits at the main gate?

His swim across the lake had convinced him that the depth was possible and that the bottom was all gravel—not mud. That was the plan. Now he had to live with the reality.

He glanced down at the top of Tshombe's helmet at his feet.

'Take it slowly, don't lose the traction,' he muttered.

Tshombe was concentrating so hard on driving that he could only nod fractionally in response. His hands gripping the two levers for the tracks and his feet on the accelerator and clutch pedals were all feeding back minute signals to his brain about the feel of the terrain. His teeth were gritted in fear and sweat beads stood out on his brow. It was all down to him.

Alex checked the compass bearing; it was the only way they could tell where they were going.

'Ten degrees left,' he muttered.

With the greatest hesitation, as if he had to push a great weight to do it, Tshombe's hands moved the track levers fractionally.

296

They felt the tank jerk. The engine raced behind him as the tracks slipped and spun.

Alex's heart stopped. They were in the deepest part of the lake. Three minutes of air left.

Tshombe forced the words out between his teeth. 'We've lost traction.'

* * *

The fighting raged on at the main gate.

A hellish red smoke drifted across the battlefield, lit up by stabs of tracer and the bright flashes of explosions.

All the BMPs had been in and out to attack twice but the howitzer bunker was still operational and resistance was mounting from inside.

A 106mm recoilless rifle on another Unimog and the 23mm AA gun on a truck were both pouring fire out at them. They were further back in the complex, dodging back and forth behind burning barrack blocks, making them hard to counter.

The defenders had set up mortars and were bringing down accurate airbursts over the BMPs. Shrapnel rattled down on their top armour. A soldier standing up in the back of Kilo 3 was slashed across the neck by a piece just above the collar of his body armour and collapsed screaming into the troop compartment behind Col.

'Close up! Sort him out!' he shouted over his shoulder as he concentrated on watching the battle and gauging when to order the vehicles to advance and retreat.

'Reverse!'

The incoming fire was getting too hot and they

needed cover again.

The troops banged the hatches shut over their heads and Col dropped down inside his turret. It reduced their firepower considerably; they only had the 30mm cannon now.

The soldiers in the trenches along the perimeter sensed the slackening of their fire and inability to pierce the defences. They began to get bolder, standing up straight to take clearer aim at them with their shoulder-held RPGs, the rockets screeching out at them through the razor wire.

It was getting light. This couldn't go on much longer.

'Alex, where the fook are you!' Col banged the side of the cabin with his fist.

The anti-aircraft guns were still intact so they couldn't launch the helicopter assault. The whole attack was beginning to grind to a halt. He could feel the battle tilting over to the opposition.

He couldn't even remember the pattern he had been trying to follow to vary their attacks.

'Kilo Two!' he shouted angrily; sending Rennie back into the fray.

It was the wrong choice. The howitzer was lined up on his sector. As the sharp snout of the BMP nosed through the red mist the huge gun roared out.

The shell exploded on the thick armour plate of the front glacis, but was heavy enough to punch through it, decapitating the driver and setting the front of the vehicle ablaze.

Rennie was standing up in the turret so his legs and stomach were riddled with shrapnel from the blast inside the driver's compartment. The crew cabin behind caught fire. Hydraulic power for the main doors failed, trapping the men inside. Col could hear the screams from the burning men and the groans from Rennie as he slumped down in the turret. The driver's foot was wedged on the accelerator so it continued to trundle out of control towards the minefield.

'Kilo Two! Kilo Two! Rennie! What's happening?!' Col shouted over the RT.

'Forward!' he shouted to take his own crew in again.

They emerged from the smoke in time to see the burning BMP drive up to the minefield. Fire slackened across the whole front as all eyes were drawn in by the hideous inevitability of the spectacle.

The blundering, blazing wreck drove onto the gravel. A spring mine popped up as it went over the trip wire. The explosion sent a hiss of ball bearings over the ground.

Then it hit an anti-tank mine. The huge flash blew the front of the vehicle up into the air and split the underside wide open. It crashed back down, a smoking ruin, its terrible advance stopped at last.

Col buried his face in his hands at the sight of the death of eleven men, which he had caused. All his usual vigour had gone.

'Reverse,' he said bitterly and they pulled back into the swirling red fog. If Alex didn't come soon they were finished.

*   *   *

It was dark on the bottom of the lake.

Alex sat still, buried under metres of water; he

didn't know how deep they were. The engine ticked over quietly behind him. Each of his hoarse breaths used up more of their precious air supply. Everything depended on what he chose to do next.

His life. The lives of his men.

If they swam for it they would either drown or be shot to pieces in the water by the defenders in the bunkers on the beach, and the attack would be lost.

In the utter blackness he was forced to dig deep inside his heart, trying to find some light in the dark.

'Let it settle. Let it settle,' he whispered to Tshombe.

He waited for gravity to press the tracks into the gravel.

If he waited too long would they get bogged down?

Then quietly, 'OK, forward gently.'

He heard the engine note behind him rise as Tshombe's foot pressed the accelerator and then let in the clutch.

The tank jerked.

'Traction.'

Alex took a deep intake of breath through his nose and breathed out slowly. They were moving again.

He checked the bearing—on course.

He had had some experience of deep-wading in other operations in Africa, and they had practised in the Ubangi River before they set off on the ferries. The Red Army had developed the technique and the T-72 was designed to wade to a depth of five metres, the metal pipe sticking up from the surface sucking air into the engine. He promised himself now that he would never do it again.

The air in the cabin was getting stale. They couldn't stay down much longer.

'Come on, come on,' he muttered to himself, willing the tank on. He wanted to get on dry land again and regain his freedom of action. Dawn was breaking up above and he needed to get into the fighting.

He thought he felt himself being tilted slightly backwards in his seat. He looked across at the spirit level next to him.

Yes. The bubble had moved to the front of the tube. They were heading up the slope into shallower water.

Now they could really get going.

'Speed up!' he called down to Tshombe, more confident now.

The tank emerging from the water was a strange sight to the soldiers in the bunker. The snorkel gradually rose higher and higher. The barrel of the long gun broke the surface first and then the massive metal monster erupted out of the lake, pushing a bow wave up the beach and shouldering aside torrents of water.

They roared forwards.

It was daylight now. A glance at his normal periscopes showed Alex brown beach and the smoke from burning buildings drifting in front of him.

'Half right!'

They spun and drove along the shoreline.

Target indicator on the bunker at the far end.

'Fire!'

Chunks of concrete blown outwards by the

instant shockwave, Alex already turning his attention to the houses along the shoreline in front of him. Kalil had insisted that they kill the mine director.

He fired into the first wooden bungalow. The shell punched through it and exploded on the second one behind it. The tank crashed into the white veranda, ripping it off and throwing splintered planks into the air.

They drove on past the burning second house. Through the smoke Alex glimpsed the man in the tie scurrying back past him, bent double and moving stiffly, clutching a briefcase in his left hand.

'Half left!'

The tank slewed between the houses to go after him. As it did so, Alex glimpsed a more important target behind him: the truck with the AA gun on the back. They had to destroy it, and the other one by the gate.

He let the man go and acquired the truck as a target. It was moving from behind a barrack hut and opened fire on the BMPs.

'Fire!'

The punch of the recoil and the truck disintegrated.

One more to go.

He steered them through the burning buildings and drifting black smoke until he saw the AA embrasure near the gate and then blew it up with another round.

'Anti-aircraft guns are down! Arkady go! Repeat go!'

Infantry jumping up from their trenches by the gate as they heard the tank behind them, Colonel

Ninja running out of the back of the bunker through the red smoke, muscular torso wet with sweat.

12.7mm onto him and a burst slammed him back against the concrete wall.

Sights onto the bunker and high-explosive round pumped into it. Concrete split open, dust billowing out from the gun slits in the front.

*   *   *

'Arkady! Pull power! Pull power!' Alex's shouting came through over the RT.

They had been waiting for forty-five minutes; rotors turning and the aircraft jiggling on the ground with frustration to get airborne. The troops had been standing, packed into the cargo bay, staring at the man in front, and trying not to think about the urge to urinate.

Arkady leaned back in his pilot's seat and shouted through the door to them, 'We go!'

He pulled the collective and they went rapidly through transition, lurching forwards and over the trees. Yamba and others held on to cargo straps on the sides to steady themselves.

He took them in a wide loop to build up speed; he did not want to be over the target area for a second longer than necessary. His was a very complicated flying machine with many vulnerable points and no armour; there would still be a lot of ground fire flying around on the landing zone.

Yamba was standing right on the edge of the ramp at the back, looking down at the treetops swinging vertiginously underneath him. The thunder of the rotors and the rush of air flapping his clothes felt good after the tension of waiting. He saw the blue glint of the lake half a mile away behind the refinery shed as they banked and dropped down into their final run.

Col ducked involuntarily into his hatch as the huge helicopter roared over his head at tree height, battering the branches with its downwash.

Fighting was still going on around the gate and troops looked up at them, rifles swung and ground fire started hitting home.

The door gunners and men on the back ramp all shot back with long bursts of suppressive fire but they were too big a target to miss. Bullets were coming in from all sides, blowing out puffs of insulation as they burst through the thin aluminium walls.

A man screamed and clutched his shattered knee; another was dashed against the man behind him with a bullet in his brain. The overhead fuel tank was holed and jet fuel started spurting out over them.

'Cease firing!' screamed Yamba, realising what muzzle flashes and hot shell casings would do to them right now.

Red lights flashed angrily at Arkady in the cockpit.

'Fuel line hit!' his co-pilot shouted across at him. Their hands were a blur over the switches, shutting down systems.

He saw the LZ in front of him next to the hangar and flared the chopper heavily to take the speed off it; the troops lurched in the back. Then came the thump of the heavy landing, the undercarriage bending under the force.

Ramp banged down onto the dirt.

They were out, at last.

Legs pumping across solid ground.

The three lines of soldiers streamed out, rifles pointing, running fast for the refinery through the maelstrom of dust from the rotors, eyes searching out their assigned doors.

Yamba at the front of Bravo Fireteam.

Run up to the door on the side of the building.

Locked.

Small charge attached. They stood flat back against the metal wall.

Sharp crack and burst of smoke. Two grenades in through the hole—never mind Kalil's orders about taking it intact—he wasn't going through the door.

Wrenched open and long bursts of fire poured in.

No resistance so far.

They streamed inside. A storage room: yellow plastic drums with toxic chemicals symbols stacked up to the high ceiling.

The teams fanned out inside the building, clearing the rooms systematically. The crack of grenades and their shouts echoed off the metal walls.

'Clear!'

'Secure!'

'Go!'

Past the rock crusher unit and into rooms filled with gleaming machinery. White-coated technicians running through the smoke. Stabs of gunfire and bodies slammed against machines and pipes.

In the centre of the building Yamba came up against a high stainless-steel wall. They blew the door open and he went through.

He stopped dead. He had never seen anything like it.

This was not just a mine.

From outside came the noise of a helicopter taking off.

*　　　*　　　*

Yuri led the charge through the main gate.

As soon as the howitzer bunker exploded the fight went out of the remaining defenders. They knew that with their heavy artillery down they had lost and they began running out of their trenches, back through the complex.

Col ordered the three remaining BMPs after them. Yuri switched on the speakers welded to the top of his vehicle and blasted out 'We Are the Red Cavalry'.

He charged down the main road and smashed through the wire gate into the complex, closely followed by Col and Josiah. They fanned out inside, chasing the enemy through the maze of burning barracks, troops standing up in their hatchways, firing at anything that moved.

Alex radioed for the rest of the Battlegroup to approach and five minutes later the remaining trucks poured in through the main gate. The infantry spilled out and swept through the complex systematically, alternatively firing and taking prisoners.

'Troop commanders secure perimeter and RV on me at hangar now!' Alex shouted happily.

Arkady shut down the damaged helicopter and ran over. The BMPs' engines roared with victory as they rendezvoused with Alex. Troops jumped off them and ran over to the tank, its barrel jutting jubilantly up into the sky. Alex hopped out of his hatch and stood on top of the tank, arms punching the air to welcome them.

Col scrambled up and slapped him on the back: 'You fooking did it, mate!'

Yuri and Arkady bear-hugged him, shouting incoherent oaths in Russian. A cache of beers, liberated from a hut, were cracked open and sprayed around. Yamba cackled with delight and began a victory dance in front of the tank, kicking up the dust and singing.

'We did it! We bloody did it!' Alex shouted at Col, clenching his fists and then shaking the older man by the shoulders.

Col looked up at him, glad to see his commander reap the reward for his labours. With his black beard, smoke-streaked face, unstrapped helmet and body armour he looked like an ecstatic modern-day pirate. To see him so happy now after all his struggles for the mission was pure joy.

Alex was elated. It felt great to stand on the tank surrounded by his men, with a beer in one hand and just gaze around at their victory: the drifting smoke, the smashed buildings, the pile of rubble that had been the howitzer bunker.

I've made it! His heart sang up to him and the words washed through him; soothing and cooling the old hurts. No one can ever take this away from me! I will always know now that I conceived and organised this campaign against the odds and won.

Where was that snarling hyena now? Sent packing, back into the darkness.

Alex turned to Yamba and laughed, 'God, it was

grim on the bottom of that lake. We lost traction.' He shook his head at the memory.

Yamba laughed. 'Yes! And I was standing in that bloody helicopter, thinking: where the hell is that boy? What is he doing sitting around on the bottom of a lake, when *I* have a job to do?'

Alex convulsed with laughter, his stomach muscles clenching and shaking off the tension. He wiped his face and looked up to see the signals truck driving through the main gate at speed. Kalil was here.

A ragged cheer of welcome went up from the crowd as it arrived. Alex jumped down and stood under the tank's gun, ready to greet his boss: feet apart, beer in hand and a motley crew of battle-stained mercenaries standing on a tank behind him, waving machine guns, grenade launchers and beer cans.

Kalil jumped down from the cab and walked over. Even at the end of a tough jungle campaign he somehow managed to look preppy: Timberland boots, chinos and blue shirt still smart, black hair slicked back.

Alex grinned in expectation of another celebration. Then he looked more closely. Kalil wasn't smiling.

*   *   *

'Kalil!' Alex shouted joyfully as the slim man walked towards him.

The Lebanese's face was dark and tense. Alex looked down at him, his grin gradually slipping away.

Kalil stood close to him, rubbing his chin

anxiously.

'Did I hear a report on the radio of a helicopter taking off?'

'Yeah, it was that Mi-8 they used for the diamond run. We didn't realise it was inside the hangar at the start of the attack and then it took off halfway through.'

Alex shrugged. OK, so they hadn't achieved every objective, but there was no need to get upset about a detail like that.

Kalil's eyes narrowed. 'Did you see the old guy in the tie?'

'Well, he did run past me.' Alex remembered seeing the scurrying figure and felt a twinge of guilt.

'So what did you do?' Kalil said accusingly.

'Well, I . . . I let him go.' Alex hurried to justify himself: 'The anti-aircraft truck was right behind him and was a much more important target.'

'No, it was not!' Kalil shot out.

The men on the tank quietened down and looked on awkwardly at what was becoming a bad-tempered exchange.

'Where was he running to? Which direction?'

'Towards the helicopter hangar.' Alex jerked his thumb over his shoulder.

Kalil flinched. 'Did he have anything with him?'

Alex thought for a second to recall the figure bent double and moving in an old man's crabbing run.

'He was carrying a briefcase.'

Kalil looked sick and placed a hand over his eyes. He drew his palm down until it was over his mouth. He paused for a moment to recover his poise and then snapped back into action.

'OK, we need to get after him quickly! Come on, let's go!'

'What?' Alex looked at him, annoyed at this nitpicking at his moment of victory. He had just come through the riskiest battle he had ever fought in; against the odds they had won and were celebrating.

Kalil was immune to all this. Alex was beginning to feel that this ignorance was ingratitude. His irritation increased. Besides which, the battle was not yet wrapped up. There were a hell of a lot of things that needed sorting out: wounded men needed attention and they had to dig in and secure the perimeter against counterattacks.

He turned towards the smaller man and tried to keep a positive tone.

'Look, come on, we got the mine. We screwed them!' he smiled encouragingly.

Kalil's face went white under his tan. He sounded almost hysterical.

'We need to get in that helicopter *right* now!' He pointed over at the big troop carrier, bullet holes dotted along its sides and puddles of aviation fuel underneath it.

Alex's anger flared up. He squared his shoulders, one hand on hip, the other jabbing the beer can at the smaller man to indicate objections.

'Look, Kalil! The chopper is shot up, it's got holes in the fuel tanks and the cargo bay is full of it. It's a flying bomb! It'll take a couple of hours to patch it up and refuel. I am not ordering my men to fly it! So he got away? *We've* got the mine!'

Kalil ground his teeth in fury and looked down. He realised that they had reached an impasse. He looked up and said quietly, 'Alex, I need to speak to you in private.' He jerked his head to indicate the signals truck.

Alex composed himself. 'OK,' he said, trying to sound calm.

He turned to the men on the tank. 'Col, Yamba, can you look after things for a minute?' He turned and followed the fuming Lebanese.

They climbed up the steps at the back of the truck. Kalil yanked the metal door open, walked to the other end of the large cabin and then turned to face Alex as he came in and closed the door behind him.

Alex stared at him, prepared for a confrontation. 'Kalil, *what* is going on?' he asked in exasperation.

Kalil looked at him strangely. He seemed to be coming to a momentous decision inside himself, considering if it was the right thing to do. He took a deep breath, folded his arms across his chest and drew himself up.

'My name is not Kalil. I am not Lebanese. I don't work for a diamond cartel and this is not just a diamond mine.'

Amir's upbringing was painful.

Caught between the two strong forces of his parents in conflict, he was at the same time energised yet confused by it.

Aisha loved him and nurtured him intensely, turning him into a sensitive, studious, mummy's boy.

For his father he alternately felt awe and terror.

The combination of the two people made him feel that he should be something great but also embittered him so that he felt that he was somehow always bound to disappoint.

He was further confused by his relations at school in Bonn. With his dark skin and black wavy hair he was an outsider; the only non-white child there. He was quiet and hard-working but never accepted into any social group.

Once, when he was twelve, he found himself sitting on the edge of a playground discussion about what Germany should do to oppose the USSR. He longed to be able to chat as freely as the German children did with each other.

He suddenly thought of a way to try to gain acceptance and declared out of the blue: 'I think we Germans should attack the Soviets!' It was the sort of sweeping generalisation his mother sometimes came out with. He had stuck his neck out and tried to speak on behalf of the German nation.

There was a pause as others turned to look at him in surprise. For a second he thought that his audacity had allowed him to get away with it.

Then a tall, sour-faced girl called Elke frowned

and said quizzically: 'But you're not a German. You're a horrid foreigner.'

It was not said aggressively; to her it was a simple statement of fact. De-Nazification programmes faced an uphill struggle in 1950s Germany. The others in the group smirked and Amir flushed.

He was not one of them and had been caught red-handed trying to sneak into their gang. Amir knew this and he never tried to gain acceptance again, but skulked in the margins of society.

He became withdrawn and fascinated by machines. He loved them because they were so unemotional, so easy to understand and control, unlike the terrifying world around him.

He always remembered holding the Luger in his father's study; the way that it had terrified him and then, when he had been given control of it, it had conveyed its deadly weight and power into his hands.

As he grew into a teenager, Amir became more and more withdrawn. His mother tried to hold him more tightly still but he pulled away and further into himself. He focused his efforts on his work and began to come top in maths and sciences.

The rejection and torment of his upbringing hardened into a visceral hatred against his father and Germany. As a sensitive, intelligent child, Amir had taken on Otto's tremendous latent rage but, being frail, had never had the means to express it physically.

Instead, as he grew older he began to look for intellectual vents for his anger. Any argument would do that he could pick up and throw at Otto and the society that he came from.

In the sixties, when he went to university to study

313

Material Sciences, it was a heady time to be an angry young man. The winds of decolonisation were sweeping through Africa, and left-wing student activism was flexing its muscles. He took in a powerful mixture of Che Guevara, Jean-Paul Sartre, psychoanalysis, Marx and Mao.

At university, his ethnicity finally became a bonus. People were fascinated that he came from Libya. Amongst the cigarette and dope fumes of anti-imperialist gatherings he at last found what he had always sought—social acceptance.

This encouragement made him want to know more about his roots. He had never had any contact with his family in Tripoli; they had cut Aisha off and she had never turned back to them. So he studied courses in Arabic and wrote letters to his grandfather. The old man held no grudges against the innocent child and a spasmodic correspondence grew up.

Amir was particularly drawn to the books of Frantz Fanon, whose personal story he sympathised with. A black man from Martinique, he had been a Francophile at home but was radicalised by the racism and rejection that he experienced when he actually visited France.

His work, *The Wretched of the Earth*, was filled with the anger of the downtrodden and oppressed. Its call for the use of violence against Western paternalism was manna to Amir. It articulated his personal grievances and gave the young man a cause to dedicate his life to.

Amir completed his Ph.D. and then continued his research in atomic metals, all the while brooding on the injustice of the world.

Then, on 1 September 1969, came the news that

314

changed his life. Amir heard it on the Deutsche Welle radio news.

That evening, a light entertainment show on the Kingdom of Libya radio station in Benghazi was interrupted by military music. Listeners turned to their sets and tried to adjust them.

King Idris had been overthrown in a bloodless revolution by a group of young army officers. After half an hour of confusion the music was finally broken by the voice of Captain Mu'ammar al-Gaddafi.

'Your armed forces have toppled the reactionary, backward and corrupt regime. With one strike, your heroic army has overthrown idols and destroyed them in one of Providence's fateful moments. As of now, Libya shall be a free and sovereign republic under the name of the Libyan Arab Republic.

'We shall not be oppressed, or deceived or wronged, no longer master and slave; but free brothers in a society over which, God willing, shall flutter the banner of brotherhood and equality. And thus shall we build glory, revive heritage and avenge a wounded dignity.

'Sons of the Bedouins, sons of the desert, sons of the ancient cities, sons of the countryside, sons of the villages, the hour of work has struck and so let us forge ahead!'

As he heard those words, Amir knew that Gaddafi was speaking directly to him: 'sons of the ancient cities . . . we shall avenge a wounded dignity . . . the hour of work has struck!'

This was the spark that flashed across the disparate hatreds in Amir's head and connected them into a coherent circuit at last. From then on his being hummed with the dark power Gaddafi's words generated.

He resigned his post the next day, wrote a brief goodbye letter to his mother and caught a flight to Tripoli. He volunteered to work for the new government and, as a highly educated scientist, was welcomed with open arms into its most secret research project.

Alex stared back at Kalil—or whoever he was.

Each of his strange denials had hit him like a shot from a stungun.

The other man sighed and looked him straight in the eye.

'What I am about to tell you is classified information. I am relying on your professionalism as a former British Army officer not to divulge this information to anyone.' He paused and then said more insistently, 'Do I have your word?'

Alex continued to look at him but nodded fractionally. He had no idea what he was getting into but he wasn't going to find out unless he assented.

The man relaxed slightly, feeling that he had at last found a confidant that he could share some great burden with.

He took a deep breath. 'My name is Kamal Maqsood. I am a Syrian-American. This entire operation has been funded by the Central Intelligence Agency of the United States of America.'

He stopped, knowing that what he said would take time for Alex to absorb.

Alex looked at him blankly; the words had just hit him and bounced off, not settling in enough to explain anything.

Kamal continued regardless, 'We are not here because we want to take over a diamond mine. We are here because we want to capture a renegade Libyan scientist called Amir Hofheim. That's the guy in the tie that I said I wanted terminated.'

317

Alex needed to stop the flow of confusion. He held up his hand. 'He's a what?'

'He's a renegade Libyan scientist—he's an expert metallurgist working on uranium refinement. The soldiers were Libyan, you know, the ones in the strange campattern uniforms that you couldn't place. That's why they were tougher to fight— they're professionals. They've been out here for years, hence the faded uniforms.'

Alex looked at him astonished; Kamal mistook his incomprehension for disbelief.

'Look, I'm not lying to ya!' His accent was coming out even more strongly now that he had abandoned any pretence of being Lebanese.

Alex wasn't listening to him. He was distracted by thoughts coming together in his head. When they had had their first briefing on the mission, he had told Col that it was strange that Kalil had said that he had never been to Africa—when he worked for a big diamond cartel there. However, he had been so keen to get on with the job that he had just pushed those doubts aside.

His expression cleared and Kamal took it as a sign that he could relax a little. He raised both hands in front of him, palms flat in a placatory gesture, and took a deep breath.

'OK, let me explain. Gaddafi set up this plant years ago when he was still the bad guy and trying to build a bomb. He was playing around in CAR, sending troops into the country and taking minerals out of it. He was particularly after uranium to refine. The French originally built the mine on the volcano,' he nodded his head towards it, 'years ago, when they ran French Equitorial Africa. They used their expertise from the Alps to

318

put the hydroelectric plant in to power it.

'It fell into disuse when they pulled out but covertly Gaddafi got it going again when his troops were in the country during the civil wars. He built the refinery shed under the guise of the place being a diamond mine.'

He checked that Alex was following him.

'A few years ago he came clean on his nuclear research programme and dismantled it, but this was his *ultra-secret* location and he didn't tell the UN about it as it would have made him look even more of a shit than he already was. Nuke facilities are bad enough in your own country let alone in *other* sovereign states.

'Because it seemed to be just a mine in CAR we never suspected that it was part of a Libyan nuclear research programme. So, what seems to have happened was that when he came clean to the UN he tried to recall his men here on the quiet, just close it down and sneak off home and no one would be any the wiser. However, by then the whole lot of them—Hofheim, the soldiers and the North Korean technicians that he had been using—had been out here in the jungle for years and had all gone a bit crazy; they were making a lot of money from the diamonds and Hofheim was playing God building bombs. So they refused.'

Kamal shrugged. 'Not much that Gaddafi could do about it—couldn't come back in and get them, couldn't complain to the UN, so he had to leave them alone.'

By now Alex had heard enough to begin rationalising what was happening. He frowned and shook his head. 'But why did Hofheim carry on with it?'

319

Kamal rubbed his face with both hands and then looked up.

'Well, having a nuclear bomb in your hands seems to do funny things to people—they start getting a God complex, particularly out here. I mean, A. Q. Khan was the father of the Pakistani bomb. He was a national hero with all the money he could want, but he was still covertly selling off the technology to North Korea and Libya, the most irresponsible countries he could find. Why? I don't know. I think some scientists just get carried away with their power.

'Hofheim has a grudge against Germany and the years out here have made him unstable—at least that's what our communication intercept guys say. Apparently they've heard him ranting about some Dark Heart Prophecy that he believes in. That he's the culmination of some medieval prophecy.' He nodded in agreement with Alex's expression of disbelief.

'Ya, I know, it's crazy,' he shrugged. 'It's all wrapped up with his father who was a Nazi and who he hates, for some reason. Something about a great threat to Germany. I don't get it.

'The first we knew about the whole operation were some radio intercepts that mentioned uranium oxide. They were picked up by chance by a computer-monitoring programme on a surveillance satellite. That got people at Langley interested and it seems that he has been refining uranium oxide ore to make weapons-grade fissile material.

'Uranium oxide is a black glassy mineral. They pull big lumps of it out of the volcano.' He held up his hands with fingers extended to indicate the unusually large size of the pieces. 'It's apparently the most concentrated location of the mineral in the world. It emits radioactive radon gas, which is why all the workers in the mine keep dying of radiation sickness. He does also get green diamonds out of the volcano—' he held up a placatory hand—'I wasn't bullshitting you completely. The crystal structure of the diamonds turns green in the presence of the uranium radiation. And it does make them worth a hell of a lot more money than white diamonds, which he then uses to fund the operation. But ultimately what he is really interested in is the uranium oxide. It's the purest natural form of U-235 available. All you gotta do is crush it, leach it, filter it a bit and then bake it to get the uranium hexafluoride you need to start the centrifuge process.'

Kamal was a lot more familiar with the technology than Alex. He realised this and finished off quickly, 'That's basically what's going on in the refinery shed. He's got the crushers and chemical beds, and then cascades of centrifuges spinning away and purifying it into a weapons-grade isotope.'

These were the gleaming banks of stainless-steel machines that Yamba had walked in on and stared at in disbelief.

'From intercepts we know for sure that he has enough material to produce a small nuclear device.' He paused to emphasise the point. 'I don't just mean a dirty bomb; I mean a proper nuclear bomb. They're not hard to make once you've got the weapons-grade uranium—that's the difficult bit. They're very simple devices—just a metal tube with a piece of uranium and some explosive at each end.

321

You blow the explosive and it smashes the two lumps of uranium together to start the nuclear fission explosion. It's a small device, just one megaton—the kind of thing that you could fit into . . . a briefcase.'

He was partly relieved to have unburdened himself but also appalled at the reality of what he had just said. He slumped down in a seat.

Alex at last understood why he had been so angry outside. He too sat down, looking at Kamal silently, the whirl of facts beginning to settle in his head.

One thing was bothering him.

'So why the hell didn't you just do it yourselves? Why did you get me involved?'

Kamal sighed heavily. He felt like he had done enough explaining already.

'Well, after Iraq, the United States does not exactly have a great reputation for intelligence on Weapons of Mass Destruction programmes in foreign countries. Langley was *very* sure that something bad was going on here but they couldn't prove it. They tried intervening on the quiet by approaching the central government but as you have noticed, there isn't really one. They have no control outside the capital.

'We weren't getting anywhere with that approach so we tried a private military company. We use PMCs a lot in Iraq and Afghanistan, and they have the great advantage of being completely deniable if it all goes wrong.

'It was a good plan: no protracted bullshit getting UN resolutions. The battle would look like just another skirmish between diamond producers in Africa. The mine gets taken over and quietly shut down and the name of the USA is never even mentioned.'

He cleared his throat and then continued in a self-justifying tone, jabbing his finger at Alex, 'The United States takes the threat of nuclear terrorism very seriously. Very few of our "allies" are as concerned about it as we are because they enjoy the irresponsibility of powerlessness. They have limited military power so they just rely on us to do things and then sit back in judgement, crapping on about international law because they know that in the final analysis the buck *won't* stop with them. They aren't the world's policeman, *we are.*' He pointed at himself.

'We had a job to do here and this was a much more ... direct solution than a multilateral approach. It was a good plan,' he repeated emphatically to justify it to himself again.

Alex sat back and sighed; all his questions had been answered for the moment.

What they were going to do now he hadn't a clue.

Kamal took the initiative.

'Look, Langley have been watching this whole battle on a surveillance satellite. We'll need to agree any further action with them. Let me get them up.'

He turned to the bank of satellite communications equipment linked to a dish on the roof, punched in a code and then pulled the conference call speaker unit onto the table between him and Alex. He was about to press the live button when he thought he ought to explain something.

'By the way, the Director of the CIA is there.'

Kamal looked at the black speaker unit on the table, like a large upturned dinner plate. It was the link to a plush conference room in Virginia where a group of very powerful men were focusing their full attention on him. He was excruciatingly aware of the fact that he was about to be the bearer of very bad news indeed. He swallowed and pressed the live button.

'Director Nordhof, sir, this is Agent Maqsood. We have secure communications.'

Alex looked at Kamal in alarm. Director of CIA Jack Nordhof was someone he had seen pictures of and read about in newspapers. 'Tough' was the only word that could be used to describe the cropped-haired, steely-eyed man. Alex had not expected to be having a conference call with him right now.

A resonant voice came back, crystal clear, as if he were speaking from across the table. It was calm but only due to massive self-control. It was the voice of someone very much used to getting to the point and being obeyed. 'Mr Maqsood, we have a helicopter on the satellite heading northeast, we think towards Khartoum. What is the situation on the ground there? Is Hofheim dead?'

'No, sir, he is not.' Kamal swallowed and got ready to deliver the really bad news. 'Sir, we have captured the complex but I regret to say that Hofheim has escaped and was seen carrying a briefcase shortly before this happened.' There was a silence from the other end.

Kamal cringed.

The rejoinder was sharp.

'Mr Maqsood, can you explain why you are not already in pursuit of this helicopter?'

'Er, sir, at this point I think I need to hand you over to Major Alex Devereux, formerly of the British Army, the operational commander. I have had to explain the background to the mission to Major Devereux,' he gulped, realising what this breach of security meant.

There was a grunt of surprise and annoyance from the other end.

'He'll give you an accurate appraisal of our assets on the ground here, sir.'

Having put Alex on the spot, Kamal pointed at the unit for him to speak.

Alex shot an angry look at him but his army training kicked in: giving situation reports to brass was something he was used to. He cleared his throat and adopted his best deep, authoritative tone.

'Sir, we have one Russian Mi-17 troop carrier here, but it sustained ground fire on the way into the LZ. It has a punctured fuel line and fuel tanks. To repair it and refuel will take two hours at least.'

'Hmm,' came the rumbling reply. Then the tone softened slightly. 'Major Devereux, from what Mr Maqsood has just told me, I guess that you are not best pleased with us right now. We have dropped you in a very large crock of shit and I apologise for misleading you. However, we are where we are.'

Nordhof was a skilled diplomat as well as spymaster. He realised that he had to rely on Alex and needed at least to acknowledge the fraud that had been perpetrated on him. Having cleared this out of the way and brought him into his confidence, he was now able to proceed.

'As I believe you understand, we are facing a very difficult situation here.'

Alex nodded; he was beginning to accept responsibility for what was happening; like it or not he would be held accountable for the deaths of a hundred thousand innocent German civilians if they didn't sort it out. The problem needed to be resolved and he had to get on with it. Arguments about why it had happened would have to wait until later.

'We have a highly unstable individual with a grudge against Germany who we have reason to believe is armed with a nuclear bomb. The consequences of that being detonated in a city in Germany are . . . unthinkable.

'Now, I am afraid to say that for various . . .' he paused to choose his words carefully, 'political . . . reasons we are not going to be able to go to the German government for help on this. This is solely a CIA operation; we haven't even shared information on it with other US departments: Army, Navy, Air Force—nobody—so as to keep security on it tight.

'Any contact on this operation would have to go right to the top: President to Chancellor, which takes a lot of time. The Chancellor is currently in Japan on a diplomatic visit and the President is in Mexico. Apart from which we have not informed the Germans of this threat so far because we didn't want them bringing the UN into it, which means we can't really go to them now. So, to put it simply, we have caused the problem and we are going to have to try and solve it.

'Now, the issue we have is that Hofheim will certainly be travelling under false papers. We have no idea what identities the Libyan government cooked up for him when he was working covertly for them, so we can't track him on normal immigration systems.

'Major Devereux, you are the *only* person that has ever actually seen Hofheim in the last few decades. He left Germany as a young man and disappeared into a very secretive programme in a very secretive regime. We have no photographs of him at all. So you can see we can't really go putting out an all-units call in Europe to go look for an old guy with white hair who might be wearing a tie and carrying a briefcase—there are quite a few of them in Europe. Apart from which, our Psy Ops people think that any sort of general newsflash alert in the media would simply provoke him into detonating the bomb straight away. We don't want to spook him.

'I understand you got a good long look at him when you swam across the lake on your reconnaissance mission?'

Kamal had obviously been filling him in; Alex shot him another glance.

'That is correct, sir, I did see him on his veranda for about ten minutes.'

'Good. We are going to have to rely on you getting close enough for a visual ID on the suspect before we approach him.'

Having explained the background and satisfied himself that Alex was taking responsibility for his role, Nordhof changed his tone to something more menacing.

'Major Devereux, you are a man of the world who understands the realities of power. Assuming we can stop the appalling threat of a nuclear explosion, we also have to ensure that this story does not leak. *If* it were to get out into the press then there would be a . . .' again he paused to choose his words, 'kerfuffle,' he said with deliberate understatement. 'The good name of the CIA and United States would be besmirched around the world, and our enemies would be emboldened—I don't just mean Al-Qaeda; the *New York Times* would dine out on this for decades! More pertinently, I would be put in front of a Congressional Committee and taken apart, and you two would also be looking at considerable spells in prison. So, this is not a story that can be allowed to go *any* further than this. That means that you and Mr Maqsood are going to have to solve this issue between the two of you. *None* of your other operatives can be informed. Is that understood?'

'Yes, sir,' the two of them muttered, trying to think how they could overcome the problem.

'Now, we will support you with as much intelligence as we can get but we don't have any operational assets on the ground near you because the whole point of this op was that no US forces would be anywhere near there.

'We will track the chopper to Khartoum and ask them to intercept it but, as you know, the government in Sudan despises the US and we won't be able to get them to co-operate.

'Security at Khartoum airport is pretty lax so Hofheim will be able to get the briefcase onto a plane just by putting it in the hold—they don't scan baggage there. The case will have a lead lining so it won't trip the radiation sensors when it comes into Europe. He'll probably just land inside the EU somewhere and then hire a car or get on a train and effectively disappear.

'So, gentlemen, you can see that we have a mission on our hands!' Having delivered his summary in reasonable tones he was now ending on an urgent note. 'I want that chopper patched up, you two on it and heading to Khartoum ASAP!'

FRIDAY 30 JANUARY, DORTMUND, CENTRAL GERMANY

'Maqsood, this is Ritter. I'm the station chief in Berlin.'

The American voice was businesslike and blared from the tiny mobile phone loudspeaker on the dashboard. Kamal and Alex listened so intently they almost clutched at the sound.

'Hi,' Kamal replied, trying to make out that he was relaxed and confident.

Ritter was slightly taken aback by his casual tone. 'OK, we have some better news for you. We have traced a house in the name of Hofheim in Bonn. House was left to an Amir Hofheim by his mother after his father died years ago. His mother then died a few years back and so it's still in his name, hasn't been touched since then. Apparently the personality profiling people think this guy will return to his childhood home so the Director wants you down there.

'The address is forty-three Robert Koch Strasse, Venusberg, Bonn.' He spelled the words out and Kamal wrote them on the back of the hire car documents.

'You gotta satnav in the car?'

'Yeah, yeah, we can work it out.'

Kamal's overconfident tone was beginning to annoy Alex. Things had been very tense between them over the last twenty-four hours since Arkady flew them out of the mine.

'OK, good. I'm getting a team of field operatives together in Berlin at the moment but it will take them a while to catch up with you guys. Langley is being *very* secretive about all this and doesn't want me to involve any military. I'm afraid we just don't have SWAT teams on standby. We normally rely on the local police for that but for obvious reasons ...' He didn't need to finish the sentence.

'Now, Langley's analysis is that we have a window of opportunity to strike the target immediately if we find him. He won't suspect that we could get on to him so fast and he won't have been able to get a gun through the airport scanners and arm himself in such a short time. Given his mentality, he will probably try to detonate the bomb as soon as he can, so orders from the Director are to proceed quickly and tackle him if you locate him. I'll call you if I get any updates. Good luck.'

'Thanks.'

Kamal hit the off switch and sighed.

Alex gripped the wheel and stared ahead, thinking over all that they had heard.

The last twenty-four hours had been frantic. Whilst patching up the Mil, Alex had given hurried orders to Yamba and Col to secure and hold the complex. Pavel's mutilated body had been discovered in a cell, but the other prison workers had been released unharmed. Then Arkady had flown them out, eight hundred miles northeast to Khartoum. Nothing had been said to the Battlegroup as to why; the soldiers just had to accept the sudden alteration of plans.

Alex had grabbed some civvy clothes from his kitbag, as well as his mobile, passport and a stash of $6,000 cash from the operational funds. Arkady knew the Khartoum route from his gun-running experience, and stopped off halfway in the desert town of El Obeid to refuel.

After a six-hour flight he dropped them in Khartoum on the outskirts of the airfield and they ran over to the stinkingly hot and crowded terminal to try to find the next flight to Europe. By then it was mid-afternoon but they were able to pick up two seats on an Air France flight to Paris that night.

They slept fitfully on the flight. Alex was quietly furious at Kamal.

They arrived in the middle of the night, grabbed the first hire car they could find and took it in turns to drive the six hours to Bonn. ETA was 9.30 a.m.

Apart from the appalling pressure of the mission, Alex was suffering from reverse culture shock. A few hours ago he was the victorious commander of a powerfully armed battlegroup in the middle of the steaming African jungle, able to direct fire from tanks, helicopters and men at will. Now he didn't even have a pistol.

He was in nice, clean, efficient Germany, driving a new BMW along the autobahn. He looked around at the darkened early morning landscape as they whipped through it: grey clouds hung low over dead fields, patches of snow, bare woods interspersed between small industrial towns.

He was only just beginning to come out of the shock of being handed the new mission. He had tried rationalising his change of circumstance but had given it up as pointless. This really was something completely beyond his control. He couldn't be blamed for it—all he had to do was solve it.

However, the old self-doubt was creeping up on him, snarling and relishing the bitter irony of how he had been so pumped up on his victory only to have it overturned almost instantly.

Sitting next to him, Kamal looked haggard. He stared out of the window to avoid looking towards Alex and found himself inadvertently reading the logos on the back of trucks as they swept past: Transworld from Warsaw, Grimm, Ntex, Zorbel.

He was completely out of his depth and tried anything to stop thinking about the horror of what might occur. He had been an enthusiastic recent recruit in the War on Terror, his Middle Eastern background making him perfect for the new focus of operations. But he had always been too attracted by the idea of being the international playboy spy. He liked being the smart guy with all the answers.

Now he had none.

He was about to be that thing that Americans detest most—a loser. One of the biggest losers in history, in fact: the guy who caused the deaths of a hundred thousand civilians.

*   *   *

Those German citizens were going through their morning routines when Alex and Kamal reached Bonn. They followed the signs for Stadtzentrum and drove across the tatty Kennedy-Brücke over the Rhine, the duck-egg-blue paint peeling off its massive metal spans. It was a nondescript, grey day; underneath them the wide swathe of the river oozed its way downstream.

They turned left along the tree-lined Konrad

Adenauer Allee, and drove south along the river, past tramstops, buses, and modern office blocks: WHO and UNESCO, the old Bundeshaus building, the new Kunstmuseum and the huge *Deutsche Post* tower block next to it.

Around them new Mercedes and BMWs moved along at the calm pace of a prosperous provincial town. Women on old-fashioned bicycles cycled past with Germanic earnestness.

It was all so unremarkable. Alex was acutely aware of the contrast between the street scene outside and the bubble of lethal knowledge inside their car as it moved through the traffic. If the people around him had any inkling of what he knew, they would have run screaming out of the town.

He saw three secretaries walking out of an office block for a break. They were huddled together discussing something, one of them lighting up a cigarette as she left the building with a gesture of relief. They were young and attractive, flicking their long hair out of the collars of their coats and laughing conspiratorially.

His mind cut back to a history lesson at Wellington on Hiroshima. The master had dramatically recounted the facts of the explosion: the blinding flash of light, how people near the epicentre had simply been vaporised and those further out reduced to piles of ash or dark stains burned into the pavement. The thought of those girls reduced to that was too much to bear. He switched his eyes forward and resolved to do all he could to stop this man with his mad Dark Heart Prophecy.

What was he on about? Who believed in

prophecies these days?

The satnav interrupted his thoughts with its calmly engineered female voice: 'At the next junction, turn right onto Graf-Stauffenberg-Strasse.' He could see the sign pointing towards the suburb of Venusberg.

This was it; they were getting close. Alex's heart rate picked up.

They drove up into the line of hills running along the edge of the Rhine. The road wound through a wealthy suburb of nineteenth-century villas, what had been the perfect retreat for government bureaucrats when Bonn was the capital. The houses became more and more spread out, with patches of woods interspersed between them, the grim winter light hanging like lichen in the bare boughs of the trees.

'Turn right onto Robert Koch Strasse.'

Alex wanted to shout at the annoying machine. Kamal shifted uneasily in his seat, turning his head to look around them.

The road was long, wide and rambling, twisting along the contour line of the hills. The houses were set back behind trees and shut off by high gates across their driveways. The whole area was deserted; everybody was either out at work or snug inside.

'OK, let's drive past, recce it and then think what to do.' Alex said it as an order; his operational instincts were coming back to him. The other man just nodded, dreading what was coming.

Alex drove along at a calm, suburban pace, counting off the house numbers on plaques on the gateposts.

'Thirty-nine, forty-one . . .'

This was it.

He drove past, trying to glance casually at the house; they had no idea if Hofheim was there.

It was an imposing Gothic villa separated from its neighbours by a stretch of tangled woods on either side. A high metal railing ran across the front. Two tall grey stone columns were set in the centre, with an ornate iron gate hung between them. Up a flight of stone steps on a raised ground floor was a heavy wooden front door set with metal studs.

In its heyday it would have had a grand, imposing feel, with its three storeys, decorated stone pillars, small tower and balconies. Now it just looked sinister: the metal fence was rusting and the front garden overgrown with brambles, wild roses and dead trees. The building was covered in dark green ivy; it had grown over most of the windows as if blinding the eyes of the house. It was completely deserted.

They parked at the roadside several houses further on.

'Right, we'll go in through the woods at the side and look around. It doesn't seem occupied—I think we've beaten him to it. We've got to get close to him to get to the bomb so we'll try and get in, stake it out and take him when he comes in.'

Kamal nodded, still looking sick.

They set off along the neat grass roadside, looking like men charged on pain of death with appearing relaxed.

When they reached the woods, Alex gave a quick glance round. No one in sight; they darted into the trees.

Creeping through the dim tangle of branches,

Alex felt his senses come alert. His breathing sounded harsh in his head, his eyes picking up on little details of bark showing in patches of light. Kamal hunched along behind him.

Alex came up against the metal railing that ran down the side of the house. It was lower here, easy to jump over. He scanned the side of the building. The sunken ground floor was built of heavy blocks of rough-cut stone; the windows were barred with ornate grilles. No way in there.

The tradesmen's entrance was down some steps near the front of the house. The door didn't look heavy.

They moved along the fence to look at the back garden. A large lawn was completely overgrown: dead yellow grass with small saplings sprouting up from it. In the middle of the lawn stood a huge bare chestnut tree. A large terrace ran across the whole of the back of the house on the raised ground-floor level, a set of stone steps ran down from it onto the lawn.

'Right, I'm going to go in through that door there,' Alex crouched next to Kamal and whispered, pointing through the bushes to the tradesmen's entrance. 'I will sweep from the front of the house to the back, making sure it's clear. I want you in the back garden behind that tree in case anyone appears.' He pointed to the chestnut tree.

What Kamal would do if Hofheim did appear he didn't know.

They both clambered awkwardly over the railings, keeping clear of the spikes. Kamal jumped down and Alex pointed him towards the back garden. He bent double and disappeared round the side of the house.

Alex was on his own.

He glanced up at the ivy-covered windows above his head. There wasn't sight or sound of anyone. It was deserted.

He stepped carefully down to the side entrance; the well at the bottom was filled with dead leaves and mud. The door was old and flimsy and rotten along the bottom; he could kick it in easily.

Everything was silent.

He paused, weighing up the plan. Was he about to get one up on his enemy and set a trap for him or provoke him into a nuclear apocalypse?

He stood back, raised his boot and smashed it into the door. The lock came away with a bang and the door lunged inside, crashing back against the wall.

In the study upstairs, Amir Hofheim looked up with a start.

*   *   *

Amir had flown from Khartoum straight into Frankfurt. He had got a taxi to drive him the two hours to the house, arriving late the night before.

He had kept the house keys from when Aisha had sent them to him in her last letter from her hospital deathbed. The house was exactly as she had left it. His greatest regret about leaving Germany was that he had not seen her again before she died. But he had been running on pure hatred then, and it had not let him turn aside from its purpose.

He had inherited his father's fixed will but it was now directed against him and the system he represented. He felt sure that he was the

338

fulfilment of the prophecy that his father had explained to him. It was all too much of a coincidence. He remembered his father looking at him contemptuously in this very room and laughing at the little boy: 'Maybe you will be the great threat to Germany, eh?'

Well, now he was.

And that great threat to Germany was in the briefcase open on his father's desk. He looked at the thick metal cylinder lying diagonally across the case.

It was the culmination of decades of work. Every molecule of the U-235 inside it had been created because of his ingenuity, his creativity and hard work in that stinking jungle. He was loath ever to give it up—had resisted the call from Gaddafi when it came. This was his life! The fruit of the rebellion that he had led since he left Germany. It was to pay them back for all they deserved: his father's cruelties, all the petty slights of his childhood, the hurts of the West on the developing world. They were all one in his mind.

He looked at the arming switch on the red box attached to the cylinder. Such a simple thing to press it.

Before he walked down into town to do so, he wanted to spend time in the house, sensing the place again, brewing up his hurts into a fresh head of self-righteous anger, as he did when he watched the black-and-white film of his parents together in Tripoli.

Aisha had sent him the key to the house safe as well. He had removed his father's Luger, still carefully greased and neatly wrapped in oilskins.

He had taken it apart and reassembled it once already, loving the precision and power that the pieces of metal gave him. That had been the beginning of his love affair with the bomb— magical machinery that solved human problems. Quickly, cleanly, in a flash of blinding light, just like the prophecy had said.

A crash came from downstairs.

His eyes widened in fear. He looked at the case and then at the pistol.

He wasn't ready. He couldn't detonate it here on the outskirts of town. It had to be in the centre, right by the old Bundeshaus, the parliament building in the heart of the Germany he had known.

He shut the case lid, fumbled the magazine back into the pistol and cocked it. He paused to listen. The noise was from the front of the house. There didn't seem to be any other sounds; he could escape down the servants' stairs at the back.

He picked up the heavy case and slipped away along the corridor, the pistol held out in front of him. His heartbeat raced. He could hear someone moving in the front of the house, pushing open doors and checking rooms.

Amir was down on the ground floor. He stuffed the pistol into the pocket of his sports jacket and slid the bolt on the back door. He tried to open the door quietly but the frame had warped with age and he had to wrench it. It gave a loud judder. He slipped out onto the large back terrace.

Alex had just closed the door of the drawing room when he heard the sound from the back of the house. His head jerked towards the noise. He froze.

Then he crept slowly along the wide parquet-tiled hall towards the back of the house.

Kamal also heard the sound of the door opening from where he crouched in the bushes across the lawn. He saw a figure emerge stealthily from the back door onto the terrace.

An old man in a sports jacket and tie, white hair neatly trimmed. He had the briefcase.

Shit! This is it. Why did it have to come down to me? Alex, where are you?

But he could see that Hofheim wasn't armed. The man was coming down the central steps from the terrace towards him.

Just run across the lawn and grab him. Simple as that. He's an old guy. Before he sets off that fucking bomb. I can do this! I can be the hero! We can all get out of the shit!

Kamal stood up hesitatingly and then ran out from the bushes.

Amir saw the man stand up and then run towards him. He was at the bottom of the steps. He dropped the briefcase and fumbled the Luger from his jacket pocket. The man was halfway across the lawn when he saw the gun. His eyes widened in fear but he could not stop and turn in time.

Amir shot him twice in the chest.

Kamal flinched with the impact, stumbled onto his right knee and then went down.

Alex heard the shots as he ran out of the back door. Looking down from the balcony he took it all in instantaneously. The body sprawled on the lawn, the figure at the bottom of the steps with his pistol arm outstretched in front of him. The figure turning towards him at the sound of his footsteps, raising the gun.

Alex threw himself down the steps and onto him. The old man was knocked over but held on to the gun. He twisted it towards Alex, the muzzle looking at him.

Alex grabbed at his wrist and pushed it down away from him. The crack of the shot was muffled, caught between the press of their bodies.

Alex felt the hand go limp in his grasp; the gun sliding away onto the ground.

The old man groaned. Alex stood up and looked to see what had happened. The old man was lying back on a patch of muddy ground at the bottom of the steps, a red stain spreading over his shirt from the bullet hole in his side.

Alex stood over him, suddenly unsure what to do. He picked up the gun and tossed it away.

The bomb!

He picked up the case and moved it away from the man. He looked at it. *Is it going to go off? Should I open it?*

'*Es ist jetzt egal, es klappt nicht.*'

The faltering voice caught him off guard. He looked at Hofheim. His head was twisted over, looking at him. The small face was dark-skinned but pale now with shock and loss of blood. He waved his hand dismissively at the case.

Alex flicked the catches and opened it. He recognised the type of simple arming switch. It was not armed. He sighed and shut the case.

The man cleared his throat and spoke again.

'*Sprechen Sie Deutsch?*'

Alex looked at him uncomprehending.

'*Sie Sind Amerikaner, oder? Nee, Sie sehen eher Englisch aus.*'

The tone was flat and without malice, as if he were losing interest in life as the blood drained out of him.

Alex couldn't speak German but got the sense of what he was being asked. 'English,' he said.

'*Ach, so?*'

He grunted.

'Do not worry about the bomb, now it is finished,' he said with a heavy accent, sounding tired. 'What is your name?'

'Alex Devereux.'

'Hmm,' he said without interest.

'Look at my blood.' He took his hand away from his side and held it up, drops of red running off it and dripping onto German soil.

'Blood and soil, hey?' he said, thinking of how that simple, powerful idea had crawled through time like a snake, out of the darkness of the Middle Ages, twisting its way from one troubled heart to another.

From Eberhardt to Himmler to his father to himself: they had all succumbed to fear and sought protection in a defensive, hateful ideology.

Now, though, he had had enough of fear. He rested his head back down on the ground and looked up at Alex standing over him. An expression of calm came over his face.

'You know, I didn't really want to kill all those people.' He frowned. 'Have you heard of the Dark Heart Prophecy?'

Alex stared down at him and nodded slowly.

'It's all about fear—we are afraid of failing and we take it out on those nearest us and pass it from one generation to the next. Are you afraid of failure, Mr Devereux? Of the darkness in your heart?'

Alex felt a bond of intimacy with the man he had shot; he was compelled to be honest with himself. His own angry words rang in his mind: 'I am not a fucking failure!'

He kneeled down, his face close to Amir's.

'Yes.'

'Were you ever afraid?'

'Yes.'

'Don't be. You are a good man, Mr Devereux.'

There, at last, he had managed a final benediction. His heart had broken free of the fear, of the prophecy, and he could feel a light inside him.

Alex looked at him as the man's life ebbed away, his frail body in shock, trembling and curling up. All he could do was kneel next to him and put a hand on the old man's shoulder so he knew he wasn't dying alone. He slipped into a coma and after a while the tremors ceased and the body lay still.

Alex finally took his hand off Amir's shoulder and closed the old man's eyes. There was a sense of absence from the departed life.

He stood up, covered his face with his hands and drew in a deep breath. He could feel a heavy weight in his heart.

Read on for an exclusive Author's Note.

Author's note

Legacy came about because of a number of interests I have, both in terms of periods of history and ideas I wanted to investigate.

I have always found the Early Modern period, starting in 1500, a fascinating time because it is the transition between the medieval and the modern worlds. In religion there is the change from faith and certainty to rationalism and doubt. In economics the world shifts from a subsistence economy to capitalism and finally in politics there is the move away from medieval political entities like the Holy Roman Empire to sovereign, nation states.

All of this flux created a lot of intriguing conflicts and characters. The historical background details in the book are factually accurate. The Knights War of 1521-2 and the Peasants War of 1524-6 happened as described. Eberhardt von Stelzenberg is based on a real character and Ulrich von Hutten was a poet and romantic German nationalist who co-led the war with Franz von Sickingen. Von Hutten survived it but died of syphilis the year after, in exile in Switzerland.

Thomas Müntzer is based on as much historical detail as we have about him. The speech he gives to Eberhardt in the hut in the forest is adapted from his 'Sermon to the Princes at Allstedt' in 1524. Later on, Friedrich Engels lionised him in his 1850 history of the Peasant's War, as the leader of a prototype communist rebellion. He was anything but a Marxist atheist but it did not stop him being pictured as a proletarian hero on banknotes during the East German regime. The communists also decided to celebrate the 450 anniversary of the war with a huge painting of the whole event and the final battle. This is housed in a specially built circular building on the site of the Schlachtberg battle and is a staggering 14 metres high by 123 metres long. Well worth a visit if you are in the neighbourhood—despite the Stalinist emphasis on size, it's actually very good.

Himmler, Wewelsburg castle and the Ahnenerbe are all accurately described in the book. The unit was set up to research Geistesgeschichte, or 'spiritual history', using a pseudo-scientific, inter-disciplinary programme. Genealogy, musicology, archaeology and linguistics were all combined and bent towards finding historical justifications for the Nazi ideology. Research was done into Nordic sagas, runes and German folk music as well as experiments on concentration camp prisoners. Archaeological expeditions were sent to Bulgaria, Croatia, Greece, Poland and Tibet to research pagan sites. Himmler himself enthusiastically supervised excavations on Lüneberg Heath in Northern Germany.

The details of the SS regiment Leibstandarte *Adolf Hitler* and their WWII campaigns are all correct. The details of the desert war in North Africa are based on Count László Almásy's book *With Rommel's Army in Libya*. Almásy's life was the basis for *The English Patient*. His book is an intelligently observed memoir written as Nazi propaganda after his return from the desert to Hungary in 1943.

In terms of the Central African Republic details, the French originally prospected a uranium mine at Bakouma in Mbomou province in the 1970s but never developed it commercially. However, it is now working under the control of a South African company.

Libyan involvement in C.A.R. is as described; petrol sellers in the country are called 'Ghaddafis' after him. Uranium oxide is a black glassy substance as described and does produce green diamonds because of the high levels of radiation it emits.

As for the ideas behind *Legacy*, what I was trying to do was to link the personal and the political. I was interested in the origins of conservatism, a fearful ideology with desire for order as its central belief. I tried to parallel these with Alex's personal struggle against his own fears.

During my research, I came across a difficult but fascinating quote in Thomas Mann's *Dr Faustus* that seemed to sum up what I was trying to get at. The quote is a bit dense but is worth persevering with:

'The scientific superiority of liberal theology, it is now said, is indeed incontestable, but its theological position is weak, for its moralism and humanism lack insight into the daemonic character of human existence.

Cultured indeed it is, but shallow. Of the true understanding of human nature and the tragic nature of life the conservative tradition has at bottom preserved far more.

For that very reason it has a profounder, more significant relation to culture than has progressive bourgeois ideology.'

349

The point from this that I found interesting was the question of why is man constantly drawn back towards his darker side? Why is it that modern liberal society, though so obviously more rational and superior, still does not satisfy mankind? Why do we have this need to seek identity in older conservative beliefs?

For instance, after the collapse of the Soviet Union the modern world was supposed to have reached the 'End of History' and a new world order. Yet there was then an eruption of older beliefs and conflicts—nationalism in the former Soviet republics and Yugoslavia, ethnic hatreds in Rwanda and now extremist Islamic ideas.

It seems to be that, whilst liberalism is great at creating a framework for a free and tolerant society, this is by its very nature anodyne and bereft of feeling. Humans still seek identity in groups and older ideas and this can lead to problems. So in the book, Eberhardt hankers for a German national identity and this 'blood and soil' feeling is transmitted down through the ages to Himmler and Otto and finally comes up against Alex and his conflicts with his own past.

Anyway, whatever you make of that, the book was an opportunity to explore these themes in more depth and I hope you enjoyed it.

JS
2010